PASSION'S STORM

"David, you cannot come in here like this." My voice, against my will, sounded like a plea.

But he continued his advance toward me. Lightning flashed, illuminating his face into a strange and unfamiliar mask

"I will do as I please," he said. "No one could be aware of my presence here. This wing of the house is deserted, and the storm is growing more intense."

I tried to run past him toward the door, but David moved swiftly, catching me from behind and pulling me against him. He turned me to face him and I was trapped against the bed with no chance of escaping.

"Don't do this, David," I whispered. "You don't want it to be . . . this way."

His lips came down on mine, shutting off any protest. The taste of his lips, sweetly familiar, was what I'd dreamed of, what I'd longed for in my darkest hours. It was as if we had never been apart.

"Yes," he whispered gruffly against my mouth. "I want it exactly this way."

CLARA WIMBERLY

LADY OF THE MISTS

ZEBRA BOOKS
KENSINGTON PUBLISHING CORP.

ZEBRA BOOKS

are published by

Kensington Publishing Corp.
475 Park Avenue South
New York, NY 10016

First printing: March, 1991

Printed in the United States of America

This book is dedicated with love to my parents, Frank and Verna Rogers, who taught me so much. Mom and I share a curiosity about almost everything, as well as a love of history and travel. And Dad, who passed away November 6, 1989, taught us what love and goodness really mean.

Heart! we will forget him!
You and I—tonight!
You may forget the warmth he gave—
I will forget the light!

When you have done, pray tell me
That I my thoughts may dim;
Haste! lest while you're lagging
I may remember him!

—Emily Dickinson

Chapter One

"Le Pendu!" The dark-skinned woman placing the cards on the table disregarded the crowd of people that surrounded us and looked directly into my eyes as I sat across from her.

"Le Pendu?" I asked, smiling at the Creole woman. Monteen Valognes often read the cards in the evening for the entertainment of our guests at the El Dorado. But tonight was the first time I had allowed the card game to include me. My guests had insisted, laughing and coaxing me to allow Monteen to read my fortune in the tarot cards.

"The Hanged Man!" Monteen hissed the words dramatically through her clenched white teeth.

The crowd murmured ominously. I tried to hide the smile that I felt upon my lips. For I knew how seriously Monteen took such matters as her cards and her superstitions and I did not wish to insult her.

"Should I be worried?" My words were lightly teasing as I asked the question of the attractive dark-haired woman across from me. But Monteen was not in the mood to be teased about her reading of the cards and her interpretation of my fate.

She looked steadily at me, letting her dark gaze peer seriously into my eyes.

Monteen Valognes was a French and Indian Creole

from La Place, Louisiana who had worked for me since the first day I opened the El Dorado Bathhouse in Hot Springs. But she was more than an employee to me. She had become a skilled therapist and trusted member of my staff. I also regarded her as my friend and I knew she felt the same about me. There was, and had been from the first, a special bond between us; probably because we both had lost someone we loved before coming together at this place.

But tonight Monteen regarded me almost as a stranger and I knew she was totally focused on her reading as she began to delve into my so-called destiny.

"A great change is coming to you . . . you must be prepared for it." The gaslights in the parlor glimmered on the satiny golden brown contours of her face and upon the golden earrings that jangled at her ears. Her black eyes flashed with warning.

The guests murmured and some of them laughed uneasily. The game had taken a somber turn and it obviously left some of them feeling a bit uncomfortable.

"But Monteen," one called. "Julia already had a great change . . . a year ago when she came back home and bought the El Dorado."

The guests laughed and some nodded in agreement.

But my friend ignored their remarks and continued to stare into my eyes as if to warn me that I must take her words seriously.

"This change could be a violent one . . . you must be on your guard."

"All right, Monteen," I said slowly, taking note of her grave look. "I will do as you suggest. I will be on my most vigilant guard. Does that satisfy you?" I started to rise from the table, for her words had begun to make me uneasy.

"Wait . . . I must finish the reading," she said.

I sat back down and moved restlessly in my chair. This was not something I could take seriously and I

10

certainly did not enjoy being the center of such speculation. But I had agreed on the spur of the moment. Now, all I wanted was to complete the game and go upstairs to bed. It had been a long, busy day and there was a full schedule of appointments in the baths tomorrow.

"Go ahead," I sighed, silently reminding myself it was only a game meant for the amusement of our guests.

Monteen flipped another card over and held it out for me to see before placing it face up on the table. On the card was the picture of a blond woman, dressed in a white Grecian gown which was tied at the waist with a golden cord. She was bending to grasp the jaws of a snarling lion.

"La Force . . . the Fortitude," Monteen said, nodding wisely. "You are a strong woman, but you must use all the strength you possess in the days to come. It is not clear if the courage you need will be spiritual, physical, or moral. Perhaps all three."

I raised my eyes to Monteen's face and bit my lips to keep from grimacing my disapproval at her. For I was still skeptical. But I said nothing, watching the dark, slender, beringed fingers as they turned the last card onto the others.

The gathering of people about the table laughed and winked knowingly as the card fell into full view. This was one they knew and the picture seemed to tell the story. It was a man and woman walking together, while Cupid hovered from a cloud above them aiming his dart toward the couple.

"The Lovers," a woman's voice cooed meaningfully.

"Yes, *Amoreaux*," Monteen whispered. "But it is not as most of you think . . . or wish." She looked away from me and addressed the guests for the first time. "She must make a decision soon . . . a difficult decision. It could be anything, but this card says it shall be one between the passions . . . those physical and

11

those of intellect and security."

The watchers spoke among themselves, some laughing and others merely looking on smugly. They seemed to know there was only one choice a young widow such as myself would make.

"Ah, Julia," one of the women said. "It does not sound like so difficult a decision to me!"

Their silly remarks and laughter irritated me and I grew suddenly impatient with them and with the game. I rose from the chair, picked up the cards, and turned them all face down.

"Enough for tonight, Monteen," I said. I had not intended my words to sound so irritated or on edge. But I was a private person and did not enjoy this casual bantering with guests I hardly knew . . . guests who for the most part were wealthy patrons who came and went each summer like the migrant locusts. It was one of the reasons I usually did not participate in such nightly entertainment. I didn't know why I had allowed it that night except that I'd been particularly uneasy and restless, and in need of some distraction.

It was not the predictions that disturbed me. For I of all people knew better than to believe in any such spiritual powers. As long as I could remember I had been told I was *gifted,* that I had the vision of sight into the spiritual world. And while it was true that I sometimes experienced premonitions, I knew there was nothing mystical or spiritual about them. I believed it was simply some quirk of nature, perhaps a trait that some sensitive people such as I sometimes possessed. I refused to make anything more of it than that.

I often thought it was my ease with the patients who came each year, or my gentleness as some often said, that made them think I had the *gift.* And I did feel great sympathy for those who came that were truly in need of help. Not all our patients were bored wealthy people such as those in the parlor tonight, in search of summer distraction.

I had worked in the baths even as a young girl, carrying towels and wrapping sheets to the therapy rooms . . . doing more when it was allowed. It had interested me even then and given me great pleasure and a sense of accomplishment when the treatments gave relief to someone. I suppose for me, working at the baths had taken me away from home and the babblings of a father often drunk and piteous. He had never been able to accept the fact that his wife had left, saddling him with a young daughter to raise alone.

It destroyed him that the woman he loved preferred the bright lights and bawdy ways of Memphis to the serene, isolated countryside of our home in Hot Springs.

Years later, in 1878 when the yellow fever epidemic swept through Memphis, we received word that Mother had died. But by then I was a young woman of eighteen and had already been sent away to school. My father grieved even now and had hardly been sober since that day. And I rarely saw him.

Tears quickly sprang to my eyes, taking me by surprise. I didn't know what was wrong or why I had been so emotional all day. I walked quickly outside to the end of the long porch and stood in the shadows of one of the huge white columns that supported the roof. There were still a few people outside, sitting in white wicker rocking chairs and chatting quietly. An owl hooted softly from the ridge behind the house. The air felt cooler on the porch, fresher than the smoke-filled parlor.

I looked up at the expanse of sky between the surrounding mountains. Stars twinkled dimly through late evening mists and a warm wind rustled faintly in the trees that surrounded the large three-story house. The gas streetlamps wavered through the swaying tree limbs. I could still see a few couples strolling down the brick walkways and hear the clip-clop of hooves in the street . . . people out taking advantage of the warm

13

August night.

"Julia," a voice murmured quietly behind me.

"Penny!" I said, turning to face my petite brunette friend. "I didn't hear you." Quickly I ran my hand underneath my eyes to erase the tears before I smiled at the young woman who approached.

"Is anything wrong?" she asked. She bent her head and looked worriedly into my face. Thankfully I was partially hidden by the shadows. But I knew she'd seen the trace of tears on my cheeks before I could wipe them away.

"It's nothing," I assured her. "It must be the night . . . the time of year . . . I don't know. Just some unexpected memories."

"Your mother?"

"No, that was long ago . . . and I hardly remember her, I was so young when she went away. It's these last busy summer days . . . before the ember days of autumn begin. It was when Father sent me away to school, almost ten years ago." Against my will my lips trembled and I turned away from her once more to look back toward the street. Whatever was wrong with me? I reached across the porch rail and pulled a blossom from the cranberry-colored crape myrtle.

"Away to school . . ." Penny asked gently: "And away from David Damron?"

I did not answer, but raised my chin slightly and took a long, deep breath. When I turned to Penny my eyes again shimmered with tears in the glow of the streetlamps. I could not help myself.

"One would think the ache would go away after all this time," I whispered. "I was only a girl . . . only eighteen. And yet . . . on nights like this, it seems like yesterday."

"Perhaps it's because you're back home now that brings it all back . . . being here at the springs. I'm sure it was very different in St. Louis."

"Oh yes, very. The air here even smells different . . .

14

sweeter, more familiar somehow. And I'm happy to be home. But perhaps you're right . . . perhaps the atmosphere contributes to my melancholy."

"Julia . . . ," Penny began uneasily. "I know it's late, but could we sit for a moment and talk? There's something I've been wanting to tell you."

"Of course," I said.

I looked down into the dark eyes of my friend. Penelope Malvern and I had been childhood pals, walking to school together each day and exploring the nearby forests and meadows in summer. The only obstacle in our friendship had been the status of our families. Penny's father owned the largest, most exclusive hotel and bathhouse in town. I smiled. It was ironic that my own place now sat right next door to the Malvern Hotel. I was accepted now, treated with respect. But back then Mr. Malvern had not approved of his daughter's relationship with Julia Crownwell . . . a girl who wore faded and patched clothes to school . . . the girl whose father was the town drunk.

But true to her loyal nature, Penny had never abandoned me. She was still my closest friend. I'm sure my gratitude must have been reflected in the smile I gave her.

"What is it, Penny? You sound worried. Sit here where it's quiet." I motioned toward two of the wicker rockers that sat near the end of the porch. The fragrant crape myrtle cast its shadows against the porch and the side of the house.

Penny sat down and leaned forward on the edge of the chair. She took my hand in hers and looked at me worriedly.

"Julia . . . I suppose you heard that they're opening the house at Stillmeadows again?"

Just the sound of that name caused my stomach to tighten. "Yes," I replied stiffly. "I did hear that."

"You know everyone assumed it had been sold . . ."

I frowned and looked at her curiously. What was she

15

trying to say?

"Yes . . . ," I began.

"Well, Father says it has not been sold—that it's the Damrons who are moving back there."

I felt my chest tighten with a swift involuntary intake of air, as if I'd been burned.

"You . . . you mean David's mother?" I asked almost hopefully.

"Yes . . . but Julia, David will be coming back also . . . and his wife."

A sharp pain stabbed through me as I leaned back in the chair and closed my eyes. I began to rock softly back and forth. Why was this happening now, just when I thought I had my life in order again? I opened my eyes and watched the delicate spidery shadows that fell across my new blue taffeta gown. It highlighted the expensive cream lace trim on the skirt and bodice, making it bright in the darkness. I tried to concentrate on that . . . on anything except what she was telling me.

"I thought I'd never see him again," I whispered. "But today . . . and tonight . . . he was so much on my mind. I tried to tell myself it was the weather, the scent of the night air, but it was him all along; it was David."

Penny looked at me with sympathy. "One of your premonitions?" she asked. She knew all about David and my past relationship with him. I knew she was probably worried about me.

I shrugged my shoulders. "I suppose. Although for the last few years when those feelings come I've tried to ignore them, push them away. I was probably doing that tonight."

"I'm sorry," Penny offered. Her face looked so sad as I turned to her.

I stopped rocking and leaned quickly forward to take her hand. "No, don't you feel badly for me. I'm only having a night of melancholy . . . that does not mean I will be despondent forever. Tomorrow I'll be

16

back to normal." My words were brisk and full of confidence—a confidence I did not really feel.

"I know you will." Penny smiled. "You have a will of iron when you wish it."

I was grateful she did not mention that the handsome David Damron was the only person to ever challenge that will.

"I suppose it was inevitable that you and David would meet again," Penny added.

"Yes," I said. "Inevitable. That's the same thing my husband Richard told me when . . . when he was dying. He said it was inevitable that I would come back home and that I would meet David again. And now his prophecy will come true it seems."

"You loved him very much, didn't you? Your Professor Van Cleef? I wish I could have known him."

"I wish you could have too," I answered. "And yes, I did love him. He was the kindest, most decent man I've ever known. He was so good to me."

We sat for a while quietly rocking until the other guests had gone in and the streets in front of the El Dorado lay silent and empty.

"Well, I really must be going," Penny said, bringing her chair to a stop. "Sam will think I've abandoned him just as he was putting the children to bed."

I stood when Penny did and put an arm about her shoulders. We walked to the wide steps that led down from the porch.

"Thank you for coming, Penny. I'm glad it was you who told me," I said.

"I wanted to be here when you heard about it," she answered. "Everything will turn out right, Julia. You'll find someone soon, someone with whom to share . . . all this." She waved her hand to indicate the beautiful, elegant surroundings.

"I'm perfectly content with things the way they are," I told her firmly. "I don't need a man to make me happy or to fulfill my life. I am content . . . that is enough."

17

"No, of course you don't. I didn't mean . . . well . . . good night, dear." Penny touched my shoulder kindly as she turned to go.

I stood watching her go down the walk and through the great iron gate leading to the street. She was a mere shadow as she turned to walk toward the Malvern Hotel next door. Then I sighed and turned to go inside.

The huge entry hall was empty. The marble floors shone dimly beneath the crystal chandelier that hung overhead. The prisms jingled back and forth, set in motion by the evening wind that wafted through the door as I came in.

I walked back into the parlor where one of the maids was busy putting the chairs back in order, making the room ready for the next day. I was particularly fond of this girl, for I had met her on one of my trips to the valley. The colored girl had taken her ailing grandmother to the springs there, the one the Negroes called the Corn Hole. When her grandmother died a few months ago, Mary came to me for a job.

"Evenin', Miz Van Cleef," the girl said.

"Good evening, Mary," I answered. "The parlor looks very nice."

I looked around with pleasure at the beauty and elegant orderliness of the room. It was just as I'd wanted it to be. Every piece, every decoration had been chosen with care. I had made it the place I'd so often dreamed of as a girl.

This should be enough, I told myself, enough to make me happy and content. After all I was no longer a little girl to only dream helplessly of things I could never have, of a position I could never attain. I was able to hold my head up now, thanks to Richard. There was no need for me to feel inferior to anyone in this town . . . not even the wealthy and powerful Damron family.

I walked to the card table and turned over the cards. *"Amoreaux,"* I said aloud.

"What's that, ma'am?" Mary asked.

I looked up in surprise, having forgotten the girl was in the room. "Nothing, Mary. Good night."

"'Night, ma'am," she replied, looking oddly at me as I passed.

I went back to the entry hall and the marble staircase that stood at the center of the room. Its ornately carved banisters curved outward on both sides at the bottom floor and narrowed toward the second level of the house.

My private quarters lay to the right of the stairs on the second floor. They were included in the right wing that ran toward the back of the building.

As I approached my room I saw that a light had been left on for me. A soft glow spread from the hurricane lamp's rose-colored globe, and lit the feminine room and its large bay window. The lace curtains there at the opened window filled with wind and belled out into the room. There were no rugs, for I'd had them rolled up in the spring and stored in the attic. I enjoyed the cool gleam of the bare pine floors. I removed my shoes, letting the feel of the smooth wood soothe my hot, tired feet.

The large mahogany bed dominated my room. A half canopy was delicately draped with white silk banners, tied back at the tall, gracefully carved headboard. The bed was the one item I had brought with me from the house in St. Louis. All the other furniture at the El Dorado was new.

I stood for a moment, looking at my reflection in the mirror above the dresser. I smoothed my hands over the fashionable blue taffeta gown that I knew matched the color of my eyes. I unpinned the blue aquamarine brooch at the throat of the lace-covered bodice and laid it on my dressing table. Then I took the pins from my long, blond hair, no darker now than it had been when I was a girl. It fell, full and straight, almost to my waist.

I stared at myself for a moment. Richard had often

told me I was beautiful, trying to convince me, I always thought, to think more positively about myself. David had been more likely to tease me and call me "blue eyes" or his china doll. But when he held me and kissed me, the teasing would leave his voice and his entrancing eyes would grow warm and full of desire.

I turned quickly from the mirror and my troubling thoughts. After I had readied myself for bed I undressed and turned out the lamp. I slid my feet between the cool sheets and pulled the soft material up about my breasts.

I was tired, but my mind still whirled with a hundred thoughts that left me wide awake. My neck and shoulders ached with a tightness as I lay back against the pillow. I tried to focus my thoughts on the soft breeze as it whispered through the window, caressing my skin and making a light swish as the curtains fluttered in the darkness.

I thought of Richard, my husband. I had told Penny I loved him. And it was no lie; I had loved him. But only here, alone, could I admit that the love in my marriage to Richard had never been the wild, tumultuous excitement I'd experienced with David. And Richard knew it . . . knew all about David Damron in fact.

That summer, nearly ten years ago, I had gone to Stillmeadows to work. The house there had its own private springs and so my experience in the baths had assured me a position with the Damron family.

I was eighteen and David twenty. We fell desperately, impetuously in love almost at first sight. It was the willful love of youth, untamed and uncontrollable, requiring that we be together every minute we could manage.

I had not cared if Mrs. Damron looked at me with disapproving eyes, or if the other servants giggled and made remarks. Some had even told me I would never be allowed into the realm of the wealthy household in any other capacity except that of a servant.

But I paid little attention, caught up only in the long looks from David and the thrill I felt whenever he was near. His dark brown hair had become streaked with gold beneath the hot summer sun. His gray-green eyes were amazing in the darkness of his tanned face. And I'd thought him to be surely as beautiful as the Greek Adonis.

I sat up in bed, willing my thoughts back to the present. My hands were tightly grasping the sheet, twisting the fine lace-trimmed edging. I took a deep breath and unclasped my fingers from the smooth linen. Even now David had the power to make me feel emotions I thought had long ago been forgotten.

My heart felt heavy as I remembered how that summer ended, with my father coming for me, sober for the first time in months. I had wondered at that strange interlude in his drinking, for as far as I knew, it had never happened again. He had ignored my pleading cries and taken me from the house at Stillmeadows. The next morning he placed me on a train to St. Louis, telling me I would be going to one of the finest schools for young women in the country. There was nothing I could do to change it.

At school I wrote daily to David, but received no replies. Finally I received a short, terse letter from Mrs. Damron who informed me that David was in Europe where she hoped he would meet someone he could bring home as a bride. A girl, she added, with wealth and position, one worthy of the Damron name. And so the servants at Stillmeadows had been right after all.

My face burned at the memory.

I had truly hated them then . . . hated them all. I realized all too painfully that I was only a summer distraction for David. Not the kind of girl he could ever marry. I doubted anything would ever hurt me again as that realization had.

Then I met Richard Van Cleef at school. He was one of my teachers, and a kind, sensitive man, who seemed to know right from the start the pain I carried in my heart. He became my mentor. He gave me books to read, the classics, he said, and then took the time to discuss them with me. He diplomatically taught me the social skills I'd never been privy to at home. Then he kindly placed me in the capable hands of his aunt, who saw that my clothes were fashionably suitable, and that my speech was ladylike and cultured.

In that warm atmosphere of love and concern I blossomed. I'd never have believed such a life could exist for me. If I had not forgotten David, if the pain had never completely vanished, I had at least gained a certain measure of contentment and happiness.

I was twenty when I graduated and Richard asked me to marry him. It had seemed the most natural thing in the world for me to say yes. He was a dear, kind man, marveling that I would ever consider marrying a man twenty-five years my senior. But I came to love him for all his goodness and to depend on him for a security and peace of mind I'd never known at home.

At the sweet memories, tears rolled from my eyes and fell onto my pillow. I had seven wonderful years with Richard until he died of a heart condition a year ago. My only regret as far as he was concerned was that I had never been able to love him as completely, as romantically, as perhaps he did me. But he knew it and accepted it, he said. Still, especially now that he was gone, I wished I could have given him more.

We'd had a comfortable life, living modestly, but well. And so I was shocked after his death to learn how very wealthy he had left me.

Then, as Richard predicted, I returned home to Hot Springs. Perhaps I'd always secretly harbored a perverse wish to flaunt my newfound confidence and wealth before the people who had shunned me in my childhood. Show them that I was just as good, just as elegantly gowned as any one of them.

So, I had come home and bought the prestigious El

Dorado. And if at first I was a novelty, a curiosity, I knew I was one no longer. I'd worked hard, proving myself the past year with the success of the spa. But I never wanted to forget the people like myself, children who grew up with so little, and I was proud of my work for the poor of the community. Yet when I hosted a ball, it often became the most sought-after invitation in town. No one could question now that the El Dorado was the showplace of the city, even outshining my rival neighbor, the well-known Malvern Hotel.

Everything had been going so well. I thought I'd never see David Damron again, never have to face the mockery or the power of those hazel eyes. But now he was back. And tonight I was again little Julia Crownwell, the daughter of the town drunk, pulling at tight, worn clothes and avoiding the eyes of those who scorned me with their looks. Lying there in the dark, in the elegance of my room, I found myself a child again, trying to hide the pain I felt inside from the rest of the world.

Chapter Two

After a restless night I was up early the next morning. I knew the guests would soon begin to fill the bathing and therapy rooms, but Monteen would simply have to manage on her own today. I had too many chores awaiting in my office to even make my usual perfunctory visits.

I dressed hurriedly and went downstairs, pausing only long enough to ask Mary to bring tea to my office. I suppose I thought if I kept myself busy enough the dreams and images that had disturbed my sleep would soon vanish.

I was already deeply immersed in work when Mary brought a tray to me. Her black eyes shone brightly in her coffee-colored face. She was a sweet girl, anxious to please, and I, as always, was touched by her caring manner.

"Thank you, Mary," I said as she placed the silver tea tray on my desk. She had brought more than the tea I'd asked for. There were crusty hot corn fritters, one of our cook's specialties. They were dusted with sugar and served with a small pitcher of warm syrup. She'd also placed a shiny red apple on a delicate fluted plate. I looked up into her smiling eyes as she waited for my comment.

"You should not have gone to so much trouble,

Mary," I told her.

"Oh, no trouble, ma'am. Besides, Miz Monteen say you need more than tea for breakfast. And she also say I best not bring this tray back with anything on it!"

I laughed for I should have known Monteen played a part in this. Sometimes I thought she'd made herself my own personal guardian.

"All right, Mary," I said. "I promise when you return there shall be an empty tray."

"Yes'm," she said, smiling as she left my office.

I placed the apple in my desk drawer and began again to pore over the account books, sipping the strong black tea as I worked.

Time passed quickly and when Mary tapped on the door later I could have sworn she'd only just left.

"Excuse me, Miz Van Cleef, but you have a visitor . . . a Miz Damron from out Stillmeadows."

Mary must have wondered at my stunned expression. But I was not prepared to meet David's mother again so soon, and certainly not this morning.

"All right, Mary. I suppose you should take this tray back to the kitchen as you go." I looked at her apologetically as I realized I had forgotten to eat.

The girl looked timorously at the tray and the plate of fritters still untouched. Shaking her head she carried it outside. I heard her voice in the hallway.

"You can go in now, Miz Damron."

But the woman who entered my office was not Grace Damron, David's mother. In fact I'd never seen this strikingly beautiful woman before.

"Good morning, Mrs. Van Cleef," she said. "I'm Millicent Damron."

For a moment my heart plunged sickeningly. Then I was immediately ashamed that I should be envious because David's wife was so stunningly beautiful. I rose to greet her.

"Mrs. Damron," I said. "Please have a seat and tell me what I can do for you."

The lovely young woman seated herself in one of the tall winged-back chairs across from my desk. There was an air about her of arrogant restlessness and a slight scowl that kept her features from being perfect. Then she smiled and her dark-lashed violet eyes seemed kinder and more friendly. She wore her luxurious black hair in an unswept fashion and it caught the morning sunlight that stretched through the windows and across the floor.

"Mrs. Van Cleef, I've come to ask for your help."

"How can I help you?" I asked, curious about what she could possibly want from me.

"My brother-in-law will be arriving momentarily from Boston. He's bringing his wife home to the mineral springs as a last effort to try and restore her health. You see, several months ago, she suffered a fall in a riding accident, after which she lost the child she carried. Needless to say both she and her husband were devastated by the tragedy. But to compound matters, she has been unable to walk since then. The doctors in Boston are puzzled about her deteriorating condition; they say there is nothing more to be done." She paused and looked questioningly at me.

"Well . . . I'm terribly sorry, Mrs. Damron. But exactly how do you think I might help?"

"The Damrons are not people to give up easily." Her beautiful full lips curved smugly as she spoke. "David wanted his wife to at least try the so-called healing waters of the springs. He—"

"David?" I interrupted. I was confused, having been under the impression that this beautiful creature before me was David's wife. "But I thought you were . . . aren't you . . . ?"

"David's wife? Me?" She laughed merrily. "Oh, my dear no." After she stopped laughing, her expression changed and the wistful restlessness again marked her features. "My husband is James, David's younger brother. No . . . although even I must admit David is a

27

most appealing man. Why, he—." She looked at me then, seeming astonished by her own words. She shook her head slightly and continued. "Well . . . I'm sure you're hardly interested in hearing trivial family gossip." She smiled and went on. "I am here only to try and find a therapist for David's wife, Allyson. One of the servants at Stillmeadows, a local man, told us that you are highly esteemed for your work with patients at the . . . what was the quaint name he used—?"

"The Corn Hole," I said quietly, watching the nervous gestures of her hands as she spoke.

"Yes, that's it. It's in shantytown, isn't it . . . up in the valley?"

"Yes, it is," I replied. "Mrs. Damron, I certainly sympathize with your family's dilemma, but I rarely work with patients . . . even here at my own spa. I have a staff—"

"Oh, yes. I understand that. I certainly did not mean to insinuate that you make your living as a *therapist.*" Her brow wrinkled and her nose twitched distastefully as she apologized. I suppose that gesture angered me as much as any words she could have spoken aloud.

"No, no," she continued. "We would be honored if you could come to Stillmeadows and stay for a while as our guest . . . only until you could make your recommendations for Allyson's treatments and of course supervise the work. She would not, of course, expect you to do any of the drudgery." She smiled, obviously pleased with herself and her explanation.

Again my heart stumbled against my breast. Go to Stillmeadows? Be subjected every day to David's adoring eyes upon the woman he loved and had chosen to marry? Millicent Damron obviously had no idea what she was asking of me.

"I have no qualms about work, Mrs. Damron—of any kind. And hydrotherapy is certainly an honorable work. I simply meant that I do not take private patients any longer. That is all done by my staff. I'm much too busy with the running of this place to do that." I waved my hand at the ledgers which lay beneath my elbows on the desk.

She seemed taken aback and blinked her great violet eyes in confusion. "But if it's a matter of money . . . ," she sputtered.

I looked at her coldly and shook my head. "No, Mrs. Damron, it has nothing to do with money. I simply cannot do it. Of course if the patient would wish to come here, she would be most welcome."

"Oh, no. Allyson would never agree to that I'm afraid."

"Then, I'm sorry."

"Then you're . . . you're saying you will not come."

"Yes, that's exactly what I'm saying." I rose from my chair and she, seeing my action, followed. But she did so reluctantly and in that brief moment I actually felt sorry for her. She seemed genuinely stunned that anyone would refuse a Damron's request.

"But there are many people in the area who are qualified, Mrs. Damron, many much more than I. I'm sure you'll find someone."

I walked around the desk, hoping she would take my hint that she should go. She turned at the doorway with a troubled look upon her face. "But . . . but we especially wanted you. Why, the people here regard you almost as a saint. They've even given you a name. What is it . . . I can't quite remember what they say you are called, but—"

"Mrs. Damron," I sighed impatiently. "That is only a local folk story. You should not listen to gossip. The rumors about me have very little, or nothing, to do with who I really am. I'm sorry, but I cannot help your family and David's . . . Mr. Damron's wife."

I walked her to the door in the entryway. She turned and smiled somewhat diffidently at me as if she might make one more plea.

"Good day, Mrs. Damron," I said firmly, closing the

29

door quickly behind her.

She stood on the porch and glanced back through the cut glass panels in the door. Her face was puzzled as she turned and swung her skirt out of the way. She walked swiftly down the steps, the bustle of her white summer dress flouncing as she moved her curvaceous hips.

I continued to watch as a young man jumped down from a waiting carriage on the street and walked around toward her. I knew he must be James, David's brother. I had never met James. He was several years younger than David and had been away at boarding school that summer at Stillmeadows.

The man did not look very much like his brother. His hair was darker and he seemed not as tall. And the way he rushed to his wife's side so eagerly was certainly nothing like his proud, confident older brother.

As James reached toward her, Millicent Damron moved her shoulders slightly, shunning his touch. Her actions were angry with that transient energy I'd noted before. Her husband stood there only a moment with his hands out in an imploring gesture before he hurried to help her into the carriage.

In that moment I felt such sympathy for him that I wanted to rush outside and call to them, tell them I'd changed my mind. I felt guilty that I had caused her to be in such an impatient state with the sweet-faced man I watched.

I continued to watch them until the carriage pulled away and moved hurriedly down the street. As I turned to go back into my office Mary entered the hallway on her way upstairs.

"Mary, did you tell me your cousin has gone to work at the Damron estate?"

She turned, her eyes wide and curious. "Why yes, ma'am. They opened the house up again you know since the family was coming back home. My cousin Jess has been there this past month workin' to have the

30

place ready."

"Can you come into my office?" I asked. "I'd like to ask you something."

"Yes, ma'am." She followed me in and laid the freshly laundered towels she'd been carrying on my desk. She continued to stand, her eyes wide and anxious.

"Oh, Mary," I said quickly. "There's nothing wrong. I only wanted to ask about Stillmeadows. Please sit down."

She sat slowly, her eyes never leaving my face, as if she still did not quite believe my words.

"Does your cousin Jess like working for the Damrons?" I asked.

"Oh, yes, ma'am. He says it's the best job he ever had. He's got a nice clean room near the stables and he gets to take care of Mr. Damron's beautiful horses. Jess always liked horses."

I smiled. "So . . . he's happy there . . . I'm glad. Has he said much about David Damron, who's coming home with his wife?"

"Only what he's heard Mr. Woolridge say. He's the caretaker, you know."

"Yes. And what has Mr. Woolridge said?" I asked.

She glanced up at me, her dark eyes uncertain.

"It's all right, Mary. . . . I know you're not gossiping and whatever you say will go no further than this room. I only ask because Mrs. Damron has just invited me to come to Stillmeadows for a while." I felt a twinge of guilt that I let her believe I might go.

Immediately her eyes cleared and she smiled. "Oh, yes, ma'am. Well, Mr. Woolridge told Jess what a fine man Mr. David is and that he's always treated all his people kindly. But I think he's worried about him."

"Worried . . . about David? But why?" I asked.

"Oh, I'm not sure about that. Just that Mr. David has changed so much over the years and that he might not be happy." She smiled blankly and raised her

31

eyebrows in a gesture of disinterest.

"Oh, I see." I frowned for I could not imagine David being unhappy. He was an emotional man, I knew, given to moods and a quick temper. But our summer together had been full of fun and playfulness. We had often raced impulsively across the meadow and into the coolness of the dark woods. . . .

"Miz Van Cleef?" Mary's voice came to me through a haze, bringing me back to reality with a jolt of embarrassment.

"Oh, Mary . . . I'm sorry. Just daydreaming, I suppose. That will be all for now."

After she'd gone I looked at the ledgers on my desk, certain now that I could not concentrate on the complicated figures before me. I decided to visit the bathhouse in spite of my earlier thoughts that I could not.

The rest of the morning proved to be an extremely busy one as I visited and chatted with the guests and spoke with Monteen about one of her elderly patients.

Finally most of the guests were in their rooms, resting before the noonday meal. And a few were still lying quietly, wrapped in sheets, in the cooling rooms.

I walked through one of the rooms in the bathing area. My heels clicked loudly on the tile floor and echoed across the empty room. A large decorative pool lay in the middle of the room and the sound of water trickling from its cherub-adorned fountain was quiet and pleasant.

I glanced up at the ceiling, where a delicate light spread through the circular stained-glass skylight. Small beads of moisture still clung to the colorful panes of glass as well as to the bronze statue in the pool. I thought this was one of the most beautiful and peaceful areas in the spa.

I lifted a hand to my forehead and brushed away the sheen of dampness on my skin. I wished I had worn a cooler dress than the black silk. For as fashionable as it might be in France, as my dressmaker had so smugly informed me, it was much too hot for an August Arkansas day.

I loved beautiful, fashionable clothes and felt lucky that as the mistress of the El Dorado I could wear them often. But I could never seem to keep myself uninvolved with the steamy bath area and I often swore to forgo fashion for the simple cotton day gowns that Monteen and the others favored. In fact I decided that was exactly what I would change into then, before the staff began serving lunch.

As I entered the cooler entryway to go upstairs to my room, Mary again came to find me.

"Miz Van Cleef," she said, smiling timidly. "I was just lookin' for you. You have another visitor, ma'am, in your office."

She nodded toward the office just across from the parlor.

I hesitated. It was probably only someone inquiring about our services, but still I wished I'd had time to change into a cooler dress and pin my falling hair back into place.

"Who is it, Mary?" I asked casually. I smoothed the material of the black silk gathers that pulled snugly across my hips. I walked on toward my office without waiting for Mary's reply. But her words behind me stopped me like some impassable wall.

"It's Mr. Damron, ma'am. Mr. David Damron that we talked about." Her words were whispered.

Instinctively my hands clenched at my side as I stood for a moment, not knowing what to do.

"Is anything wrong, ma'am?" Mary asked.

I straightened my shoulders and took a deep breath. "No, Mary, nothing at all. Thank you."

David . . . here? Now? I could not see him now, a voice shouted inside my head. I'd wanted to be prepared for our first meeting, wanted to have him see me in a dazzling gown of white with diamonds

33

glistening at my throat. Not now, like this, with my hair falling in straggly wisps about my neck, my skin flushed and shiny from the steamy heat.

I bit my lip thoughtfully, knowing there was nothing to do but go in and face him. I lifted my chin and muttered to myself. "Julia, my girl, get a grip on yourself. You have absolutely nothing to prove to this man!" My self-administered scolding seemed to help and I marched resolutely to the door. Mary had left the door open a few inches. When I touched it lightly with my fingertips, it swung silently open on its oiled hinges.

I stepped onto the velvety soft carpet and stopped just inside the door. My breath caught in my throat at the sight of the tall man who stood, his back to me, as he gazed out the window. He had not heard me come in and I took the opportunity to compose myself further and to study him for a moment before he discovered my presence.

He was so different from the slender young man I remembered. He had grown taller and broader, with powerful muscles that rippled beneath his tan riding jacket. He stood with his feet apart and continued to gaze out the window. In his hand he held a short riding crop which he tapped restlessly against the soft leather of his top boots.

I allowed my eyes to open wide as I took in every inch of him, from his head to his muscular calves encased in black boots. Strong brown fingers clasped and unclasped the riding crop. He *was* different; he was a man now instead of a boy. But I would have known him anywhere.

"David?" I said, my choked voice almost a whisper across the silence of the room.

With a catlike movement the man whirled gracefully to face me. His brow wrinkled as he looked at me and his hazel eyes were wary.

I should not have expected him to know me. There was no reason to connect Julia Van Cleef with the

34

young girl named Julia Crownwell that he had once known.

He was staring at me, his lips open slightly as if to question who I was and why I had addressed him by his first name. I was immediately conscious again of my appearance as I brushed the wispy tendrils of hair back from my face.

I took a step forward, causing the light from the desk lamp to reflect fully upon my face. And it was my turn to stare at him.

My glance moved across his face, a more solemn face than I remembered. But time had not changed the handsomeness of those proud features, the straight arrogant nose and sensual mouth. And his eyes . . . those unusual gray-green eyes that could change as suddenly as a storm cloud and were now looking at me with a dawning realization.

In one instant rush he expelled the breath from his lungs as if he'd been kicked in the pit of his stomach. The noise was loud in the small room.

"Julia," he whispered in disbelief.

A smile leapt to his eyes and he stepped forward as if to draw me into his arms.

I moved back, frightened of what I saw in his eyes and even more of the feeling it evoked deep within me. This could not be, my mind warned. He was a married man now and I was not about to be charmed again so easily into his fascinating spell as I had as a girl. My look must have warned him away, for he stopped still, a puzzled frown upon his face.

"Why are you here?" I asked bluntly, keeping my voice steady and impersonal.

His jaw tensed and the warmth left his dark-lashed eyes as he looked at me. I could see that he was changed more than just outwardly. He seemed hardened somehow by whatever his life had become. And now he stared at me heartlessly as if he had never cared. And the brief happiness I thought I'd seen flare in his eyes at seeing me was now gone.

"I can see I've intruded," he said. His voice was now deceptively quiet, the quirt in his hand held stiffly and unyieldingly. "I assure you, Julia, I had no idea it was you that my sister-in-law spoke to earlier. I never knew your married name."

I assumed by his remark that he would not have come had he known my true identity. I glared at him coldly, trying to draw my eyes from the stormy gaze that held me prisoner. So easily . . . as it always had.

"Did you think to change my mind?" I asked. "To charm a lonely widow perhaps into doing as you ask?" As soon as the words were past my lips I knew I should not have spoken them. David's hooded eyes gleamed at me dangerously and I felt threatened and terribly vulnerable.

"You flatter yourself," he murmured coolly. "I came only to ask if you might help my wife. But as Millicent has already warned, it seems I'm only wasting my time." He stood staring at me angrily, then stepped suddenly toward me.

A glint of fear stabbed at me before I stepped quickly out of his way. "Do you know who I am?" I asked. I did not intend for my angry words to sound so haughty, but I knew they did.

He turned to me then, his eyebrows drawn together slightly, a light gleaming knowingly within his expressive eyes.

"The *Lady of the Mists* I believe is the name I've heard bandied about." His voice dipped sarcastically.

I felt a flush to the roots of my hair. How had he heard that ridiculous name so quickly? The same one which Millicent Damron had referred to. And what must he think of me that I would wish to flaunt such a pretentious image?

"That's not what I meant," I said, quickly turning from him to walk around behind my desk. Somehow I

36

felt safer with the wide expanse of polished wood between us.

"What I meant was, I am no longer a girl who works at the bathhouse, one to be hired out for the summer by one of the wealthy families. I *own* the El Dorado and I no longer do therapy work. I thought I made that clear to your sister-in-law. I assure you it's nothing personal." My voice was as cold and accusing as his looks at me.

"Oh, I'm certain neither of us wishes this to be personal . . . do we?" he said slowly. "So it isn't true that you go to the valley and work with patients at the springs there?"

My attempt at a cool, undisturbed facade disintegrated at his words and my mouth moved silently. "I . . . I do go to the valley, it's true. But that's quite different. Those people have no one else to help them. They are the poorest, the most needy. . . ."

"And do you really believe that only the poor and neglected can suffer, Julia?" His tone was one of disbelief, his sneering words almost a challenge.

"No, of course I don't. That isn't what—"

"You may be the elegant grande dame of the city, the proprietress of the El Dorado," he said through clenched white teeth. "And I'm certain you no longer need tend to any patient you do not wish to. But I suppose when I saw you I hoped there was still a spark of that girl inside your fashionably draped body . . . the girl who could comfort with only a touch, who cried at the deformed limbs of a cripple, and whose greatest ambition was to help whomever she could." He looked straight into my eyes for the longest moment. "But I can see I was wrong. Wrong to come here and wrong to think that person really ever existed! I'm sorry to have taken so much of your valuable time, Julia." His softly spoken words were clipped and angry.

I stood speechless as he stalked out of my office, his

37

bootted heels ringing across the marble floor of the entryway. The front door rattled as he closed it behind him.

I closed my eyes and fought back the feelings that came flooding over me. Then almost against my own will I walked quickly to the windows facing the street and pushed aside the dark green velvet curtains.

The street was crowded and several men stood near the stone entrance pylons, talking. But I had no problem picking David out in the crowd. His dark sun-streaked hair gleamed in the noonday sun. After he passed through the gate I could still see his head and shoulders above the stone fence.

He paused for a moment and glanced back once toward the house. His face was still tight and angry. Then swiftly, with one fluid, graceful swing, he was into the saddle astride a shining chestnut horse with a star-blazed face.

I watched him until he was out of sight. Then I could only stand silently as if paralyzed. Slowly I felt my eyes fill with hot, bitter tears. This was not the way I had wanted it to be. I raised my hands and impatiently wiped my eyes, letting my fingers remain to massage my aching temples.

"David," I whispered. "Why did you have to come back now? Just when I thought I'd forgotten you."

Chapter Three

I had surprised myself with my emotional reaction to David. Even Millicent Damron's smugness had not disturbed and frustrated me the way he had.

And David . . . how angry he had become with me . . . such a sudden, fierce anger. I thought he must love his wife very much to want so desperately to help her.

Suddenly I was filled with an unexplainable curiosity about the woman David had married. Even though I knew I had no right to wonder about her at all. I imagined she was very different from myself, certainly with a more educated and sophisticated background. I found myself visualizing them together—David and the woman he loved in a passionate embrace.

I closed my eyes tightly until the vision disappeared. My head pounded furiously as I paced restlessly before the windows. But I hardly realized what I was doing.

I berated myself over and over for my rudeness to him. I should not have behaved so, or pointed out to him how my social position had now changed. David had never seemed to care about such things . . . at least I didn't think he had. I was so confused. One meeting, one look at the man, and I became a muddleheaded fool. All my past intentions of hurting him, of some sweet revenge, had vanished, and I found that I was the one left upset and bewildered. I was not accustomed to being out of control like this and it was not a feeling I liked.

When Monteen stepped into the room almost half an hour later I was still deep in thought, still pacing back and forth.

"Julia?" she whispered. Her dark eyes were wide as she saw the look on my face. "Is anything wrong? We wondered why you did not come for lunch."

I looked at her in surprise, for I'd been so lost in thought that I had not even heard her enter the room. I forced a smile toward the Creole woman.

"No, nothing's wrong," I assured her. "I had something on my mind, that's all. And I wasn't very hungry. Besides, it's too hot to eat."

"Umm . . . and I suppose it was too hot to eat breakfast too."

"What? What do you mean by that?" I asked as I walked briskly to my desk.

"Oh nothing. I only wondered if perhaps this *something* on your mind had anything to do with the man I saw Mary bring in here earlier today. He was a handsome devil at that."

"Monteen, sometimes you forget yourself!" I muttered.

She laughed, a short derisive sound. "Don't bother trying that high-and-mighty manner with me, *mon ami.* I know you much too well to be put off by it. And you know I shall only keep asking until you tell me what is wrong." To prove she meant what she said, Monteen plunked herself down into one of the chairs in front of my desk.

I could not help smiling at her for I knew she meant exactly what she said. And we were surprisingly alike, even though she was probably ten years older than I. I could never really be sure, since Monteen refused to discuss her age. But in our friendship during the past year I had managed to piece together enough of her history to make a logical guess.

40

We both had a hard, poor existence as children. But whereas I escaped via school and Richard Van Cleef, Monteen had run away from her abusive father with a riverboat gambler. She stayed with him for years, traveling the length of the Mississippi, until a year earlier, when her lover was killed in a gunfight in Natchez.

I probably would never know how Monteen found her way here of all places, but I did know she now wanted a different kind of life than the riverboat circuit. And I was grateful for that, because this strong little Creole understood me as no one else could. She sometimes joked that we had known each other in a past life. I could tell Monteen about things that my innocent Penny might never understand and I often did just that.

Monteen waited with growing impatience, watching me closely as I sat thinking.

"The man you saw was David Damron," I told her quietly.

"Oh . . . *chère* . . . ," she said with understanding. "But what did he want?"

"He wanted me—or rather Mrs. Van Cleef—to come to Stillmeadows and try to help his wife, who is crippled."

"You mean he did not know before today that Mrs. Van Cleef and Julia Crownwell were one and the same?"

"No, he didn't," I said, looking into Monteen's warm black eyes.

"Ah, I'm beginning to understand. And you quarreled, no?"

"It's impossible, Monteen! If he had known beforehand who I was he probably would never even have come here!"

"But you . . . it would not bother you to help his wife would it? I mean, you have never before discriminated in your selection of patients. I thought you had rid

41

yourself of this man's influence upon you long ago."
Monteen's face was passive, and much too innocent.

"I have . . . of course I have. But I've told you how
his mother felt about me. Why should I subject myself
to her snobbishness again? You tell me, Monteen, why
should I?" My voice grew louder and in my agitation I
began to pace again behind the desk. It angered me that
I could not seem to stop my chin from trembling
whenever I talked about David.

Monteen frowned. I knew she had never before seen
me this way and she had never seen me cry.

"Of course I would not tell you to do that, *chère*. But
perhaps this would be a perfect opportunity to show
the Damron family who you really are . . . what you're
made of."

"No, I couldn't. It would not be right." I thought for
a moment. "But if I went . . ." I whirled and with one
finger raised into the air to emphasize my point I said,
"Only *if*, mind you . . . it would be to help this woman.
And for no other reason. It would not be right to
punish her for something that happened long ago and
in which she played no part."

"You are entirely right, my dear," Monteen declared.

"I would not do it with any thought of revenge," I
said firmly.

"Of course not."

"David Damron no longer has any control over my
emotions!" I continued.

"I can see that."

I looked skeptically into Monteen's face and saw the
wide, innocent look she directed at me. Then her teeth
flashed brilliantly against the darkness of her skin. I
should have known I could not fool her.

I sat down heavily in the chair and ran trembling
fingers through my disheveled hair. "What shall I do,
Monteen?" My voice came out flat and weary.

"Follow your conscience, *chère*," she advised, her
smile now gone. "You *do* have the healing hands and

you must do what is right, but not at the expense of your own happiness. And who knows, perhaps after you become reacquainted with this man, you will find he no longer holds such a dangerous fascination over you."

I did not reply for I could not admit aloud what was in my innermost thoughts: that after seeing David today I could not imagine he would ever be absent from my heart again. My mind was awhirl and I felt a need to be outside, away from the business of the spa and the noise of the city.

"Perhaps I shall ride out to the valley," I said. "It will give me a chance to think."

"Shall I come along?" Monteen asked.

"No . . . no, you go ahead with whatever you have planned. But thank you, Monteen . . . for everything."

"You will tell me what you decide?" she asked, as she rose to go.

"Yes, I will . . . soon."

Moments after Monteen left I changed into a simple bottle-green skirt with a green-and-white pekin satin blouse.

I walked briskly across the front porch and saw that my new carriage had already been brought around. Our handyman stood quietly holding the bridle of the sorrel mare.

"I shall be right back, Harry," I told him, walking past to the Malvern Hotel.

I fairly burst through the elaborately carved double doors to the hotel lobby and walked quickly toward Penny, who sat behind the huge curved desk.

"Penny," I said, catching my breath. "Do you suppose your father could spare you for a while? I thought I'd take a short ride and I wish you would go with me."

Penny was obviously surprised by my brusque manner, especially since I usually made a point of appearing calm and unhurried. She looked about briefly, not hesitating to help me.

"Of course. Let me find one of the girls to stay at the desk. As soon as I tell Sam, I'll be ready."

I breathed a silent sigh of relief and paced the floor. My black boots shone beneath the hem of the long dark green skirt as I walked. I was so tense; I only hoped this ride would help me to relax.

As soon as Penny came back we walked outside and toward the entrance to the El Dorado.

The afternoon sun gleamed on the pale yellow metal of the elegant lady's carriage. Its dark green fringed top shaded the tooled leather seats. I'd had the carriage custom built and never tired of seeing it hitched and ready to spirit me away. But today it seemed to matter little.

Penny did not speak, but I was sure she knew something was on my mind. She always seemed to know. But she was patient, waiting until I was ready to speak.

I slipped soft kid gloves on my hands, took the reins from Harry, and guided the sorrel out into the tree-lined street.

As we drove I began to talk, never taking my eyes from the road. "David came to see me this morning. It seems his wife has been crippled in a riding accident. He wants her to try hydrotherapy and he asked me to help." I glanced at her. "I refused."

"You did? But why?"

"I would be staying at Stillmeadows, at least for a few weeks."

"Oh, I see. Well, I can certainly understand your not wishing to become involved with the family again."

But she looked curiously at me from her expressive brown eyes.

"I'm afraid I was terribly rude to him," I said.

"It must have been an unnerving experience," Penny said noncommittally. "Are you . . . are you having second thoughts about your decision?"

44

"I . . . yes, I suppose I am." I said nothing more, trying instead to concentrate on the road before us.

It felt good being outside with the wind whistling past us, the trees a blur of green as we raced past them down the dusty road. Just ahead on our right I could see the road which led into the foothills and on to the northern valley of Hot Springs Mountain. Impulsively I pulled the sorrel to the right and with hardly a break in stride we began the ascent.

About halfway up the mountain I pulled gently on the reins, slowing the mare to a more leisurely pace. The horse was still ready and threw her head up, pulling impatiently at the bit in her mouth. Her eyes rolled wildly back toward us in the carriage.

"Whoa, girl," I said quietly, holding the reins firmly so she would not bolt.

After the horse had quieted, Penny and I marveled at the primitive, untamed beauty that surrounded us. The forest was dark and still. The sound of birds could be heard, their varied songs echoing through the trees around us.

Soon the slope leveled off and the little mare cantered with renewed spirit. I knew she could feel the tenseness, the impatience in my hands on her reins.

We drove past large clumps of blooming purple asters and black-eyed Susans which drooped over into the little-used roadway. When we reached the overlook I pulled to a stop and tied the eager mare to a nearby sapling. Penny followed and together we looked down into the valley.

"Was I wrong to refuse him, Penny?" I asked, the anguish of my decision causing an actual physical ache within me.

"That's entirely your decision to make . . . one you must decide, dear. But certainly no one would expect you to put yourself in such an untenable position, Julia," Penny said quietly.

I looked at her quickly, for something in her tone

made me wonder what else she wanted to say.

"But?"

"But . . . it's obviously bothering you. The fact that you refused him. Why do you think that is?" Penny looked directly into my face as she asked the question gently.

"Do you think it's because I want to be near him so badly?" I asked sharply.

"No . . . I did not say that." She placed a calming hand on the sleeve of my blouse. "In fact it could be just the opposite. Perhaps you're even afraid to be near him, living, though temporarily, in the same house."

I thought for a moment about her words. They were certainly true enough. I was terrified of being near him, and of feeling my resolve to forget him weakening. But I had not wanted to admit that, even to myself.

My eyes betrayed me as I faced Penny and she nodded knowingly.

"Have you ever refused to help anyone who asked for your help . . . anyone here at the springs?" she asked quietly.

"No . . . but this is different . . . I know it would not be wise to go there . . . to be near him. And yet—"

"And yet, you feel guilty that you cannot help her, as you try to help everyone else who asks."

I shrugged my shoulders, finally admitting what I was feeling. Besides, I didn't seem to be hiding it very well. "Yes, I do. I'm so confused . . . knowing I should help her and afraid I'm only doing it for my own selfish reasons."

Penny smiled widely at me and shook her head. "Nonsense, Julia! You are the most *unselfish* person I've ever met. And you're strong enough to get through this. You always do what you must do . . . and this will be no exception."

At her words, I felt my spirits lift for the first time since speaking with David. Perhaps she was right. Penny always had a knack for breaking a problem down to its simplest terms.

"Besides, if you did not feel you should go, would you be having these agonizing second thoughts about what you told him?" she asked.

I smiled at her. "You always manage to see things so clearly, Penny . . . to get straight to the heart of a problem."

"And so do you . . . it only takes a bit longer. But that's because you are a much more discriminating thinker than I!"

We laughed and stood for a moment enjoying the view of the valley and the cloud shadows that dotted the countryside.

Penny pointed to a house far away on the east side of the valley. "That's Stillmeadows, isn't it?"

"Yes," I answered quietly.

Just then a huge dark shadow from the fast-moving clouds passed over the house, and I shivered. The house looked different in the dusky light, with a vaguely uneasy appearance. And suddenly I felt a deep unreasoning fear wash over me.

"We'd better go," I warned, turning back to the carriage and the grazing horse. "I think it might rain."

But Penny grasped my arm. "Look, Julia—over there on the next ridge. That rider is going to kill himself!"

I saw the man and horse at once just as they plunged over the edge of the mountain and down the dangerously steep slope. Through the trees we could see them moving with heart-stopping speed in and out of the sunlight and shadows. The chestnut's powerful hindquarters were bent low to the ground as it fought to maintain its balance down the precipitous drop. The rider's left arm was thrown out for balance. Their movements were frightening and graceful at the same time, as if in a strange, slow-moving dream.

Penny and I were both stunned silent by the spectacular stunt we watched. Finally we saw the horse

47

emerge from the sun-dappled forest at the bottom and with a leap of triumph begin to run flat out across the grassy meadows. The rider leaned low over the horse's neck, as if urging it on. His exultation seemed obvious in every move of his controlled body as horse and rider seemed to merge into one magnificent creature.

Penny's eyes were opened wide with delight and she clasped her hands to her breast in a breathless little gasp. "Oh my . . . but he is extraordinary! I wonder who he is?"

But I knew, had known the moment I saw him across the forested gap which lay between us.

"David," I whispered, unable to take my eyes from the horse and rider. "It's David Damron."

Penny turned quickly to me and I saw there a momentary astonishment. Her dark eyes were wide and her lips were parted as if she might warn me about something.

Perhaps I should have tried to hide the look on my face . . . the great well of emotion I felt each time I saw David. But the power and excitement of his ride opened little bittersweet memories in the deepest recesses of my heart. I remembered the wildness of him, that quality that I found so exciting, almost irresistible. He did everything in an uninhibited, dangerous manner. Even as I watched him, I felt a weak tremble begin in the pit of my stomach and move over me.

I thought I had so thoroughly schooled myself in self-control these past few years. But I was as surprised as Penny by my reaction and afraid that I was losing that ability to hide my feelings, at least where this one man was concerned. And I knew if I expected to help Allyson Damron, I would have to guard against what I felt today. For it would take all the strength and resources I possessed to conceal my feelings for her husband.

Suddenly I remembered Monteen's words from the night before as she had read the tarot cards. I'd tried to dismiss them from my mind, but now I struggled to remember. She warned of a change and a need to be strong spiritually, physically, or morally. But which? All of them? And the difficult decision I would be called upon to make? Was this it—the decision to go to Stillmeadows?

But I knew it was too late for such questions and doubts. For even if time proved me wrong, the decision was already a *fait accompli*.

Chapter Four

As we drove back toward Hot Springs the gray clouds moving from the west had already covered the entire sky, blocking out any traces of sunlight. The mare whickered softly, tossing her head in alarm as lightning flashed in the distance. I flicked the reins, urging her on before the rain set in.

Penny and I were both silent, watching the storm clouds roll nearer. And I wondered if she too was still recalling the vision of the horse and rider we'd watched. It was the vision of a man pursued by some inward demon, a man who seemed to welcome, even to taunt danger.

I pulled the carriage to a halt at the stone pylons just as Harry came rushing forward to take the reins. He'd obviously been watching for our return.

I said good-bye to Penny hurriedly just as the first large raindrops plopped loudly onto the dusty street.

"So, you're going," she said quietly.

"Yes," I replied. "I am."

"Julia, I know you'll be careful, but after seeing David today, I . . ."

"What?" I asked.

"I think he's a dangerous man . . . in many ways."

"I'll be careful," I said. "And as soon as I'm settled I will send a note to you letting you know how everything is going."

We embraced quickly and parted, each of us intent on rushing up the sidewalk to our home. As I reached the porch of the El Dorado, the rain had become a noisy deluge, a wall of water that fell about the house and trees until the street could hardly be seen.

I rushed inside, shaking the water from my skirt and blouse. But I had much to do and so I did not take time to change. I sent one of the maids out back to the carriage house.

"Please tell Harry to come to my office when he's finished with the carriage," I told her.

I went into my office and sat at the desk, pulling stationery and pen from the drawer and placing them on the smoothly polished wood surface. I felt strangely calm, having made my decision to go to Stillmeadows, and I would not allow any doubts to invade my thoughts now.

Almost without conscious thought I began to write my message to the man I'd once loved, the man who'd been so much on my mind of late.

David:

After you left today I thought for a long while about what you asked. I realized that I've never before refused help to anyone. And my conscience will not let me refuse your wife. If you still want me to come, I will, doing whatever I can to help her. I hope you understand that at this point our attempts might be futile. With your permission I would like to bring Monteen, our best therapist, and Mary, one of our housemaids. I understand Mary's cousin Jess is in your employ. If you are still agreeable that I should come, I will arrive day after tomorrow. We shall require no special accommodations.

Julia

I was just finishing the note when Harry appeared at the door.

"You needed to see me?" he asked, taking his cap off as he entered the room.

"Harry, would you mind driving out to Still-meadows as soon as the rain lets up? I'd like you to deliver a message to Mr. David Damron." I sealed the envelope and handed it to the tall, slender man before me.

Harry watched solemnly, his face blank and unreadable as he waited for further instructions. His pale blue eyes were as noncommittal as ever. I knew him not one whit better today than when I first opened the spa. He was one of the employees who stayed on at the El Dorado when I came. And I felt a sudden twinge of shame that I had made no attempts to know him better.

"Yes, ma'am, be glad to," he replied. Harry was never one to waste words, or to spend unnecessary time asking questions. It did not seem to matter what was requested of him; he was always quietly willing to accommodate me. Others might have found that quality in him unmanly, but it was one I appreciated.

"You will probably need to wait for a reply."

"Yes'm," he said, turning to go and placing his cap back atop his graying sandy-colored hair.

"Oh and Harry, if you see Monteen on your way out, would you tell her I'd like to see her as well?"

I watched with amusement as his fair complexion turned a rosy pink, for I knew he would make a special effort to see her. He was intrigued by the dark, fiery Creole; I had noticed that much about him. And I was sure he'd never once said anything to let her know it. Still it amazed me that a man in his middle age was so timid where women were concerned. It had never entered my mind until then to wonder if he'd ever been married. I watched as he moved his lanky frame through the door and out of sight.

53

When Monteen came in a little later, I was already making a list of the things to be done before we left, not the least of which was finding someone to manage the El Dorado while I was away.

Monteen's face was expressive and I could see she was trying to be patient, even though she was dying of curiosity.

I smiled at her and leaned back in my chair.

"I've decided to go to Stillmeadows. And I would like you to go with me."

Her dark eyes grew large and curious. "Of course, *chère,* if that is what you wish. But are you sure this is what you want? It seems you've changed your mind quite hurriedly since this afternoon."

"It isn't as if it's a lifelong commitment, Monteen. And no, I'm not that certain it's what I should really do. But I suppose it's the way I've always done things . . . quick decisions . . . instinct, whatever you want to call it. I just felt it was the right thing to do and if it doesn't work out, then we'll come home." My voice sounded much more bright and self-assured than I felt.

"All right," she answered quietly . . . too quietly. "When do we leave?"

"Day after tomorrow, if David agrees. And Mary will also be going with us. I think it will be good for her. She will have a chance to visit with her cousin and I'd like her to see what goes on inside a great country estate like the Damron home. Who knows, one day I might build a home in the country and I shall need someone like Mary to see to the running of it."

Monteen nodded but did not reply.

"Monteen, what's wrong?" I felt a touch of irritation. But I'd found that with my Creole friend directness was the best way of finding out what bothered her.

She looked up at me from where her eyes had been studying her hands in her lap. The look she gave me was innocent, one I knew well. I crossed my arms and waited, raising my brows with impatience.

"Julia, I don't want to frighten you, or even influence your decision. I'm almost afraid to say anything . . ."

"But . . . ?"

"I have a very bad feeling about this. Have had since you left this afternoon. Then, this storm came up, almost like some terrible omen. I don't know . . . I can't explain it."

"You, my friend, are too superstitious. And you're also a worrier. You need children so you might worry with legitimacy." I tried to tease away the worried look in her eyes. But it didn't work.

She did manage to smile weakly. "I know you're probably right. Besides, you're the one with second sight, so if anything were wrong, you would sense it . . . wouldn't you?"

"Monteen . . ."

"All right. All right," she said, raising her hands in protest. "I will say no more about it. If you think it is what we should do, then that is good enough."

"I think I should try and help," I assured her. "So don't worry. It was probably only the storm that made you jittery . . . you know how you hate them."

"Well . . . perhaps you're right," she answered.

"So," I said, hoping to change the subject, "I need a manager for this place while we're away. What's your opinion of Harry?"

"Harry?" she asked, looking puzzled. "My opinion? I suppose it's something I had not given much thought to." She pursed her lips into a thoughtful moue.

"You know he's madly infatuated with you?" I said.

"Harry? Infatuated with me? Why, he hardly speaks to me . . . or even looks at me for that matter." Her dark eyes were wide and disbelieving.

"He's only a bit shy I think," I said.

She put her hands at her small waist and looked thoughtfully into the distance. "Infatuated?" Then with a lift of her brow, she grinned broadly. "Why Harry, you sly devil you."

"Monteen!" I scolded. "If you dare go and embarrass that sweet man, I'll never tell you another thing!"

She laughed, but I could see she was obviously pleased at hearing of Harry's attraction to her.

"I would not dare," she said, the broad grin now only a smile. Still her eyes twinkled with pleasure. "Harry is a fine man . . . the kind of man I should have pursued rather than Rafe . . . my dashing riverboat man." Her eyes grew distant at the mention of her lost love and I knew she still missed him.

"Being quiet and settled is not necessarily a bad thing," I said.

She turned to me and smiled rather wistfully. "No, it is not. It certainly is not a bad thing at all." Then her eyes twinkled again. "And who knows . . . our Harry might not be so shy in the dark seclusion of a bedroom."

"Monteen!" I said, pretending to be scandalized. But I could not keep from laughing heartily with her.

She continued to preen and pose, swinging her hips about until I was laughing hysterically and holding my aching sides.

"Oh stop it, please," I said, wiping my watering eyes. "I'm completely serious about this. Harry knows everything about this place and we probably won't be gone longer than a few weeks at the most. What do you think?"

Finally she stopped her outrageous act and turned her head thoughtfully. "I think it is a splendid idea. Harry will handle it very well, just as he does everything else around here."

"Good," I said. "I'm glad you agree. He's gone now to deliver my message to David. So I should know shortly if we are still wanted."

"Ah, but *chère,* I'm sure you shall still be wanted." Her voice insinuated something entirely different than what I meant. Partly the mood of the moment, I surmised.

Still, I grimaced at her, unable to laugh about this particular subject. "This will be a professional visit, Monteen. David is happily married now and even if there were anything left between us, I certainly have too much respect for his wife and his marriage to ever consider such a relationship."

"It is good to see that the thoughts troubling you earlier today have vanished." She looked at me as if she knew that statement was untrue.

When I did not answer her, she smiled and rose to leave me. "As you say, there is much to do, so I think I will begin. I will see you at dinner?"

"Yes," I replied with distraction.

After she left I leaned back in the chair and stared unseeingly out the windows. I was aware of the rain that continued to fall heavily, but my mind was a blank and I felt strangely relaxed after our interlude of laughter. I sat for a long while until the room grew dark. The atmosphere was muggy and storm filled. An angry flash of light nearby lit the shadowy room and drew me back with a start to reality.

Through the din of the storm I heard the muffled clang of the dinner bell. I realized I was hungry. In fact I couldn't recall the last time I'd eaten. And it seemed days since Monteen had read my future in her tarot cards. But in reality it had only been a few emotion-filled hours.

The dining room was already filled when I arrived. This was always a pleasant time of day at the El Dorado. At dinner our guests and those who assisted them during bath hours met on equal terms. Together we enjoyed the good feeling of rest and food after a day of hard work.

I spoke to many as I made my way through the islands of linen-covered tables to the front of the room. Monteen was seated at our regular table where we rotated guests each night until I'd had a chance to become acquainted with each person at the hotel.

As night fell the storm could be heard raging on above the big sturdy building. But unlike Monteen, I did not find it frightening. If anything it made the gathering feel even more cozy and intimate than usual.

I decided I would not make the announcement of my departure, lest it seem out of the ordinary. Instead I would let Harry handle it after we'd left, in whatever manner he chose.

When the dessert dishes had been cleared, most of the guests made their way into the parlor or out onto the porch to watch the last flicker of the dying storm. But I was exhausted and had not even changed out of my rain-dampened skirt and blouse, so I chose to go directly to my room.

The stairs and hallway seemed unusually dark as I hurried to the sanctuary of my quarters. I even began to unbutton my blouse just outside my doorway. But something stopped me suddenly and I felt my heart begin to beat furiously against my ribs.

There was someone there; I could feel a presence even before the smell of smoke drifted through the open door into the hall. In the dim flicker of light, I saw the outline of a man standing before my windows. I could not make out his face, but the glowing tip of a cheroot shone eerily across his features.

"Who are you?" I asked, my voice echoing in the hallway.

The man did not answer, but leaned toward a table to turn up the wick in the hurricane lamp.

"David!" I gasped. "You should not be here . . . in my room." I walked into the room, leaving the door behind me open.

His cool eyes moved to the front of my blouse, where I'd unfastened the top buttons. Then he smiled, his eyes mocking me. "Oh, come now, Julia. We're both adults, beyond such false modesties surely."

"What do you want?" I asked nervously. I found myself unsure of how to stand, or of what to say to this man who was now practically a stranger to me.

He saw my edginess and he laughed. The sound was quiet and familiar in the closeness of the room.

"Only to thank you," he said. He placed the cheroot back in his mouth and his teeth gleamed whitely in the darkness of the room.

"There was no need . . ."

"And to tell you how beautiful you've grown. Even more beautiful than before . . . if that is possible." His voice was low and soft as he gazed at me over the lamp.

My breath caught in my throat at his look and his words so I could not speak.

He made a small sound, almost of laughter. "Besides, I enjoy riding through the wild fury of a storm. It makes me feel strangely alive."

"Yes . . . I remember," I said without thinking, the intimate words betraying me.

"Do you?" he asked softly.

I noticed his hair, which looked almost black with the wetness of the rain glistening on it. I wondered again if he rode to banish some anger or frustration. It was the same thing I had wondered when I watched his wild abandoned ride down the mountain earlier. I met his dark, hooded gaze and wanted with all my heart to ask what was wrong . . . what was it that caused that troubled look in his eyes? But I knew I dared not.

"Then there is no problem?" I asked instead. "No reason why we cannot come to Stillmeadows as planned?" I looked away from his searching eyes.

"No. No reason. I have made arrangements so that everything will be prepared for you and your two companions."

He was not, it seemed, going to mention our earlier bitter conversation, and neither would I. Perhaps this was even his way of trying to put all that aside. And no matter how curious I was about his treatment of me so long ago, I thought it was best if we began our relationship anew. We were more strangers now than friends.

"I'm looking forward to meeting your wife," I said stiffly.

His eyes narrowed as he gazed at me, almost as if I'd issued some challenge. Then his mouth curled into a crooked smile and he bowed, a slight, rather formal movement.

"Yes," he said. "As I'm sure she is you." The mockery I'd seen before was hidden as he quietly moved toward the door.

"David," I said, halting his steps.

"Yes?" He turned to meet my question. His eyes met mine with a dark, inscrutable hardness, a coolness that had not been there before. He let his gaze wander quickly over my face, focusing for only an instant upon my lips.

"Is anything wrong? Anything else you wanted to tell me?"

He smiled and his eyelids closed for a moment, shutting off his eyes from my view.

"No . . . nothing," he murmured. "Now that you've agreed to come to Stillmeadows, everything is fine indeed." He met my look then and once again his eyes were cool and mysterious. Whatever emotion I'd glimpsed only a moment ago was now gone, hidden so expertly that I thought he'd somehow schooled himself to do it.

"Good night, Julia," he said.

I walked to the door and watched his tall, masculine form move gracefully into the shadows and down the stairway. He did not turn again to glance back at me and I quietly closed and bolted my door.

I found that my legs were trembling as I sank slowly into a chair near the bowed window. Impulsively I leaned forward and raised the window a few inches, stretching my hand out to catch the lightly falling rain. I drew my arm back in and splashed the sweet-scented water upon my warm face.

I sat there that night for the longest time until the rain-dampened wind wet the curtains and finally caused me to shiver. Still I could not make myself move. I stared at nothing, seeing not my room, but the vision of the man who'd just been there, crowding my room with his disturbing presence. I closed my eyes and breathed in the lingering spicy smell of his tobacco as if I could make him reappear.

Soon the house around me grew silent and the streets outside as well. And I felt entirely alone with the sound of the rain falling gently on the leaves and upon the windowpanes. Still his face, his eyes, would not leave me, and neither would my doubts.

But now, more than ever, I wanted to go to Stillmeadows. And not only to help Allyson Damron. Now I felt a compulsion to find the reason for the pain I'd briefly glimpsed in his gray-green eyes and to learn what had changed him so much since that summer long ago.

Chapter Five

It continued to rain off and on until the morning we left. Mary could hardly contain her excitement, as if she were embarking on some great adventure instead of just going over into the next valley. Even Monteen was unusually happy and cheerful once she became reconciled to the fact that she could not keep me from going.

We all laughed and chatted as we drove away from town and toward the pine-scented mountain.

I drove the little yellow carriage while Mary and Monteen, seated beside me, kept up a constant exuberant chatter. And I laughed right along with them.

The rain had brought a coolness to the air, even though the sun was shining brightly down on us. We crossed the mountain and made our way down the other side toward the valley where Stillmeadows lay.

A while later we reached the turn in the road where the long drive began onto the Damron estate. The house was still more than a mile away, but we began to catch glimpses of it as we drove along the curving road. Its white exterior moved in and out of our vision through the regal old trees that lifted their branches high in the air. The entire estate was as beautiful and majestic as I remembered. Moving through the trees and well-kept grounds where the air was filled with birdsong and a gentle breeze always made me feel as if I were entering a magic kingdom.

As we reached the bottom edge of the long sloping lawn, I pulled the carriage to a halt. I wanted a chance to study the house before anyone became aware we were there. The women beside me did not question my actions or seem surprised. They were as intent as I was, it seemed, on studying the magnificent house and acreage that lay before us.

Stillmeadows was not a large house, at least by the grand Boston scale to which the Damrons were now accustomed. Over the years there had been additions made symmetrically to each side of the original structure. It stood quiet and stately with its white exterior gleaming in the morning sunlight. The large trees that lined the road and dotted the grounds, as well as the towering lilacs and azaleas about the gracefully landscaped yard, made it obvious the house had stood here for many years.

The wide expanse of lawn that led from where we sat up the sloping hillside was green and well tended. Away to my left and behind us was the lovely meadow for which the house was named. It was surrounded by dark, dense forest and far beyond that the steep rise of the mountains which encompassed the entire valley.

"Très magnifique," Monteen whispered as I urged the mare onto the short circular drive leading directly to the house.

We stopped near an arching walkway that led to the front. The house towered above us cool and serene in the sunlight. It was constructed of brick, painted a brilliant white, its two stories elaborately trimmed just beneath the rooftop and again about midway of the house. Dark green shutters hung on each side of long-paned windows. A two-storied portico stood at the center front of the main structure with double columns at the end of each level. Curving handrailed steps led down both sides of the lower portico to the walkway.

We were met immediately by servants, some of whom carried our trunks inside, while an older gray-haired woman escorted us into the house.

"I'm Mrs. Woolridge, the housekeeper," she said curtly. Her eyes, a pale, flat blue, looked at us with little interest.

"It's me you'll be needin' to ask for anything you might want while you're here. Mrs. Damron need not be disturbed."

"Yes, of course," I told her.

Her eyes turned to Mary, who stood nervously twisting her fingers together. "This be your servant girl?" Mrs. Woolridge asked.

Something in her imperious manner irritated me, especially where it concerned Mary. And I suppose I spoke more quickly than I normally would.

"Mary *works* for me, Mrs. Woolridge, but she has come here in the capacity of a friend as well. I trust you will make her stay as pleasant as ours."

Mary looked at me imploringly, for I knew she did not wish to cause trouble. But I would not stand by and let this rude woman treat her with such cold disdain.

The woman's lips twisted into a thin straight line as she looked away from my gaze.

"Certainly, Mrs. Van Cleef," she answered. "As you wish."

I knew that Mrs. Woolridge and her husband had acted as caretakers here for the past few years. I suppose it was possible that they would begin to think of the house as their own since the family had been away so long. Perhaps that accounted for her curt manner and the look of resentment I saw on her unsmiling face.

Mrs. Woolridge summoned two of the house servants. Mary followed them upstairs to find our rooms and see to our trunks while Monteen and I were shown into a small parlor to the left of the

65

wide entryway.

The house was the same; nothing had seemed to change. I was surprised to find that I'd forgotten the familiar scent of roses and lavender until now. For it was so much a part of my memories of this house, one I'd thought never to forget.

The stern-faced housekeeper silently poured each of us a cup of coffee. "Mrs. Damron will be with you shortly," she said, leaving us there in the parlor alone. Again I was confused, unsure if it was Millicent Damron or David's mother Grace who would be greeting us. But I had to admit the prospect of seeing either of the women did not fill me with great enthusiasm.

The small, cozy parlor, a room of striking contrasts, felt pleasantly familiar. Deep jade-green walls were complemented by a white carved mantel and fireplace at the end of the room. Built-in sideboards, also the unusual Chinese green color, had white marble tops. These pieces extended from each side of the fireplace to the opposite walls.

A silver tray and coffee service sat on the small round oak table before the now cold and empty fireplace. Monteen and I sat in two English Regency armchairs which were upholstered in a rich mandarin-red brocade. Overall it was a warm, inviting room, seemingly appointed for the comfort of its occupants.

I realized, more now than when I was younger, that Mrs. Damron had a certain flair for providing just the proper atmosphere throughout her home. I did not like the woman, had deeply resented her in fact. And I found it odd that the cold, undemonstrative woman I remembered would be inclined to want her guests to feel at ease in her home.

"This is a beautiful old house," Monteen murmured as we waited.

"Yes," I said. "It seems exactly as it was when I was here before."

"Ah, but *you* have changed, and perhaps that will make a difference in how you are welcomed this time." She had almost read my thoughts.

We heard voices outside the parlor and I immediately recognized one of them as Grace Damron's. This would be the first time I'd seen her since my father sent me away to school. I hoped David had already told her who Julia Van Cleef actually was. Nervously I took a sip of the strong, black coffee just as the woman entered the parlor.

She came forward energetically, her gray eyes scanning us briefly. I placed the delicate cup and saucer on the table and rose to greet her.

"It's nice to see you again, Mrs. Damron." I extended my hand to the tall slender woman. I had deliberately chosen my words so that we could get our earlier acquaintance out in the open right away.

Grace Damron stopped immediately and her gray eyes, so keen and piercing, appraised me sharply. She did not recognize me and that fact seemed to startle the usually cool, insouciant woman. She took my hand nonetheless as she gazed with a puzzled frown into my face.

"Have we met, Mrs. Van Cleef?"

"It was a long time ago; I worked here one summer. My name was Julia Crownwell then." I was aware that Monteen practically held her breath beside me.

Mrs. Damron's face turned pale and she took a small step back, removing her hand from mine as if she'd been scorched.

"Why, I . . . I did not realize. You are . . . Julia Van Cleef, the owner of the El Dorado?" Her expression was one of incredulous disbelief. Then she forced a tight smile upon her lips and reached for the silver coffee server as she took a seat. She composed herself quickly and almost succeeded in appearing unperturbed by the discovery of whom she had invited to her home.

"Well, please . . . sit down," she said.

She sipped her coffee, smiling at Monteen and me before she spoke. But I had a feeling this was only a delaying tactic so that she might compose herself further. She was always a woman of great outward control, at least in my eyes.

"This is Monteen Valognes, our best therapist at the spa and also a dear friend of mine."

Grace Damron smiled and nodded graciously toward Monteen. I thought proudly that my Creole friend looked exceptionally beautiful today in her silk gown of pistache green with her ebony hair pulled back into a wealth of curls.

Mrs. Damron's eyes did not linger however on Monteen, but came back to rest upon me. I could see the puzzled confusion in her look, but the resentment I had expected was not visible.

"My son failed to mentioned that it was you," she said quietly.

"David did not know when he came to see me," I told her. I glanced at Monteen, who smiled encouragingly at me and quirked one eyebrow as she silently sipped her coffee.

"Oh, I see," she said. "And of course Millicent had never met you."

"No," I replied.

"Well . . . none of that matters. What is important is that you're here to help poor Allyson and we're all very grateful for that."

"We shall do our best, although as I warned David, it's possible that our efforts will make no difference at all."

"I understand. But we had heard so much about you and your work that we were certain if you agreed to try, there was a great possibility for her improvement."

"We certainly will do our best," I assured her. "Will we meet Allyson today . . . is she bedridden? There are so many questions I'd like to ask about her."

68

"I'm sure David will tell you everything you need to know. I myself have not spent that much time with my daughter-in-law since her accident. David, and Allyson's sister Anna, have tended to her needs. My son has been very strong through all of this though I must say."

"Please, Mother, no flattery behind my back." David's voice as he entered the parlor was deep and filled with fond amusement as he chided his mother.

I could feel the tension grip my body as he approached us so unexpectedly. As usual, he had the power to startle me with his confident stride and air of self-assurance.

There was an immediate spark of affection in Grace Damron's eyes as she rose to embrace her tall, handsome son. As I watched them I noted that she herself was still a very attractive and youthful-looking woman. There were no signs of gray in her auburn hair which she wore in a smooth upswept style. And her slender figure was tall and erect; she was only a few inches shorter than David's six-foot stature.

David's eyes swept to me, his look warm and friendly. There was no hint of the mockery I'd seen when I found him waiting for me in my room. It was hard to believe they were the same eyes that had blazed at me with such fury only a few days ago when I'd first refused to come. I smiled and turned to Monteen, who sat watching both of us with great interest.

"David, this is Monteen Valognes, whom I spoke of in my note." I swept my hand toward the dark woman seated near me.

David stepped forward gracefully. "Miss Valognes," he murmured smoothly. As he bent, his eyes met hers on an equal level and continued to gaze into hers as he placed a kiss upon her hand. Monteen's black eyes grew languid and a provocative light reflected briefly in their depths.

David smiled, today seeming full of all the charm of his youth and as self-confident as ever of his attraction

69

to women. I could not resist smiling myself, for I'd never seen Monteen so quickly captivated by any man.

"Would you like to join us for coffee, dear?" Mrs. Damron asked. "Mrs. Van Cleef . . . Julia was just asking about Allyson."

"I'm afraid I haven't time for coffee. I was just going to the stables to see to one of the carriage horses. Jess tells me it seemed a bit lame. But we'll have time later . . . perhaps at dinner?" He turned to me as he spoke. He was very polite and pointedly casual.

"Yes, that will be fine," I said. "It will give me time to get settled in."

After David left there did not seem to be much else to say. So Mrs. Damron rose as if to dismiss us.

"I'm sure you'd both like to see your rooms and become better acquainted with the house before lunch. Make yourselves at home, wander about all you wish. Do you remember where everything is, Julia?" I could hardly believe her solicitous attitude.

I assured her I did and after telling us where we'd find our room she bustled off again to attend to some household duty while Monteen and I went upstairs. As Mrs. Damron had directed we turned left at the top of the stairs and went into one of the newly added wings.

I could feel the intensity in Monteen as she walked beside me, although she said nothing until we were in the privacy of my room, which lay at the end of the long hallway.

"*Mon dieu,* Julia!" she exclaimed as soon as we were inside. "I thought I should die from the sheer excitement of that man's touch! He is . . . oh so handsome, so manly and . . ."

"Monteen, calm yourself," I laughed. "I've never seen you behave so irrationally."

"Well, it has been a long time since I have met such a man!" she insisted, her eyes wide with excitement. "How you can resist him I will never understand. And the way he looked at you . . ."

70

"Monteen," I warned, turning from her eager eyes that threatened to see just how very much his presence had disturbed me.

"Oh, *chère,* I'm sorry. Forgive me for behaving like an empty-headed fool. I understand that a woman cannot carry on a silly, meaningless flirtation when her heart is so seriously involved. Certainly not a woman like you."

"And who says my heart is . . . seriously involved?" I asked, walking to the window that faced the front of the house.

"I do," she said quietly.

I turned to her and smiled, but suddenly I was not so sure I should have come. I had underestimated the effect David would have on me here in the supremacy of his own home.

"Well," she murmured, "I will leave you alone to unpack. Shall I send Mary in to help you?"

"No, no, I will do it. But if you don't mind, please check on her to see if she's all right. I hope Mrs. Woolridge won't be uncivil to her."

"Yes, I will," she said. "I believe my room is just next door. I will see you in a little while and we shall go to lunch together."

"Yes," I answered. But I was already unpacking my clothes and my mind hardly registered what she was saying.

"Julia," she said, turning at the doorway. "If anything happens here we do not have to stay. I mean if anything disturbs you . . . you will tell me, won't you?"

I looked up and caught the worried look in her dark eyes. "Of course I will, Monteen. But why would you say such a thing?"

"It's probably nothing. You just seem so distracted and sad . . . so unlike yourself before David came. Is it the house or . . . ?"

"It's nothing, Monteen, really. I will be fine. We'll be here a few days and then it shall all be behind us. I don't

71

want you to spend all of our time worrying about me. It's a beautiful estate . . . we must try and enjoy it as much as we can."

She looked skeptical, but did not protest further. "All right. I'll see you in a little while."

After she closed the door I sank down on the bed, running my hand across the soft deep-rose coverlet. This room, like all the others here, was elegantly appointed with everything that a guest would find comfortable. It was spacious and bright with its rose-and-green decor. At one end of the room was a fireplace with a delicately carved, cream-colored mantelpiece and a tiled hearth painted with flowers. A small feminine rose damask chair sat near the fireplace and beside it was a rosewood tea table. On the other side was a small, colorfully painted Chinese screen which hid a copper bathtub and bathing accessories. The soft plush carpet was a deep green, splashed with touches of rose and cream. The curtains at the wide windows were of cream-colored Viennese lace.

I walked to the window and pushed aside the curtains. The view of the meadow and the mountains beyond was spectacular. I watched as the leaves of the huge old trees around the house trembled gently in the breeze. The wind seemed always to blow here as the mountain drafts were swept downward and across the wide meadows to the house. I recalled that spring and summer storms at Stillmeadows could sometimes be quite fierce.

I shivered and let the curtain fall back into place. I didn't understand why, here in the beautiful sunlit comfort of a gracious house, I should feel so cold and apprehensive. It was only a feeling, some hidden emotion I could not quite fathom. The same uneasy feeling I'd had the day Penny and I stood on the mountain above the valley and watched the dark cloud shadow move across this place.

If I could have done so graciously then I would have

left the house . . . and the man whose gray-green eyes so distracted me. I would have run down those stairs and out to my carriage to drive as fast as I could back to Hot Springs and the security of the El Dorado.

But as I had learned to do in the years previous to that, I pushed the disturbing feelings away, disregarding the intuition that warned of some underlying danger here in the outwardly tranquil house.

For I had already committed myself to helping Allyson Damron. And even if I did not know her I would not run away now like some frightened child.

So I went back to my unpacking, making my mind a blank and trying to banish the disturbing feelings that crept like ice through my veins and, it seemed, into my very soul.

Chapter Six

I put away most of my things and placed my cosmetics on a small cherry dressing table near the bed. I turned and looked into the mirror at my royal blue traveling suit with black lapels and narrow matching black ribbon trim at the sleeve and skirt bottom. I had grown warm while working so I turned to take off the short cropped jacket before going down to lunch.

My hands were shaking as I smoothed the white silk shirtfront into the high waistband of the blue skirt. I did not want to admit, even to myself, how very nervous I was about this first awkward meeting with David and his family. But I did want to look just right, neither too plain and businesslike, nor too feminine and frivolous.

My hair was pulled tightly back into a simple black chenille net. I gazed at myself for a few minutes, finally deciding to add a large gold-trimmed black onyx brooch to the neck of the blouse.

I stopped at Monteen's door, which she had left open. Our rooms were similar except for the colors, hers being of deep gold and cream, which I thought suited her very well.

She came out quickly and joined me and we made our way down the hall toward the stairway.

"Mary's already made friends with some of the girls

downstairs," Monteen told me. "I met her cousin Jess, a very nice, pleasant boy."

"Good," I said. "I think this will be good for her and I'm sure she'll learn a great deal."

"Well, she certainly seems happy to be here."

As we reached the bottom of the stairs Monteen took a deep breath. "Are you ready for this?" she asked, in a light, bantering tone.

"We shall see," I whispered tensely. "This will be the first time I've dined in the elegant dining room. We servant girls were required to always eat in the kitchen." I smiled, trying to joke.

"But you are no longer a young and naive servant girl, *chère*. You are the very elegant and sophisticated Julia Van Cleef. You will do well." She smiled into my eyes with encouragement. And I could not help feeling somewhat better, momentarily at least.

The small family dining room was just off the wide entry hall, across from the little parlor where we'd had coffee. I had seen the long gleaming mahogany table through the arched doorway as we came down the stairs.

Grace Damron was there, along with Millicent and the man I'd seen her with in front of the El Dorado. They seemed to be arguing quietly as we entered the room. But James, upon seeing us, immediately drew himself up to attention. His gray eyes, much like his mother's, grew wide with surprise as he looked directly at me. And I thought I also saw a spark of admiration in his look and the curve of his lips as he approached us.

His mother frowned at him, but quickly made the introductions as James politely took my hand and then Monteen's. But I was far too preoccupied to notice what else might have transpired in their looks. For I was only aware that David was not yet in the room.

"I must apologize for my oldest son's absence. When he deals with horses, he sometimes loses all track of time. I've sent one of the servants to remind him."

We seated ourselves and the servants brought in trays of food, placing them on the long mirrored mahogany sideboard. The table, as well as other pieces of furniture, glittered with the shine of finely polished silver and brilliantly faceted crystal. Regal white brocade curtains hung graceful and cool at the long windows and an elaborately curved chandelier hung above the middle of the table.

Just as one of the maids began to serve from the silver dishes, David came into the room. Immediately a spark of interest and awareness seemed to fill the air as everyone's attention focused on him.

He walked unhurriedly, seemingly unconscious that he was late. He looked fit and healthy; his tanned face was burnished as if he'd spent the morning in the sun. The air stirred as he passed, bringing with it the scents of leather and pine. He carelessly tossed his short riding crop upon the sideboard as he passed. He wore buff-colored riding breeches which clung to his muscular thighs, and a full billowing black shirt opened casually at his tanned throat.

"Sorry I'm late," he said. But the look on his face was detached, belying his quietly spoken words. He poured himself a glass of wine from a crystal decanter on the sideboard before taking his place at the head of the table.

As if realizing he was the focus of all our attention, he looked up, and a glimmer of amusement and surprise moved across his handsome features.

"Please," he said wryly with a lift of his brows, "continue with your conversation."

"The animal you were tending must have been in dire need," James mused. He reached forward to take several small sandwiches from one of the trays. "To have kept you so long."

"Animal . . . ?" David looked confused, then he laughed. "Oh, that wasn't what delayed me. The morning was so pleasant I could not resist a short ride."

77

His quick glance scanned mine briefly and I felt an immediate blush upon my face. How many times we had gone riding . . . sometimes separately so that no one would suspect we were meeting somewhere.

Grace Damron smiled at him sweetly, as one would at a favorite child. I was a bit surprised by her look, for she had not seemed so tender those many years ago. "You've always loved riding. I'm happy you are able to enjoy it again, at least while we're still at Stillmeadows."

David had not begun to eat, but instead sipped casually from the crystal fluted wine glass. "So am I. It makes me wonder why I ever left here . . . indeed if I ever shall again."

James looked quickly at him. "Surely you can't mean that. Your law practice is one of the most successful in Boston."

But Millicent Damron smiled knowingly and did not seem the least surprised by his statement. "Allyson would certainly not be pleased to hear you say such a thing, David. You know how she detests the country. And she detests horses even more! Sometimes I wonder whatever it was the two of you found in common."

David smiled at her, a bit mysteriously I thought, but his eyes narrowed as if her remarks irritated him.

Millicent saw his look and laughed mischievously. Her beautiful violet eyes glittered like shards of purple glass. She was enjoying the bantering between them, it was obvious, and it did not seem to matter that it made everyone else at the table uncomfortable.

"Oh, David . . . you must be getting old," she teased. "It's so very easy to make you angry these days."

David did not laugh, but continued to stare at her coolly at her as if unconcerned.

"Millicent," James warned.

"Oh, don't use that tone of voice with me, Jimmy," she snapped. "You're all much too serious. Why can't we just have a little fun once in a while?"

78

Monteen, who was seated beside me, glanced at me and rolled her eyes pointedly. It was obvious that she felt, as I did, that we'd entered into a house filled with family secrets. And neither of us really wanted to hear about them in this manner.

"Children," Mrs. Damron scolded. "What must our guests think?" Her voice was deceptively quiet, but full of authority as she glanced at Millicent. There was no misunderstanding that she meant to have peace at her table.

Millicent grimaced and twisted her mouth, much as a scolded child would do. I suspected if I dared to look underneath the table I might also see her kicking her feet in anger.

Jame tried to steer the conversation into another direction. I was beginning to see that he was the peacemaker here.

"I understand you and David knew each other previously, Mrs. Van Cleef," he said politely.

I could not help feeling sorry for him in his efforts and I smiled at him. He seemed sweet and vulnerable and it was hard to imagine that he would choose such a petulant, plainspoken woman as Millicent for a wife. In any case I found him entirely different from David.

"Yes, we did," I said. I was so disconcerted by his words and the way everyone was watching me that I could hardly eat.

"Why, darling," Millicent cooed at her husband. "Have you not heard? Mrs. Van Cleef was once a servant girl here at Stillmeadows. Isn't that right, Mrs. Van Cleef?"

She looked at me with a challenge in her beautiful eyes and I knew she was seeking revenge for that day in my office when I had rejected her. I felt my face stiffen, even thought I tried to retain a smile. My eyes stung as I met her stare with one of my own.

"Yes, I was," I replied, directing my remarks to James. "I believe you were away at school that

79

summer. I worked in the bathing rooms whenever guests were here. And the rest of the time I did whatever chore needed doing. It was an experience I have never forgotten."

"Oh, I'll wager that's correct," Millicent laughed. Her eyes widened and she smiled like a sleek self-satisfied cat. She certainly seemed to thrive on stirring up controversy, something I should keep in mind in the future.

I took a sip from my wine glass and glanced over the rim to meet David's hazel gaze. But he looked away before I could read whatever lay in the misty depths of his eyes. Millicent's remark did not seem to disturb him as it did me.

"Julia was a very young girl then and I think we must all agree she has become a beautiful and poised young woman. We are all very proud of her. I, for one, am very gratified she has so graciously consented to return to us for a while." Grace Damron's compliment surprised me more than anything could have. Unconsciously I glanced quickly at her, wondering if the words were sincere. Her quiet, almost apologetic gaze indicated they were and that puzzled me even more. For she'd always treated me quite shabbily before, especially when she realized that her son was spending so much time with a mere servant.

"I certainly agree," James added gallantly, his voice low as he raised his glass to me. There was a warm, almost provocative look in his light-colored eyes and when my glance went to Millicent, she seemed to be paying no attention at all to his flirtatiousness.

"Well I, for one, intend to take a nap. It's too hot to do anything else this afternoon," she said, rising from the table.

I felt such relief, being finished with the ordeal, that I breathed a deep sigh and rose also.

"Why, my girl," Mrs. Damon said to me. "You've hardly touched your meal. Was it not to your liking?"

"Oh, it was delicious," I said self-consciously. "I'm sorry. I guess I wasn't very hungry."

"Julia, if you'd like we can go now and let you meet Allyson." It was David who spoke as he still sat nonchalantly at his place, watching us steadily.

"Yes," I replied, happy to be away from Mrs. Damron's questioning eyes. "I'd like that." Turning to Monteen I asked, "Will you join us?"

"No, I . . . I told Mary we would prepare our herbs and lotions for tomorrow. And I'd also like to have a look at the bath area." But I did not miss the look she threw over her shoulder as she left: one of warning, I thought.

David had walked to me and indicated with a motion that I should go toward the back of the house from the dining room. Allyson's room, he pointed out, was on the ground floor, near the hot-springs room. And as I discovered, it was at the very rear of the house, close to the large French doors that led into the gardens.

I was surprised, when David opened the door, to be greeted by a dim, shadowy room, much different from the rest of the beautiful house. I glanced up at him and saw a look of irritation cross his face.

"Wait here," he told me.

Briskly he walked into the darkened interior. Loud clatters echoed in the room as he threw open wooden shutters one by one, until the room was awash with sunlight. I heard, rather than saw, him raise the windows, for my attention was captured by the woman who reclined upon the bed before me.

She seemed afraid, almost cowering, as David angrily went about setting the room in order as he thought it should be.

"My God, Allyson!" he said. "How do you stand it in here? It must be a hundred degrees! I've told you to leave the windows open. Must I have someone assigned especially to you . . . one you won't manipulate to suit your own needs?"

I was stunned. He was ranting at a totally helpless, bedridden woman. I'd never seen him this way.

But the woman did not answer; instead she looked at him with great pleading brown eyes as she watched him move about the room like an angry lion.

"I'm sorry, darling," her voice whispered weakly. "No one came to do that this morning. I'm sure they must only have forgotten. Please . . . don't be angry."

"I'm not angry," he said quietly. "Where is Anna?"

"I don't know where my sister is," she said, shrugging her shoulders.

I blinked in confusion. How could she be so docile, so patient and kind with him after the way he had berated her? I glared at David, hoping he would see how horrible I thought he'd been, but her quiet words had already hit their mark. And it seemed to leave him even more frustrated than before. But he fell silent.

"I've brought Julia Van Cleef, the lady I told you about earlier," he said, his voice now quiet and calm.

I stepped further into the sweltering room and found with surprise that the heated scent of roses surrounded me. There were vases of roses everywhere, on every piece of furniture. And all of the blossoms were white.

Allyson smiled at me as I stepped closer. She was not a conventionally pretty woman. But she had a certain sweet, wholesome attraction. Her hair, which was light brown, was cut in a short, curly style which framed her face interestingly. I guessed it would probably be easier to care for this way. A plain, wide mouth and short upturned nose kept her from being pretty, but her dark, expressive eyes with their lovely winged brows were truly extraordinary.

I felt drawn to her right away and I could see she felt the same toward me. How strange it seemed. It was certainly not something I had expected to feel toward David's wife.

"So, you have come to help me," she said shyly.

"I hope that I am able to do that," I said. "Certainly I

82

will try."

"I'm so happy you're here." Her voice was excited and happy. "It will be so good to have someone to talk with." Then seeming to think about her remarks, she looked with apology at David. "A female that is . . . someone my own age."

David's lack of response could not disguise the twisted sneer on his lips. I frowned at him. Whatever was wrong with him that he would treat this poor girl in such a way?

Seeing my look he seemed a little bemused, as if he expected me to know why he acted as he did. Then he smiled wryly and turned to leave.

"I shall leave you two to become better acquainted," he said rather curtly.

After he'd gone, Allyson spoke softly, "Don't mind David. It's terribly frustrating for him, finding himself burdened with an invalid for a wife."

"Surely no harder than it is for you!" I said.

"Oh, I'm learning to accept what's happened," she said with a sigh. "I'm certain that's the best thing for all of us . . . my acceptance. And meaning no disrespect to you, Julia, but I only agreed to come here for the baths to please David. And I'm afraid he will be terribly disappointed."

The look of quiet surrender upon her features troubled me. And I vowed silently if there was *anything* I could do to make her better, I would do it.

"You are a very courageous and unselfish person," I told her.

"Oh, no," she replied. "Not at all. 'Tis easy to appear that way when you love someone as I do my husband."

She looked at me then oddly, straight into my eyes, and I thought for a moment she did not seem shy and innocent at all. But then the moment was gone. I wondered if she knew about David and me and our summer together. Somehow I hoped, for her sake, that she did not.

We talked for a while until she began to grow tired.

"I'll leave you now and let you rest," I told her. "Is there anything I can get for you . . . shall I send someone in to attend to you?"

"No, no. I'm perfectly fine. I'm sure my sister Anna will be along directly."

"All right then, if you're sure. I will see you tomorrow morning and we will begin to try and make you better."

"Oh," she whispered. "How truly wonderful that would be."

I left her room in a quandary, not knowing quite what to make of this place and the people who lived here. Even David, whom I thought I knew. And his wife was certainly nothing as I expected. I had not thought to reach such an instant rapport and sympathy with her. Somehow I could not imagine her and David together. He was so dynamic and full of life, while she seemed compliant, almost weak. But perhaps, I told myself, that was because she was ill. Or perhaps that was the kind of woman David wanted for a wife.

In any case I could hardly wait to see Monteen and tell her about the meeting with Allyson and the way David had behaved. I knew I could depend on her practical mind to sort through the maze of puzzling temperaments we'd found here among the Damron family.

I was beginning to see that the seemingly close and happy family was hardly that at all. And it was not something that had been present that summer, I was certain of it. There was an undercurrent of hostility now that was almost tangible. Why would that be so? This family of attractive, wealthy people seemed to have everything anyone could wish for. But something was missing and I found myself desperately curious to discover what that was.

Chapter Seven

As I walked back through the house to go upstairs I was struck again by the beauty of the house at Stillmeadows. Various doorways stood open allowing bright shafts of afternoon sunlight to radiate into the main hallway.

I went upstairs and directly to Monteen's room and rapped softly on the smooth wood door. She came quickly to the door and her dark eyes lit when she saw me.

"Come in. Mary's here. We were just wondering about the mysterious Mrs. Damron. Did you meet her?"

Mary smiled shyly at me as I came in. Monteen and I sat on a small, gold damask-covered sofa near the front windows. The sun through the curtains was warm upon my shoulders.

"Shall I bring tea?" Mary asked.

"There's no need for you to do that, Mary," I said. "Why don't you sit with us awhile and rest?"

"Oh, I don't mind at all," she insisted. "Everyone is so nice and I've been told I may come and go as I please and to help myself to anything in the kitchen." I could see how pleased she was by the Damrons' generosity. Evidently Mrs. Woolridge's first response toward Mary had given way to a more generous attitude.

"Let her go," Monteen said as she smiled at Mary. "I think our Mary has her eye on one of the cook's helpers."

"In that case I'd love to have some tea," I told the girl. "Oh and Mary, please tell Mrs. Damron that Monteen and I will have dinner tonight in our rooms."

Monteen said nothing, but looked at me curiously.

"Since we must be up early," I explained, not meeting her dark, questioning gaze.

"What's wrong?" she said quickly, after Mary had left.

"Nothing's wrong," I sighed in exasperation. I turned slightly to catch the view out the front window. The meadow was bathed in a haze of muted gold as the sun sank lower over the distant mountains.

"You're worried about something . . . and there's no need to pretend otherwise."

"What could I possibly be worried about in this beautiful place?" I said lightly, glancing out the windows.

"There's no denying the beauty here, the outward serenity," she said, rising from the sofa to pace back and forth. Her dark eyes were aglow as she turned to me. "But there's something wrong, Julia . . . I can feel it . . . like the stillness in the air before a spring storm. And don't tell me you don't sense it too."

I respected my friend too much to try and brush aside her fearful instincts. But I was not ready to admit that I felt the same thing.

"I agree there's much hidden here," I said. "Just as there is in any family. And I'm sure most of it is a private matter . . . certainly none of our business. We must make the best of the situation for the time we're here."

"It's much more than that, *chère,*" she said. "And I think you know it. But . . . since you obviously don't want to discuss it, I will not interfere." She sat down beside me again. "Now, tell me about the young Mrs.

Damron. What is she like? Did you hate her on sight?" she asked with great relish.

"On the contrary. I liked her very much."

"Well!" Monteen's eyebrows lifted and her face was full of surprise. But she was no more surprised than I that I should find myself saying such a thing.

"I did," I repeated. "I liked her. She is sad and sweet . . . and quite nice. But I just can't understand. . . ." My words trailed away as I recalled David's harshness with his wife. It was not like him. He surely could not have changed so much in ten years. Or did I know him as well as I thought I did?

"What? You don't understand what, Julia?" Monteen's voice broke into my thoughts.

"David," I said. "He was abrupt with her . . . hateful even and quite impatient. I could not believe he would treat her in such a way . . . a poor bedridden girl. And she was so tolerant of him, almost protectively so. It was as if he had a right to treat her in such a manner."

"But is that so strange?" she scoffed. "After all, many men treat their wives this way. It's their dominant nature. One of the reasons I never married, as a matter of fact."

"But not David. He was never like that . . . at least I didn't think so. I just don't know what to make of it . . . or of their relationship."

"Perhaps it's for the best, seeing him in this light. Perhaps you've simply romanticized this man so over the years that you've forgotten what he was truly like."

"No," I insisted. "I don't believe that's true."

She shrugged as if not knowing what else to say. But the look in her eyes disturbed me. It was something I had not seen before. There was almost a pity in her look. Clearly she wanted to believe me, but she thought I was only fooling myself where David Damron was concerned.

"I think I'll go to my room to rest a bit before dinner. Shall we eat here, or in my room?" I asked, anxious to

87

change the subject.

After agreeing we would dine in her room, I left. I needed to be alone for a while, to think about the treatment we had planned for Allyson—and to try and put away the disturbing thoughts I had about David's odd behavior.

Later, when I came back for dinner, we were careful to avoid the subject altogether. We talked instead of the procedures we would use in the baths the next morning.

We sat silently for a moment as we watched the impressive sunset behind the darkening mountains. The clouds lay motionless above the hills, the sunlight reflecting in their depths in shades of mauve and gold.

When we said good-night I had every intention of going to my room and to an early bed. But the evening was hot and sultry with no hint of a breeze to cool the August air. Almost intuitively I turned to go downstairs, thinking to go into the garden at the back of the house. I had always loved the gardens there, with their wide brick walkways and intricately placed perennials among the rosebushes.

The house was quiet as I walked along the wide hallway toward the back of the house. I especially wanted to avoid seeing any of the family and having to explain why I had chosen to miss dinner.

I noticed a faint light underneath the bedroom door of Allyson's room. I tiptoed quietly past and softly turned the brass handles of the double French doors which led directly outside and into the fragrant gardens.

There was still enough light from the dusk-filled sky to lighten the garden. The air was still and quiet. It was as beautiful and serene as ever. The large garden was well planned, with every available space filled with various flowers according to curvature of land and light.

The garden was bordered on all four sides. The long

sides running away from the house boasted tall, neatly trimmed hedges against stone walls. On the other side of the garden, directly across from where I stood, was the carriage house, gleaming brightly in the waning light. Beyond that I knew were the stables. And of course the great house behind me formed the fourth boundary. The overall picture was one of complete isolation for anyone sitting or walking in the garden area.

I stepped down the wide stone steps to the brick walkway, breathing deeply the warm evening air and the scent of earth and growing plants. Away from the shelter of the house there was a faint wind which moved upon my face and hair and brought with it the strong scent of roses.

As I walked past the rosebushes, their white blossoms gleamed in the shadowy dimness: the same white roses that filled Allyson's room with their warm, haunting fragrance.

Even though I knew I was secure in the walled garden I felt an odd tingle of apprehension along the base of my neck. I turned once back toward the house, but I saw no one. When I turned back to the pathway I stopped still, for there before me stood a man, tall and imposing in the gathering darkness.

My breath caught in my throat and I took a step backward. Then I saw the red tip of a cigar's glow, illuminating the face of the man who stood watching me.

"David?" I said weakly.

"What are you doing out here alone?" he asked, his words quiet and low.

"It was hot . . . I . . . I couldn't sleep. Is there any reason why I should not be here?" I asked.

The cigar glittered again in the darkness as its pungent, smoky aroma drifted toward me. He flicked the cigar into the moist dirt beneath the roses and stepped toward me.

"No," he said. "No reason. I'm surprised to find you here, that's all."

He stood uncomfortably near to me and I could see the dark slash of eyebrows above his hooded eyes, the white gleam of his teeth as he spoke. I even felt the warmth of his body, which seemed to reach toward me with the faint tantalizing aroma of his spicy shaving balm. Cautiously I stepped away from him.

The gleam of a smile crossed his face and he laughed softly. The sound angered me, unreasonably, I knew. But he was so smug, so sure that he knew my innermost thoughts and fears. So sure after all these years of the power he still held over me.

"I think I should go," I said.

He moved swiftly, grasping my arm in his hand and turning me back to face him. He pulled me so close I could feel the beating of his heart against my own chest.

"Do you think to avoid me the entire time you're here, Julia?" His words, whispered near my ear, were soft yet defiant. "How long are you going to run from me?" His voice became accusing, almost angrily so.

"Let me go, David," I said, twisting my arm in his hard grip. I was trembling as he pulled me closer, refusing to let me go. But I could not be sure if my shaking was from fright, or the result of being held within those strong arms after all the nights of wondering how it would feel.

Suddenly from the house there was a noise as if someone had closed a door. David's head went up and in that moment that his attention was drawn elsewhere I pulled away and hurried back along the walkway. He did not follow and I did not glance back at him.

I saw no one ahead of me even though I was sure it was the clatter of the French doors I'd heard. Once inside the house I paused for a moment, taking a deep breath to try and compose myself. I turned and looked back to the garden where I'd encountered David, but it was completely dark now and I could see no one.

"What do you want?" The voice behind me was loud and jarring, causing me to jump with fright.

My hands went to the bodice of my dress to still the pounding of my heart. I turned and looked into the eyes of the woman who questioned me. She held a large candlestick in both hands. It was encased in a glass hurricane globe. The candle's flame flickered eerily in the drafty hallway, reflecting upon her features. She was tall, towering above me almost like a man. Masses of dark hair stood out about her head, giving her a wild, disheveled appearance. Unusual, piercing eyes, whose color I could not distinguish, stared at me, accusingly, it seemed. It was only then that I wondered if she had seen me captive in David's embrace.

"Who are you?" I asked, now more curious than frightened.

"I am Anna Jackson, Allyson's sister." There was no hint of friendliness in her words.

"I'm Julia Van Cleef," I replied, meeting her icy gaze above the glow of candlelight. "I have come to—"

"I know who you are and why you're here!" she interrupted. "And I'll tell you frankly that there's nothing you can do for her that I cannot do myself!" Her deep voice rose and she made no effort to try and conceal her resentment of me.

But strangely I could understand that resentment and I could hardly fault her for wanting to take care of her sister. I knew exactly how she must feel and I found myself wishing to assure her that I would not push her aside. It was obvious how much she cared about her sister.

"I'm sure that's true," I said quietly. "I understand you've been very devoted to Mrs. Damron. But perhaps we could both work together to help her now."

One dark eyebrow lifted, but she did not smile. Instead she studied me warily as she held the candle lamp above me. Her eyes were hard and thoughtful as she assessed me thoroughly from my face to the clothes

91

I wore, even down to the tips of my shoes.

"The colored people here call you an angel of mercy," she said. I thought it odd that even this compliment sounded like an accusation.

I did not reply, for it placed me in an uncomfortable position, as it always did when someone mentioned such a thing. I knew it was true, just as I knew it was not uncommon for those sweet gentle people to dramatize such things. Yet how could I agree without seeming to accept the unwarranted title as fact?

Suddenly she lowered the lamp, her appraisal apparently completed.

"We shall see," she said, still referring I supposed to the name I'd been given.

"Then you will come to the baths tomorrow morning, Anna?" I asked. "I'm sure Allyson will feel more at ease if her sister is with her."

"Yes, of course, if you will allow it." Her voice was still and formal.

"Of course. There's no question of that." I tried to assure her as kindly as I could. The last thing I needed in this household was another enemy.

"Then I'll be happy to come," she said brusquely, turning to go.

"Good night," I called after her.

She walked down the hallway and stopped at the next door past Allyson's room. She placed her hand on the doorknob, then turned back to me. For the first time there was the glimpse of a smile on her plain face.

"I would be careful walking about at night here if I were you. You never know what kind of dangerous night creatures you might encounter. Even in the garden." Then she disappeared into the darkness of the room.

So, she *had* seen me with David. Whatever must she think? I could not suppress the shiver that ran through me, for her words had the sound of some ominous warning. Suddenly the hallway seemed dark

92

and filled with unseen drafts and whispering noises I could not explain. Quickly I gathered my skirts and hurried toward the entry hall and the stairway which was better lighted. But I did not feel entirely secure until I had reached my room and closed the door firmly behind me.

I walked about the bedroom quietly, being careful not to disturb Monteen next door. I certainly did not want her to know the apprehension I was feeling, for I knew it would only precipitate another lecture.

After a while I realized I was not going to be able to sleep and I needed something to divert my thoughts from David and the feel of his arms about me. I took the black medicine-bag from the dresser to make a list of all its contents. I emptied the bottles, placing each item carefully upon the bed. Then I began to list each medicine and its use on a sheet of paper.

It was not often that we gave medicine to patients, but I had brought it along just in case we needed it. It was not unusual with the beginning of such exercises and water therapy as Allyson would have that a patient would feel some aches and pains. And I did not know if Allyson's crippled legs were entirely without feeling. In any case we would be prepared. I set aside the laudanum and another dark brown bottle which was filled with a bitter elixir. It contained an opiate of poppy and I was very careful with it as it was said to be most addictive. My bag contained only one small bottle, which was sealed with thick wax.

I sat upon the bed and made a note of each item before placing the various bottles carefully back into the bag. I was deeply engrossed in my work when I heard the noise outside my door.

It was a quiet, shuffling noise, as if someone walked dragging his feet. I listened for a moment, not really alarmed, but only curious. But the quiet laughter that followed seemed to echo around the room and it brought chills down my spine. It sounded to be directly outside my door. It was a low, whispered noise, an eerie haunting sound that gave me the most horrifying feeling.

I hesitated only a moment before jumping from the bed and flinging open the door. But there was no one there . . . nothing except a dark, empty hallway. Even the candlelit sconces along the wall had been extinguished, leaving only a trace of light that filtered up the stairway at the end of the hall.

My legs had begun to quake. Why was I so frightened of nothing? I closed the door, turning the key in the lock this time and pushing the heavy bolt across the wood frame. And even though I knew there was no one in the room I looked about with the most unexplainable feeling.

I closed the curtains and turned the wicks up brighter in the lamps until finally I'd banished almost all of the shadows that lurked in the room.

Even after I'd prepared for bed I left one lamp burning dimly near the windows. And as apprehensive as I was, once I was in bed I felt somehow safer.

The cool, smooth sheets were soothing, comforting to me in a familiar way. And as I listened to the loud whir of crickets outside and the clatter of the cicadas in the huge old trees around the house, I soon gave in to the weariness I felt, and slept.

Chapter Eight

I woke early the next morning, having had no ill effects from the anxieties of the previous night.

Mary was soon at my door and bustled in, all smiles, with a tray containing a steaming pot of chocolate and a plate of hot rolls. Seeing Mary so happy and unconcerned gave me a new sense of resolve and made me think I must have been imagining things last night.

"Well, you certainly seem to have spent a pleasant first night here," I said as I poured a cup of chocolate.

"Oh yes, ma'am. I like it ever so much. It's almost like bein' at home . . . here in the country I mean. Nothin' to disturb your sleep ceptin' the crickets." She took a deep breath and her enthusiasm was quite contagious.

"Then I'm happy you came," I said. "You may do as you please today, Mary. Monteen and I will be busy in the bathing area most of the morning."

"I'll be takin' care of your things just like at home," she said, her voice proud. "But if I should get through early, I might take a stroll around the grounds if you don't mind." Her dark eyes were large and luminous, hopeful as she watched me. Evidently the young man she'd met already meant a great deal to her.

"Of course, Mary. Anything you like." She could hardly contain her excitement as she fairly skipped out the door.

Monteen had not risen as early as I and was still dressing when I looked in on her. I told her I'd go downstairs alone. Indeed I was grateful for a few quiet moments to gather my thoughts and decide how I would proceed with the fragile Allyson.

In the hallway I noted that the candles were once again burning. I decided that the laughter I'd heard last night was only some of the maids putting out the lights. I breathed a sigh of relief that my fears seemed to have vanished with the dawning. I even felt a bit foolish at all the frightened thoughts I'd allowed to form in my imagination. For here in the bright, cheerful light of morning, the house was as beautiful and elegant as ever: anything but frightening.

The bathing area was dark, with not even a candle having been lit. I stepped into the darkened room and walked through the dimness to the tiled sunken pool in the middle of the floor. The Damrons were not the only local residents to pipe the steaming water from its outside source into the house for their personal use. But I doubted anyone could claim to have done it with more elegance.

I placed the black medicine-bag on a table and gently massaged my temples. My head had begun to ache slightly as it sometimes did in the moist, heated air of the springs. But today felt different. My heart began to pulse heavily against my breast as I realized what was happening to me.

"No," I said softly, desperately trying to fight the whirl of thoughts in my brain and the flashing visions that sprang before my eyes.

I looked into the pool which I knew was clear and calm when I'd first stepped into the room. But now suddenly I saw something . . . and it seemed as real as I was. It was the vision of a woman, lying face down in the water, her long, dark hair spread out about her. In her lifeless outstretched hand she clutched a single rose, a perfect long-stemmed white rose.

I closed my eyes, swaying dizzily as heat rushed through my body and to my head.

"No!" I whispered again as I raised a trembling hand to my forehead. I did not want to open my eyes again lest the vision still be there before me, as bright and tangible as before.

I'm not sure how long I stood there before I felt hands upon my shoulders, gentle and easy. "Julia?" It was Monteen and even in my distressed state of mind I was aware of being grateful it was she who had found me. At least she knew what was happening and would not think me sick or even insane.

She moved me toward a chair and I sat down, finally daring to open my eyes. I glanced quickly toward the pool. But this time it was clear; not a ripple marred its surface. The gaslights had been lit and the room was bright as the illuminations reflected against the glistening Italian marble floors.

"What is it, Julia?" Monteen asked. "Are you ill?"

I shook my head, unable to put into words the disturbing thing I'd just seen. Why was this happening to me now? Was it the emotion of being here—of being so near David—that had made this happen? It was like a nightmare . . . but I was wide awake.

"It's the first time this has happened in . . . a long while. I thought . . . hoped they had stopped for good," I told her.

"What was it, *chère?* Can you tell me?"

"No," I said, shaking my head slowly. "I can't. I don't want to think about it now. Allyson will be along any moment. She must not see me like this or she will be frightened. I don't want that."

"But Julia, you—"

"No!" I insisted. "I'm fine now. Really. I'm fine." I rose and walked to the table where the towels and wrapping sheets were neatly stacked. Their clean sun-sweetened fragrance drifted up to me and the common scent brought reality a bit closer.

When Allyson was brought in only moments later I was composed and I had everything arranged as I liked it. I hoped there was no trace of worry on my face as I turned to greet her and her sister.

Anna was as unsociable that morning as the night before. When she and Monteen were introduced she practically looked down her nose at the smaller woman. But Monteen, given her fiery impulsive nature, handled it very well, I thought. There was only a slight lifting of her brows as she looked discreetly toward me.

And whatever she thought of Allyson she kept hidden as we moved the woman from her wheelchair onto a long, padded table.

I was surprised at the woman's voluptuous figure, although she certainly would not have been described as anything other than plump. And I had noticed she was tall, like her sister. But somehow she had looked more fragile and ethereal in her dim, rose-scented bedroom.

She was dressed in thin, loose-fitting pajamas, as I had requested. She would even be able to go into the steaming water in them.

But I was most interested in her lifeless legs and their muscle tone. I was puzzled, as I knew her doctors in Boston must have been. Her limbs seemed perfectly normal, shapely, and well formed. There was no hint of atrophy as one might expect to see in someone who had been completely bedridden for several months. I could see that Monteen noticed it too.

But I was certain, by her docile manner during our prodding and poking, that there was no feeling in her feet or legs. Her face was serene and expressionless as she lay looking up at the carved molding on the white ceiling.

Anna stood nearby watching us anxiously, as if she might step in any moment and warn us away from her sister.

"What we will do, Allyson, each day, is massage your legs as we're doing now. The lotions we use are made of natural ingredients with medicinal herbs—Monteen's specialty." I looked at Allyson's smiling face as she nodded, agreeable to my words. "Then the warm baths . . . we'll increase the time a bit each day. We won't use the cold needle showers, not yet. Then your legs will be massaged and stretched again while your muscles are still warm. Then we'll wrap you in sheets and let you lie quietly until your body temperature is back to normal."

"Sounds wonderful," she murmured.

Even Anna did not seem displeased by our work and that made me feel a bit more confident about dealing with the strange, enigmatic woman.

"We will need you to help us, Anna, if you don't mind," I told her.

"Of course," she nodded solemnly. "Anything you wish."

"Oh, one other thing," I said as I recalled the medicine bag I'd brought. "If we're lucky and the therapy helps, you may begin to have feeling in your legs again. And if this does occur, it might be painful at first as we exercise your legs each day. I have brought medication with me if you require it. So let me know if you do begin to experience any pain."

"Thank you, Julia," Allyson said, reaching forward to place her hand on my arm. "Your words give me confidence . . . and hope."

It was a long, tiring morning for all of us and especially, I knew, for Allyson. But she did not complain at all. Instead she seemed to enjoy having someone to talk to and kept us entertained with stories of her obviously privileged life, most especially since she'd met and married David Damron.

I found that some of her words made me very uncomfortable, for I did not wish to hear the intimate details of her life with David. But I could hardly ask her to stop, seeing how it made her so happy.

It was well past noon when we took Allyson back to her room. I went to the kitchen and asked that a tray be sent to her. Then Monteen and I took a small tray of bread, cold meat, and cheese to the garden so that we might rest a moment. And I knew Monteen wanted to hear about the vision I'd had.

The day was cloudy, with a soft, warm breeze that wafted across the roses, carrying with it the sweet scent of rain.

We walked to a weathered wood bench beside the stone wall and set the tray of food between us on the seat. A sturdy trellis above the bench was filled with the thick, tangled vines of wisteria, its blossoms long ago faded away. Still, the vines provided a pleasant shaded spot as we sat in its sheltered bower, with the riffle of wind playing through the leaves above us and rustling the boxwoods at the wall behind us.

I looked about the lovely garden, able to see now in the light of day the many varieties of flowers. It was designed in the style of an English garden, with formally and symmetrically arranged designs. At our feet was the brick walkway and directly across it lay thick mounds of pink impatiens and blue mealycup sage. In the center of the rectangular garden was a circular herb garden, green and redolent in the warmth of the day. I could feel myself relaxing in the beautiful atmosphere, and I sensed that Monteen felt the same. I closed my eyes for a moment and leaned my head against the back of the seat.

After awhile I began to sense Monteen's dark Creole gaze upon me. I turned to face her, knowing she wanted to discuss what had happened in the bath earlier. And I also wanted to hear her opinion about the woman David had married.

"Do you want to talk about it?" she asked.

I took a deep breath and tried to recall exactly how I'd felt and what I had seen before me. It had all happened so fast I could not be sure of every detail. But one thing I could never forget was the image of that lifeless body in the tiled pool.

"I can't imagine what triggered the images this morning," I told her. "It's been such a long time. . . ."

"You were white as a ghost when I came, and so lost in thought that you did not seem to even know I was there."

"Yes," I said. "I know. It's just that it was all so horrifying . . . the feelings, the headache. And so terribly real." I paused for a moment before continuing. "I thought I saw a body floating in the pool . . . a woman. Her dark hair was spread about her head and face." I shuddered as I recalled the gruesome sight.

"Was there anything else?" she asked quietly, as if she was afraid she would alarm me.

"A rose," I said, remembering. "In her hand . . . a white rose."

"Who was the woman? Did you know?"

"I . . . no. But all I can think of is Allyson and how her room was filled with white roses. The woman's hair was dark like hers. But I couldn't see her face . . . and the hair . . . it could have been Anna . . . or anyone. Perhaps not even anyone I've met."

I rose quickly and stood looking across the garden. "I don't know. Perhaps it was no one . . . perhaps it's completely unrelated to this house . . . or any of its occupants."

"Perhaps," Monteen replied quietly.

"But you don't believe that," I said.

"No, I don't. I think it is directly related to your being here in this place. I told you before. . . ."

"I know," I said, turning from her. "Let's walk."

She immediately fell into step beside me and we walked silently around the huge boxwoods and bordering flower beds. We stopped at one of the rose-filled sections and I gazed at the thorny bushes with their ghostly white blossoms.

"Julia," Monteen said suddenly. "Let's leave here. Forget the promise you made to David. Forget the responsibility you feel to help his wife. There's something wrong here . . . I can feel it! And even though you won't admit it, I believe you feel it too."

I turned to her and looked into dark, worried eyes. They were filled with genuine fear . . . something I'd rarely seen there. The sentiments she expressed had crossed my mind too. In fact I'd thought seriously last night of leaving Stillmeadows. But it was not only the apprehension I'd felt or the coldness of Anna Jackson and Millicent Damron. I knew David's disturbing presence had as much to do with it as anything. But oddly, he was also the reason I could not go. I could feel my resolve and willpower weakening whenever he was near me and I was left feeling lost and out of control.

"No," I told her. I took her hands in mine; they felt cold even in the warmth of the day. "I must stay, but if you would be more comfortable back in Hot Springs, of course I will understand."

"No," she said, frowning at me. "It's not me I'm worried about . . . it's you! I'm afraid for you, Julia."

"Don't be. I can take care of myself."

The look she gave told me she did not believe that statement for a moment. But I could not let Monteen dictate what I should do. I'd made up my mind to stay at Stillmeadows, and for whatever reason, that was exactly what I intended to do.

And she, knowing me as she did, said no more on the subject. Perhaps her restraint was one reason we had become such friends in so short a time.

I heard someone laughing across the courtyard and turned to see who had joined us in the garden.

I saw two people step through the arched stone entryway which led from the stable area. It was Millicent and David. She looked stunning in a royal blue riding habit that clung to her curvaceous figure.

102

Her small black hat sported a blue feather which fluttered gaily in the breeze as she walked. She had her hands entwined through the crook of David's arm as she smiled up into his face. They both laughed and talked animatedly as they moved toward the center of the garden. They were so intent on one another that they had not discovered they were no longer alone.

My attention was diverted from them momentarily as I caught a movement from the corner of my eye. There was someone moving near the corner of the house. I turned just in time to see Anna Jackson standing in the doorway. Her face was dark and angry as she too watched the approaching couple. Then she turned, her dark skirts awhirl behind her, and went back into the house. David and Millicent had not seen her, nor us.

I wondered briefly why seeing them together had made Anna react so angrily. Her actions set off a small alarm somewhere in my mind and I turned to look once more at the laughing couple. This time I looked with a more adept eye and what I saw made my heart lurch with the recognition of a sickening reality.

Millicent's face had the adoring look of a woman in love; she could hardly take her eyes from him. His face was much harder to interpret; but there was no doubt that the teasing look held affection. And there was something more in his attitude that disturbed me, something which left me feeling alone and left out. There was a gentle teasing quality about the way he looked at her, the way he seemed to admire her. And there had been nothing of that in the looks he sometimes threw my way. His manner toward me seemed coldly assessing, mysterious and hard to comprehend. Seeing him this way with Millicent left me quite unexplainably with a small nagging ache near my heart.

I saw that the eyes I was so involved in remembering had turned our way. David stopped and Millicent turned about slowly, the smile leaving her face as she followed his look.

"Good afternoon," he said, politely and with more interest than I expected. He turned and walked around the herb garden toward us. Millicent did not relinquish his arm, but hurried along beside him.

They stopped within a few feet of us. David's intense look that roamed briefly over my face and hair both thrilled and perplexed me. I was so confused where the man was concerned that a simple glance threw me into a quandary and I had difficulty thinking calmly.

"How did your morning go?" he asked warmly. There was a hint of amusement in his voice and I was certain he knew how uncomfortable his look had made me. That and seeing him with Millicent irritated me more than I realized.

"Our morning was fine," I said quietly. "And if you're interested, so was your wife's."

The only perceptible change in David was a narrowing of his hazel eyes. But Millicent's lovely red lips flew open and her eye glittered with anger. She made a step toward me.

"How dare you—," she began.

"No," David said quietly, reaching for her arm to pull her back. "It's all right, Millie. Julia is perfectly correct in reminding me of my responsibilities."

With that soberly spoken phrase he turned and walked away from us. Millicent threw me a look of anger and ran after him.

"Oh, Julia." Monteen's voice was only a whisper beside me. "Perhaps you should not have—"

"I know!" I snapped. Suddenly I was so tired. Tired of being careful, tired of hiding my feelings, and tired of there always being someone near to watch my misery when I made a mistake.

What was happening to me? I, who always prided myself on gracious and dignified behavior. I was reverting back to my early days, snapping at people like

104

an angry, willful child. And I was afraid everyone could see it for what I knew it to be . . . jealousy, pure and simple. I was jealous that I was not the one clinging to David's arm and being the object of his gentle, teasing looks. That I was not the one he seemed so happy being near. And yet strangely, I did not feel this jealousy toward his wife, Allyson. In fact I liked her very much, and if circumstances were different, I imagined we might even have become friends.

I walked away from Monteen and I suppose she sensed my dilemma and my need to be alone because she did not follow me. I was not even aware when she left.

As I walked alone in the garden I had time to reflect, to rethink my feelings. I could not let anything keep me from helping Allyson and so I must be careful, outwardly at least, not to let my emotions get in the way again.

I felt somewhat strengthened as I went to my room and began to pull dresses from the wardrobe.

And when Monteen rapped softly at my door later I was sure she expected to find me dining again in my room. But I surprised her by being dressed and ready in one of my most stunning new Parisian gowns. I would face David and Millicent at dinner with a new resolve.

Chapter Nine

"Julia!" Monteen exclaimed. "You . . . you look wonderful."

I laughed and smiled at her. "You sound surprised."

She grinned at me sheepishly. "You must admit you have not been exactly yourself since coming here, my girl. And after what happened in the garden today I was not even sure you would wish to go down to dinner."

"I know." I took her arm, noting the softly flowing, jonquil-colored dress she wore. I envied her the ability to wear such bright, vibrant colors, but her dark hair and olive skin were born for it.

"Come in a moment while I finish," I told her.

I watched Monteen's reflection in the mirror as I pulled my hair back and tied it at the nape of my neck. She still looked worried. I placed a ribbon entwined with silk flowers in my hair and turned to face her.

"I'm all right," I assured her. "I won't lie to you and tell you that this afternoon meant nothing. I know I'm always dangerously close to losing control where David is concerned, but I'm confident it won't happen again." My words sounded bright and unconcerned, perhaps even hypocritical. But that facade was the only way I knew to try and get through the problems I faced.

"Oh, *chère*," she said as I turned to face her where

she sat on the bed. She waved her hand slightly, setting her golden bracelets to jangling. "Don't apologize. Not to me. I am the last one to condemn you for your feelings toward a man. It is only that I'm worried about you. I don't want to see you hurt again and . . ."

"And you think if I stay here I will be," I finished for her.

"I know it, Julia."

"No," I assured her. "I won't be. I like Allyson and I intend to help her if I can. I will not allow myself to become involved with her husband and cause her even more problems than she already faces. Besides, it's obvious that David does not still feel the same way about me as before." I looked away uneasily, for I could not deny deep within my heart that I felt this to be true. And it hurt more than I cared to admit.

"If you truly believe that, you are fooling yourself, my dear. If a man ever looked at me as he does at you, ooh la, I should probably not be able to deny him anything!"

I could feel a flush upon my cheeks and I turned to rearrange something on the dresser. "He has a wife," I said coolly.

"Oh yes, the poor, sweet, suffering Allyson." Her voice was cold and sarcastic and very unlike her.

I spun about to look at her. "Monteen! How can you speak with that tone of voice about her? She's—"

"Has she so easily fooled you then?" she asked, with a cold snap to her black eyes that was unfamiliar.

"Whatever do you mean?" I asked.

Monteen stood and strolled to the window that overlooked the meadows. "There's something about her. It's nothing specific . . . just a feeling I had when I first saw her." She turned, the motion setting her yellow skirt awhirl. "I don't trust her. I don't trust her at all. And I'm rarely wrong in my first impression of people."

Her attitude irritated me. "So . . . it's just an

intuition. You don't like her because of some silly intuition."

Once again her dark eyes flashed. "I would not expect such a comment from you, *mon amie,*" she said stiffly.

I was immediately ashamed of my curt dismissal of her words. And she was right, I should know as well as anyone how those vague intuitive feelings could be so clear and certain. I relied on mine many times where a new acquaintance was concerned.

I sighed and smoothed the skirt of my blue peau de soie gown and touched the beribboned flowers in my hair. "You are, of course, entitled to your opinion, Monteen. I should not speak lightly of your feelings. Let's just go downstairs for dinner before we're late."

I ignored her look of disbelief at being dismissed so coolly. But as usual she was not one to waste time pouting and immediately she followed me out the door and silently down toward the dining room.

As we came down the stairs we could see James and Millicent outside the dining room. He was frowning at her and I suspected they had been quarreling again. I wondered what the reason could be this time. When he saw us, his handsome face immediately cleared and he smiled a warm, friendly greeting as he pulled away from his beautiful wife.

"Ladies . . . how lovely you both look tonight."

I looked past James and met Millicent's violet eyes staring at me. She was still angry, I could see, about my rudeness to David and I found myself hoping she would not turn the evening into another unpleasant occasion.

Surprisingly, I need not have worried. Once we entered the room and took our places, everything seemed to fall pleasantly into place. And Millicent behaved in a gracious, even friendly manner.

Grace Damron sat at the head of the table with David on one side of her and his wife, Allyson, sitting in a wheelchair directly across from him. I was not surprised when Millicent went immediately to take a chair next to David as if her husband were not even in the room.

James then indicated I should sit next to him, so I found myself on the opposite side of the table from David. There was hardly any way I could avoid looking directly into his face.

He met my look with a cool gaze, his eyes then lowering from mine as if I were a stranger. I had expected him to be angry, but the iciness that sparkled in his eyes took me by surprise. I had never known him to be so cold and aloof.

Thankfully, James did not allow me to ponder David's mood for long. He regaled us all during the meal with humorous tales of his days at school and often of escapades here at his home which usually involved his older brother.

David was quiet, though he often smiled with good nature at James. But he did not offer any measurable comment.

"How I would love to have known David then," Allyson said. "Before he became so old and staid." Allyson pursed her lips as she teased her husband and her dark eyes glittered at him with mischief.

Sitting there with her wheelchair hidden by the table, she looked as healthy and vibrant as any normal young woman. And her quiet shyness had vanished, replaced by an exuberant lightheartedness which took me by surprise.

Millicent stiffened noticeably at Allyson's teasing words and did not seem to take them in the bantering way they had been given. She was certainly quite protective of David, it seemed.

"David is *anything* but staid," she said with a lift of her lovely brows. "I'm surprised sometimes, Allyson, at how very little you know about your husband."

Grace Damron, who had been quietly watching and

110

listening to her family, cleared her throat and directed a look of warning at Millicent. But the young woman chose to ignore it, gazing instead with apparent anger at Allyson.

Allyson giggled and lifted a delicate crystal wine glass to her lips. She peered across the top of the glass at David, who was watching her with a look as cold as steel. It was a moment before I realized why Allyson was acting so different. She was drunk!

"Don't you think you've had enough wine?" David asked steadily.

"Oh, don't be such an old pooh. I'll bet you weren't like that when Julia knew you before." She looked around James, who sat stiffly, obviously embarrassed for her. "Was he, Julia? You must tell us all about him when he was younger. I'll bet all the girls hereabout were madly in love with him. Were they?"

My face grew hot and I could not look at David. But I was sure he must have been as uncomfortable as I. Monteen flashed a look at me as if to say she had made her point about the woman she disliked.

"That was so long ago, I'm sure Julia does not even remember." It was Mrs. Damron who spoke, her voice firm and quiet as if to close the subject.

But Allyson would not be denied. "Oh, I doubt that. I know from experience how devastating my husband's charm can be. And that's something a woman never forgets. Isn't that right, darling?" She turned toward her husband.

"Where is your sister tonight, Allyson?" he asked.

Once again she giggled. "I have no idea." She took another sip of wine, this time sloshing some of it onto the creamy white linen tablecloth. "Oops!" she said, laughing. "Anna is probably out gazing at the clouds, worrying if it will storm. The worrier, the worker . . . that's what she is. No fun in her. Oh, she hates it when I tell her that!"

David turned to one of the servants who stood

111

silently by as if he had heard none of our conversation. "Please send someone to find Miss Anna. Tell her her sister wishes to go to her room now."

"No!" Allyson said. She slammed her glass down on the table, spraying tiny flecks of red on the tablecloth. "You shan't send me to my room like a naughty child!"

"Oh, for heaven's sake, Allyson! Stop making such a scene," Millicent snapped, her eyes flashing. "Go to your room and sober up."

The servant hesitated, but David nodded toward him, ordering him silently to do as he'd been told.

Monteen squirmed uncomfortably in her chair. Neither of us knew quite what to make of the scene we were witnessing or how to escape it.

Allyson began to cry. "Please, David," she pleaded. Her voice now lost all its defiance and was instead one of a wheedling, spoiled child.

I was stunned at this change in her, but if anything it only made me pity her more.

James, obviously trying to ease the tension in the room, made an attempt at casual conversation. "I understand, Julia, that you lived in St. Louis. I always enjoyed our trips to that city."

"Yes, St. Louis is a very exciting city."

"And your husband was a professor, I believe?" Millicent joined in. But her words, unlike James's, were not meant to soothe. I could see that in the twinkle of her eye.

"Yes," I said, pushing my plate away. I found I had little appetite now and was left with only a sick feeling in the pit of my stomach.

"And much older than you, I understand?" she smiled.

"Richard was twenty-five years older than I."

David's eyes, cold and appraising, flicked toward me and his lips moved in an odd, disapproving way. There was surprise in his look and I lifted my head rather proudly. I was not ashamed of my relationship with

112

Richard and I meant him to know that.

"Why Millicent, dear," Allyson interrupted. She'd dried her eyes and her mood had changed dramatically again. "There's certainly nothing wrong with that! Besides I find it very romantic. Isn't there a Greek fable about an older man who takes a poor but beautiful wretch and transforms her into a stunning lady?"

I could hear the intake of breath around the table, but Allyson seemed unaware and continued. "Or am I thinking of the story where Aphrodite turns the ivory statue of Pygmalion into a real live woman for the pleasure of the king of Cyprus? Oh I can't recall how it goes!"

"Allyson! That will do," Mrs. Damron interrupted.

"*Ma foi!*" Monteen said beneath her breath, her eyes blazing at Allyson.

"Oh . . . but I did not mean that Julia was a cold statue or a . . . a wretch that had to be transformed. Oh, Julia, please forgive me if it sounded that way!" Tears again sparkled in Allyson's dark eyes. "Somehow everything I say comes out all wrong."

"Only when you're drinking," Millicent muttered wryly.

"I'll take her to her room," David said, rising from the table. The look on his dark face was angry and closed. As he moved around the table toward his wife she looked up at him and there was a flash of fear upon her face just as there had been when he stormed into her room. She looked like a young, frightened animal caught in a trap.

"Let me take her," I said suddenly. I wondered again why David was so cold and cruel to her. After all, her words had been directed toward me, not him, and I could see she was in no state to actually know what she was saying.

I thought for a moment he would deny me. He opened his mouth as if to speak and his look challenged me. But with a sigh of resignation, he motioned for me

113

to go ahead.

I went to Allyson and placed my hands on the back of her chair, pulling her away from the table. She turned and gazed up at me with a look of sadness and gratitude. She was crying again and my heart turned over as if seeing a lost child seeking comfort. I touched her shoulder. I could not find it in my heart to turn against her as the others had seemed to.

As we moved from the table I was shocked at the expressions on the faces of those seated there. Why was I the only one who felt pity for this poor, miserable young woman?

Grace Damron turned her face away as if the sight of Allyson sickened her. David, still standing, looked down at his wife and there was no hint of compassion in that look . . . only disgust. Millicent's beautiful, vacant face was full of triumphant pleasure as she leaned her body slightly away from us as we passed. Only when my look swung to James did I see an expression that was full of sympathy. I found myself once again appreciative of his presence in the midst of such animosity.

Monteen followed me. She was probably only too eager to get away from the people gathered in that room. And she would support me, no matter if she approved of Allyson or not.

"Well!" Millicent said as we moved around the table toward the door. "It looks as if she's managed to spoil our dinner once again."

Did she mean that Allyson behaved this way often? And was this the reason David seemed to resent his wife so? Somehow I felt there was more to it than that.

"Eat your dinner, Millicent," Grace Damron said quietly. "I'm sure we will all enjoy a quieter, more pleasant meal if we only make an effort." She did not seem to notice Allyson's flinch at her remarks. "Julia, Miss Valognes, please return and finish your meal afterward. I insist."

114

Monteen and I exchanged glances as we took a now-subdued Allyson into the hallway. I certainly did not relish returning to the table, but when we were met by Anna just outside the door and she took her sister in hand, there seemed to be little else we could do.

"What did I tell you?" Monteen whispered before we went back in. "Allyson is highly unstable! Who knows what she might do?"

"Monteen, please. Not now." I was weary of the talk and the confusion it caused within me.

But even I had to admit that the atmosphere in the dining room was much more pleasant without Allyson's presence. Somehow that evoked memories from my past, when I was not so welcome here, and I empathized with her. What an unhappy time she must have had since her marriage into this family. Indeed it might even have contributed to her sad state of mind.

"Miss Valognes, I meant to ask you earlier. I've been told you are a fortune-teller of sorts . . . a reader of the tarot cards." It was Millicent who spoke and her interest seemed genuine.

"Yes, that's true," Monteen said, watching the woman carefully. "It was taught to me by my grandmama as was taught to her by her grandmama. An old Creole tradition."

"It sounds so exciting! Perhaps we might persuade you to read our fortunes one night while you're here. I think a bit of entertainment would be quite refreshing."

Monteen glanced toward me as if for approval; I shrugged. I had no real objection to her reading the cards so long as it did not involve me.

"I shall be happy to," Monteen said, seeming to warm a bit to the other woman.

In the brief silence that followed, thunder rumbled somewhere far in the distance, perhaps above the mountains. The atmosphere had been hot and humid most of the day and I supposed it would probably rain before midnight.

115

"Oh, let's go out on the portico and watch the lightning," Millicent suggested, looking with animation toward David rather than her own husband.

I was surprised that the beautiful, very feminine creature could be excited about so simple a thing as an approaching storm. And I was even more surprised when I felt a small tug of understanding for how she felt. I had always loved the sights and sounds of a summer storm.

James rose quickly and walked around the table, taking his wife's arm and escorting her away, giving his brother no opportunity to accept Millicent's not-so-subtle invitation. Millicent did not make a protest, but went with him toward the hallway. David pursed his lips and smiled as if his brother's obvious actions amused him.

I probably would not have joined them if I had known that Mrs. Damron would decline on the pretext of tiredness. And I should have known with Monteen's aversion to lightning that she would not relish being outside. So as it was I was left in the awkward position of being paired with David.

I did not know what to say to him after my hasty remarks in the garden. But when James and Millicent moved to the far end of the porch and out of hearing, I felt I should at least make an effort to mend fences, for I did not want the coldness that had sprung up between us to continue. For Allyson's sake, I told myself.

"You always loved storms as I recall." David's voice was low and husky beside me.

"Yes . . . I still do," I replied.

The wind had become brisk and was heavily scented with rain. It whipped the tops of the huge trees back and forth as if they were saplings. Lightning was now almost constant in the west above the mountains.

"David, I apologize for my remark this afternoon," I said, deciding to get straight to the point. "It is certainly not my place to criticize or interfere in your relation-

116

ship with your wife."

He turned to me and looked down steadily into my face. My heart began to thud heavily in my chest. He was so close . . . too close. His face in the light from the open door was serious and thoughtful.

"I won't deny there are . . . problems here, Allyson's and mine not the least of them. But I don't think you would understand." His voice was still cool and controlled, but underneath I sensed a quiet anguish that caused me to want to reach out to him. It hurt that he thought I would not understand.

"Perhaps I would," I said. "We used to be able to talk about such things . . . about everything. Remember? Our problems, our hopes and dreams."

I saw him stiffen and draw away from me. "That was a long time ago. We've both changed since then."

I did not reply. I could not find an answer or a denial. And knowing he had rejected me once should have been reason enough for me not to care. But I could not deny that I did. Where was the burning resentment I should be feeling? Something had happened to me since David's return. And standing there in his presence, with the scent of the fresh wind blowing across the meadows, I felt many things for him, but resentment was no longer one of them.

"Did you love him?" he asked abruptly, looking down at me again.

"Love him? My . . . my husband you mean?"

"Yes, your husband. Did you love him?" he demanded, through jaws now stiff and unyielding.

"Yes. I . . . I loved him."

Swiftly he stepped toward me and pulled me against him, his hands biting into my arms. "But did you love him as you once loved me?" His voice was a challenge and I could feel the bitterness.

"David . . . don't do this." I pulled away from him and stepped to the railing, clutching it to steady the trembling of my hands.

117

"Damn you, Julia! Do you know what it did to me . . . your leaving so suddenly, me hoping against hope that you would come back one day? Do you?" He turned me about, his strong hands holding me fiercely against him. I could feel the anger in him, the frustration he felt, and I was speechless. Surely he couldn't blame *me* for our parting that summer.

How could he pretend it was I who had put an end to it? When all along it was he and his mother who'd wanted a better, more profitable marriage than a poor girl would provide. And what of love? I wanted to shout. How dare he pretend it was love he'd felt for me. I knew better, had learned it with a hard and bitter lesson in fact. He'd only used me for a summer diversion . . . a mere amusement. And now that I was back—a wealthy widow, changed from the unsophisticated girl he knew—now he was ready to accept me again?

I should have hated him for that. Did he really think we could start all over again? But even as I denied him in my mind, against my best intentions I was drawn to him as always, wanting to reach up and touch his lips, those lips that could always send my senses reeling. He was like a magnet and I only a small, weightless piece of metal to be moved about as he desired.

Lightning ripped the sky above the house. The storm had finally reached us in all its fury and I had hardly been aware of it. Quickly, as the thunder rumbled about us and rattled the long windows in the house, I wrenched away from him. It took every bit of strength I had. But I ran into the house and up the stairs to the sanctuary of my room, never looking back at the man who stood alone in the raging storm.

Chapter Ten

Tears of frustration burned my eyes and I did not bother to light any of the lamps in my room. Instead I walked to the windows and wrapped my arms tightly about my body as I watched the rain splatter against the windowpanes.

As I stood there thoughtfully watching the storm raging I suddenly remembered the medicine bag. I glanced quickly about the room but it was not there. In my haste to get away that morning I must have left it in the therapy room. I turned toward the door, debating whether or not I should risk going back downstairs to retrieve it. I did not want to see David again.

A shiver ran through me as I thought of him, of his shuttered, accusing eyes and the intensity I'd felt in his strong hands. I stood motionless, unsure of what to do.

Suddenly the door opened and a shaft of light from the hallway spread across the carpet of my darkened room.

I felt a stab of alarm that traveled over me in a cold, tingling flash. I saw his outline there against the light. Then he closed the door and walked toward me. I could see his face in the flickering lights of the storm.

"David, you cannot come in here like this." My voice, against my will, sounded like a plea.

But he continued his advance toward me. His quiet

determination was frightening and I moved one step backward until my hips touched the edge of the windowsill. Lightning flashed, illuminating his face into a strange and unfamiliar mask.

"I will do as I please," he said slowly. "No one could be aware of my presence here. This wing of the house is practically deserted. And the storm is growing more intense. . . ."

"Stop this, David," I said. "You're frightening me."

"Good!" he said, moving even closer to me. "Good, because you frighten me, Julia, more than you can ever imagine." There was a hint of pain in his voice.

"I frighten you? But . . ."

"Does that surprise you?" He was dangerously near, so near I could feel his breathing and catch the tantalizing, masculine scent of him. So close I felt trapped, paralyzed by my need to be in his arms.

"I'm frightened of the power you seem to have," he continued. "That after all this time it's as if you never left. That the ache I feel for you is as strong . . . *stronger* even, than it was before." His voice became a low growl as he continued. "Frightened that I can't get enough of looking at you . . . that I want to take you right now and—"

"Stop it!" I said, putting my hands over my ears. "David . . . you know this can never be. We should not even . . ."

"Why shouldn't we," his voice whispered. "My marriage is a farce. You can see that after being here only two days." I did not answer him, did not look up at him. "Perhaps you expect me to believe you're still mourning the loss of your husband?" His words rang with sarcasm.

"Please leave."

"There was no real passion in you for the man you married. Affection, perhaps, or gratitude, but not love and passion. I can see it in your blue eyes when you speak of him."

"That's not true! I won't allow you to say such things about Richard. He was good . . . a fine decent man and I . . ." I was crying then, the tears finally spilling over and running down my cheeks.

"You what?" he growled. "Desired him, wanted him in the night when storms raged outside like tonight and you couldn't sleep? I don't believe that!"

I looked at him defiantly, wanting to hit him, wanting to run away from his words.

He grew quiet and motionless as he looked down at me. "Tell me, Julia, did you ever think of me when you lay in his arms at night?"

I gapsed and turned away, but quickly he reached for me and pulled me back to face him. Holding me prisoner he continued his disturbing questions and accusations.

"Did you ever pretend it was me . . . my lips that kissed you . . . my body that—"

"No!" I shouted, closing my eyes so that I could not see his face. And so he could not see the lie in my eyes.

"Liar!" he whispered fiercely, shaking me gently.

My eyes flew open to meet his and he laughed softly. "You're wondering how I know?" he whispered. "Because it happened to me so often that I began to question my sanity. I despised myself for allowing anyone to have such complete control over me. But at least I've never lied to myself as you're doing. I never tried to deny how much I wanted you. . . ."

"Don't, please," I said, twisting away from him.

I didn't want to hear any more, could not bear to admit the words he spoke might be true. I ran past him then, toward the door. I dared not stay there with him any longer. It was no good like this with the anger and bitterness coming between us, threatening to become a part of his desire for me. For I knew it would destroy everything.

But David moved swiftly, catching me from behind and pulling me back against him. He turned me to face

121

him and I was now against the bed, with no chance of escaping him.

"Don't do this, David," I whispered. "You don't want it to be this way."

His lips came down on mine, shutting off any other protests. His kiss was hard and punishing, meant to let me know that he could control me if he wished it. And it was true, as much as I hated to admit it . . . at that moment I could not resist him. The taste of his lips, so sweetly familiar, was what I'd dreamed of so often, what I'd longed for in the darkest hours of the night. And yes, even what I'd thought of with Richard. It was as if David and I had never been apart, as if no other man had ever touched me except him.

"Yes," he whispered gruffly against my mouth. "I do want it, exactly this way."

I began to cry again, my face wet with tears, but I made no other protest. For I was lost, adrift in the fiery, overpowering surge of desire that swept over me. It was what I wanted too. I could deny it no longer, no more than I could deny him.

His lips moved to mine again, his kiss more insistent. Then slowly, his caresses became gentle and tender, the anger seemingly replaced by something else . . . some bittersweet emotion that struck fire between both of us. And then he held me, only that, not kissing me, but holding me as if he'd never let me go. For a moment it was as if we'd returned to the sweet, warm love of our youth, when we could not get close enough to each other.

"David," I whispered, pressing against him. It was this sweet tenderness that chased away the last of my remaining resistance. I wanted him and I didn't care about anything or anyone else, just that we were here, alone together and free to do as we pleased.

His hand reached up to touch my face, his thumb gently caressing my cheeks. When he felt the wet trace of tears he pulled away and looked at me.

122

"Damn!" he swore softly. "I didn't mean to make you cry . . . I'm sorry." He pulled away from me.

I could see his outline there in the darkness as he stood apart from me. His hands were on his hips and his head thrown back as if he gasped for air.

"David?" I asked, puzzled by his reaction.

Finally I heard his ragged expulsion of air, a sound almost of defeat. "All right," he said quietly. "I can fight anything except your tears. I'm sorry if I frightened you." Without touching me again or explaining further, he moved toward the door.

"Wait," I said. "Please, David, you don't understand."

He stopped and turned to me with a puzzled look.

"The tears," I stammered. "They aren't from fright, or anger, or any of the things you think."

"What then. Disgust?" he murmured.

"No, David . . . no, never that!" What must he think of me? And was I sure, under the circumstances, that I wanted to tell him everything I was feeling? I reached out and placed the palm of my hand against his chest.

"Have we grown so far apart that you can no longer sense my feelings?" I asked. "I'm crying because . . . because I want you so much . . . and I know it can never be, not the way I want it to. No matter how much we both want it . . . it just can't. And it breaks my heart."

His eyes were dark and unreadable there in the shadowy room as he moved closer and pulled me against him. He took my hand that lay against his chest and raised it to his lips.

"I know that," he whispered. "I had not thought you'd changed so much that you might lose your principles. But I was so angry. . . ." He laughed, a sound of derision. "I even told myself I could force you to do as I wished. But I could never do anything against your will, Julia . . . you know that, don't you?"

"Yes, David. I do know that." My heart ached at the

tenderness in his voice, at the vulnerability he tried so hard to hide. I wanted to throw myself into his arms and forget where we were, forget he was married. And I might have done so if his wife had been anyone other than Allyson. Poor, pitiable Allyson with her large, baleful eyes and her sad weakness.

"I wish I could promise you this will never happen again," he said. "But I can't. I'm afraid I'm not that strong where you are concerned."

"Nor I with you," I admitted with a slight breathlessness. "So we must make sure we do not put ourselves in such a position again," I said, my voice shaking as I spoke.

"God," he said, laughing again at himself. "Why couldn't I have fallen in love all those years ago with someone of easy morals and low character?"

I was ashamed of the hope that sprang up within me when he said the word "love." For nothing had changed. And even though he was teasing me about my character, I knew it was not so easy for him either to go against the principles he held so dear. He had proven to me tonight that he was the same man I remembered.

When he pulled me against him this time he seemed to hold his emotions in check. The urgency and the anger seemed to have vanished, or at least he convinced me of it. He caressed my hair, gently pulling the ribbon away and smoothing his hand down the unbound length of it. And those brief, sweet actions were almost my undoing. I could resist his anger, his almost punishing aggression, but this . . . this sweetness was almost more than I could bear. And he knew it. As always he knew it too well.

He pulled away and put me at arm's length. He did not attempt to kiss me again, but only looked at me for a long, heart-stopping moment: a sweet, silent good-bye. Then he left my room quietly and resignedly.

I went to the door and locked it after him, then threw myself upon the bed. I cried again, great racking sobs

124

which left me breathless and my head aching. If I had thought I knew pain all those years before when I'd had to leave here, it was as nothing compared to this. I should never have come back, I told myself . . . should never have even come home to Hot Springs.

David and I needed hundreds of miles separating us . . . thousands if we were to fight the emotions that surged between us whenever our glances met across a room. I'd not felt so out of control since Richard's death.

I cried myself to sleep even while the storm intensified and raged noisily outside the house. In fact when I opened my eyes a while later I thought it was the thunder that had wakened me.

I sat up, my skin feeling warm and damp from the humidity in the air. I listened, but the storm seemed to have moved on, leaving only a gentle flicker of intermittent lightning and the quiet soft patter of rain on the roof. I got up and as I began to unbutton the dress I still wore, walked to open one of the windows.

When I pushed, it slid up easily, unleashing a wave of fresh, cool air. I sat in a chair before the opening and breathed deeply of the fragrance, rubbing the sleep from my eyes as I did. I wondered if David rested any better than I.

At first I did not realize what the flashes of white were that appeared before my eyes. I thought it was from sleeping. Then I saw that it was a movement of some kind down across the lawn. There was someone there . . . the graceful movement of white as someone ran across the yard and beneath a large elm tree at the edge of the meadow.

I rose from the chair and stepped closer to the window. It was only in the soft flicker of light that I saw the outline of another person . . . someone who'd been standing beneath the towering old tree, waiting.

The figure in white with the long flowing gown was obviously a woman. And it was just as obvious that the

125

second person, tall and dressed in dark clothes, was a man.

The woman began to dance about before him in a tantalizing, provocative fashion. Her movements were graceful and slow as if she kept beat to some silent melody. She whirled and spun there in the darkness, like a moth fluttering about a candle, moving toward the man, then away again. I continued to watch, mesmerized by the ghostly sight, and I wondered who it was and why they were there.

But as I continued to watch it became clear to me. Suddenly the dark shadow of the man moved toward the luminous firefly vision of the dancer and they whirled together there in the misting rain. I even thought I heard the trilling sounds of the woman's laughter and the low muffled answer of the man's. Then the couple stopped, their contrasting shadows merging together into one hardly visible shape. That shape collapsed to the ground and there on the thick wet grass they became lost in the dark shadow of the tree.

Even though I could see nothing, I turned quickly from the window and the scene before me. My pulse beat rapidly at my throat; my insides felt weak and trembling.

Who was the ghostly dancer and the man she'd run so joyfully to meet?

"It must be two of the servants," I whispered aloud, as if to convince myself.

But the picture in my mind's eyes would not go away: the picture of a lovely Millicent, in a royal blue riding habit, clinging to David's arm and looking up into his face with such adoration. And she had worn white at dinner.

"That means nothing," I murmured in the darkness.

I ran my hands across one of the tables until they fell upon the matches. Then lighting a candle I glanced at the clock. It was only a few minutes past midnight.

126

I blew out the light and went about undressing for bed. The storm had brought cooler air and the breeze from the window that played against my bare skin caused me to shiver. But I did not want to return to the window, did not want to see what happened below me there near the meadow.

And I knew, even if I tried to deny it, that I did not want to chance recognizing the couple who'd met beneath the tree, did not even want to think that David had left me here alone only to go to someone else. Would he leave, aroused by my kisses and warm from my arms, to seek the comfort and satisfaction of another woman?

I got into bed, pulling a sheet over my shivering body.

Was that it then? I asked myself. Was it David and Millicent who'd danced in the flickering lights of the storm, who moved together . . . who even now . . .

"No," I whispered, my words almost a prayer as I tried to banish the vision from my mind.

"Perhaps it was the Lady of the Mists," I said, trying to divert my thoughts. "Perhaps it was only she . . . or perhaps I only dreamed it."

I thought of the whimsical name the mountain people had given to this particular woman of folklore, the mystical lady in white who sometimes emerged from the mists of the hot springs to help the poor and the sick. It was told that she often rescued the injured or lost from isolated areas of the mountains. Even the Indians had told of her.

I made myself think, desperately trying to forget what I'd seen. I recalled the first time I'd ridden to the valley during an outbreak of cholera. The weather had been dreary with the mists hanging over the mountains like a thick fog. The colored people, some of them delirious with fever, had sworn I was the mystic lady come from the mists to save them. To my dismay, the rumor apparently still persisted. Millicent and Anna had both alluded to it and David had mentioned it that first day he came to the El Dorado.

David. It was always David who came back to my mind.

Could I really blame him for going to someone else? I, with my conscience and strong sense of doing what was right. *I* had caused him to turn away. Surely I didn't expect him to remain faithful to *me* . . . a woman he had not seen since his youth, and one he could not love the way he wished.

What a ridiculous, romantic fool I was! And more ridiculous still because I had to admit it was exactly what I wanted, what I'd so naively hoped for.

Yes, I longed for David Damron to want me and only me. And to love me. And even as I admitted that this was true I berated myself for forgetting the resentment I'd so carefully cultivated against him the past ten years. For I had thought to wrap myself in its cloak of protection, and keep my heart safely intact. But I was wrong and now, if he was the man beneath the elm, I was also too late.

Chapter Eleven

I overslept next morning and jumped out of bed in an even more agitated state than usual. I bathed and dressed quickly in a simple dress of dimity sprinkled with sprigs of pink flowers.

Mrs. Woolridge herself brought tea to my room that morning, explaining that Mary had been asked to gather herbs for the cook. I was certain that Mrs. Woolridge could have sent someone else and wondered why she had not.

She stood for a moment before leaving. I looked up from the table near the fireplace where I sat drinking tea.

"Yes, Mrs. Woolridge?"

"I understand you have a few medicines with you, ma'am." She sounded almost solicitous, although still not entirely friendly.

"Why . . . yes, I do."

"Well if . . . if it would not be too great an imposition, Mr. Woolridge is feelin' mighty poorly this morning. It's his rheumatism, I suspect. I wondered if you might have something you could recommend. I wouldn't ask but . . ."

"Of course," I said, not wishing to make her explain. I could see in her tired eyes that she was concerned about her husband. It had probably taken a great deal of courage for her to come to me and ask for such a favor. And I did not wish to make it any harder than necessary.

"I'm certain I can find something. Is he in much pain?"

Her brow wrinkled and she clasped her hands together at her waist. She stepped forward a bit as if my answer had given her more confidence.

"Oh, ma'am, he can hardly go this morning, 'tis so bad. The medicine he's been taking just does him no good anymore!"

"I left my bag downstairs yesterday. If you'd like to meet me in the bath area in a few minutes I'm sure I can give you something that will help him."

She managed a little smile, although I thought she did not quite trust me yet. Why she did not was still a mystery.

"Thank you, ma'am," she said quietly, backing toward the door. "It must have been the rain and cool weather this morning that affected him so." Her words sounded apologetic.

"I'm sure that must be," I said. "I'm more than happy to help."

When I smiled at her, this time she smiled widely and her eyes lost some of their closed unfriendliness.

When Monteen and I went downstairs she seemed especially quiet, looking at me from the corner of her eye as we walked toward the baths. I knew my coolness the day before had disturbed her, perhaps even hurt her. But I felt helpless to explain how I felt. And I certainly did not think it wise to tell her about my visit last night from David. Especially since she was so convinced I was the one to be hurt.

Anna and her sister were already in the beautiful tiled bath area when we entered. Allyson was lying on the table, patiently awaiting our arrival.

"I'm sorry we're late," I said, going quickly to the

130

table and smiling down at her. "I overslept."

"I'm not at all surprised," she said. "What with the terrible storm last night I did not sleep so soundly myself."

When Mrs. Woolridge stepped quietly into the room I went to the bag I'd left near the exercise tables. The black bag stood open. I did not remember leaving it that way. But I'd been preoccupied and could have done it without thinking.

I found the bottles of medicine and also gave her a lotion which her husband might rub on the inflamed joints and muscles.

"Thank you, ma'am," she said, glancing self-consciously at Anna and Allyson as she left.

"Let me know if that does not help Mr. Woolridge," I called to her.

"I will . . . thank you."

Anna watched me as I closed the bag and set it on the floor beneath a table. But she said nothing.

"You seem to have made a friend," Allyson said.

"Mrs. Woolridge? I certainly hope so. She did not seem so friendly when we first arrived," I said.

"She is a bit standoffish," Allyson said. "But I understand she's totally devoted to David."

I wondered if that was why the housekeeper had acted so rudely to us before. Did she think I had hurt David somehow?

I quickly set to work with Allyson's exercises, unable to look into her eyes. For seeing her had brought with surprising alacrity the picture of her husband as he stood before me last night in the darkness. I could almost see the flicker of lightning upon his handsome face. It was so vivid that for a moment I was afraid I might be experiencing another vision.

I shook my head to clear my mind, aware all along of Monteen's questioning looks toward me.

I stepped away from the tables, indicating that she

131

and Anna should continue the exercise. My mind was elsewhere, still agonizing over what I'd felt last night. And it especially bothered me here in the presence of David's wife. When I looked toward the three women, Allyson watched me. Her eyes were dark and troubled and for a moment I thought she must know what I was feeling about David.

"What's wrong?" I asked quickly. "Are you in pain . . . anything?"

She shook her head and the expressive look was immediately gone. "Oh no, nothing like that," she said quietly. "But I . . . I wanted to apologize to you. To both of you for the . . . the way I behaved last night."

Monteen continued to work, but her eyes met mine across the table. There was a flicker of scornful doubt on her face.

"Oh Allyson," I began. "Please don't feel you should apologize . . . not to me at least."

"I've already spoken with David."

"But I don't . . . I didn't mean that you owe *anyone* an apology. My goodness, you have enough of a problem just getting better. I'm sure everyone here can overlook your having a bit too much wine."

"I'm afraid my husband does not agree."

There it was again. The seeming evidence of David's rancor, making me wonder again. And I felt a twinge of guilt that I could still be attracted to a man who was so obviously cruel and unfeeling to his wife. Was I wrong about him last night . . . lulled by desire into believing as I wanted to? And could I think he would treat me any differently after a while . . . after the familiarity began to bore him?

"I cannot believe David would be so uncompromising in his treatment of you," I told her, with immediate sympathy.

"I'm afraid David is not the same man you once knew," she said.

132

I felt uncomfortable and I did not want to get into an intimate discussion with her, especially in front of Monteen and Anna. In fact Anna had that look I'd seen before, as if she would intervene whenever she thought the conversation might become too hurtful to her sister. I had never seen anyone so devotedly protective of anyone.

So I said nothing more, but busied myself with cleaning up as Monteen and Anna helped Allyson into the warm, steaming water.

Later, when they were drying her, Allyson looked up at me with that sweet, shy look I could not resist and said, "Would you have lunch with me today, Julia . . . in my room?"

For a moment I hesitated. I was not sure I was ready to hear all the things she might want to say about David. And I knew I was not ready to admit I was wrong about him.

"Yes, of course. I'd be delighted. I'll come right away as soon as we're finished here."

As Anna and Monteen pushed the wheelchair from the room, Monteen turned to me. "I'll see you at dinner tonight, Julia. I'm going to spend the afternoon with Mary. She wants to show me the grounds and the meadow."

I was relieved at her words for I had longed for a chance to be alone if only for a few moments. I needed to compose myself before I went in to see Allyson. The last thing I wanted was for her to learn about the emotional conflict I felt every time I looked at her husband.

Later, when I went into her room, I was again overwhelmed by the warmth and the sweet scent of roses. The glisten of white blossoms was everywhere. And for an instant I had a small insight into this person David had married.

Hard as it might be for me to understand, she was a

woman of excesses. The roses, though beautiful, were certainly much more than one would normally place in a room. And her drinking . . . I had the distinct feeling at last night's dinner that it had happened often. And I even wondered if her sweet shyness, the almost apologetic way she deferred to everyone—especially her husband—was but another sign of her intemperance.

She looked lovely; actually the picture of health as she sat propped up on the high bed, with white satin pillows at her back. There was a splash of color on her cheeks and her brown eyes shone with anticipation.

"Oh, I'm so glad you came," she murmured in that soft, shy voice that did not quite match her sturdy outward appearance. "I grow so lonesome in here day after day. That's one of the reasons I agreed for you to come, you know. Because I so longed for companionship."

Her face was alive, so childishly enthusiastic that I could hardly bear to look at her. I sat in a chair near her as we waited for someone to bring our lunch.

"If you're pleased," I said, "then I'm sure I must have made the right decision by coming."

"Has anyone told you about the cotillion we'll be having here at Stillmeadows?" she asked.

"No, I don't think so," I replied, smiling at her ebullience.

"I'm so glad you will be here. It's the end of the summer ball and I understand it was a tradition of long standing when the Damrons lived here before. Everyone for miles around will be here!"

"It sounds very exciting, and of course I would like to attend. If I'm still here of course."

"Of course you shall be here! It's only a few days from now. I think Millicent and Mrs. Damron began to plan it even before we arrived here!"

I tried to hide the uneasiness I felt. For in truth, a

gala ball in this house was not something I could look forward to. The mere thought of dancing with David set my pulses racing with anxiety; and yet the idea of not dancing with him was too painful even to contemplate.

"Then, of course, I shall look forward to it," I heard myself say.

We heard the delicate rattle of china just outside the door. I guessed the maid was having a difficult time opening the door and wheeling the cart at the same time. So I rose to help.

When I opened the door I'm sure the expression on my face was humorous. There in the hallway stood David, one hand on the wooden tea cart, as he reached forward with the other to open the door.

We stood for a brief moment, our eyes seeming unable to look away from each other. There was a look of pleasure in his gray-green eyes as his gaze wandered quickly over my face and down to the dimity dress that I wore. I knew he was thinking about last night, and so was I. But of course he could not know I had seen him and the woman he met under the elm tree.

"Julia," he said quietly.

"Here," I said, reaching forward to the cart, laden with covered silver dishes. "Let me help you."

In my haste I touched his hand and looked up into his eyes. There was no way I could dismiss the look there in the expressive depths, no way I could deny the heart-stopping spark I felt each time he was near.

I backed away from him, awkwardly holding the door open for him to come in. Then I followed him to the bed, where he placed the cart near his wife.

I felt such a conflict of emotion as I watched him set her dishes out before her. His show of graciousness toward her should have made me happy. After all, was it not his callousness toward her that had troubled me since coming here, his harsh treatment of a defenseless

135

young woman? Then why was there such a crush of agony within me now, a real physical ache near my heart?

"Come sit here, Julia," Allyson said. She had been watching me as David helped her.

The cart that David brought had three lunch settings on it. As I sat directly across the table from Allyson, David pulled a chair to the end for himself.

Allyson's looks at us and her slyly worded phrases soon brought a sickening feeling of comprehension to me. She had deliberately planned to have both of us here at lunch today. It was as though she wanted David and me to be thrown together.

"David, why don't you show Julia your prized horses . . . perhaps she'd even like to go riding with you."

David said nothing, only sipped his coffee as his eyes watched the fluttering motions of Allyson's hands.

"No . . . really," I stammered. "I don't care that much for riding." Of course David knew that was not true, but under the circumstances I trusted he would understand.

"Oh!" she said brightly. "Well, I'm sure he would be delighted to show you the grounds this afternoon."

"I . . . I have something else planned," I said quickly.

I looked into Allyson's expressive brown eyes and saw a flicker of excitement in their gold-flecked depths. I frowned at her and took my teacup into trembling fingers. I could not even look at David, knowing how angry he must be.

"Allyson," he said, almost as if reading my thoughts. "I'm afraid you're making Julia uncomfortable." There was a sternness in his deep voice, a warning. But I sensed that he was making an effort to treat her more gently today.

"Oh, now, David," she said. "Julia is a grown woman. And a principled one at that. I'm sure she understands that my meaning is completely innocent. As a matter of fact I was just telling her about the dance." Her eyes turned to me. "And I would count it as a favor, Julia, if you would be David's partner at the cotillion. It's not fair for him to have to suffer because of my poor unfortunate circumstances."

I looked across at David and the anger was evident in his stormy eyes. I shook my head slightly, hoping he knew that this was not my idea.

Allyson's eyelashes lowered against her pale cheeks in a shy gesture; then they lifted slowly, with an almost challenging look at David. The smile she gave was slow and deliberate, an intimate look that only married couples seem to share. My face grew warm and flushed and I wondered what she was hoping to accomplish.

David sighed, more a sound of disgust, I thought. He rose from the table and dropped his napkin onto the gold-rimmed plate.

"We'll discuss this later, Allyson . . . alone." Without so much as a glance at me, he turned and left the room.

After a moment's silence Allyson spoke. "I'm sorry. I seem to always do and say the wrong things, at least where my husband is concerned."

"I'm sure he was as embarrassed as I at being put in such an awkward position, Allyson," I said evenly.

"But I didn't mean . . ."

"Why do you continue to portray yourself as a burden to him, Allyson? Did you ever think he would be happy to spend a quiet evening with you at the ball, watching the dancers, listening to the music. Just being there with you?"

The look on her face stopped me from saying more. It was one of gentle amusement and quiet resignation.

"Please," she said. "I thought you, at least, would be honest with me."

"But I am . . . I . . ."

"No, Julia. No, you're not." She stopped my words, holding up her beringed hand with its neatly kept nails. "A woman would have to be blind not to see the attraction that still exists between you and my husband."

"Allyson!" I said in surprise. I could not believe she had actually said those words to me. And I suppose my face showed my absolute astonishment.

She reached her hand forward to touch mine briefly. "It's all right . . . really it is. I quite understand. David is a dynamic man and one that many of my friends in Boston find quite devastating in looks and charm. I've always known he married me only because he wanted a family. I accepted that when I married him, thinking that one day he might love me. . . ." She looked away and I thought her chin trembled slightly. "But then I was not able to give him even that . . . the one thing he so longed for. And now . . ." Her choked voice ended and she lowered her eyes. I had never felt so helpless, so unable to help anyone, as I did at that moment. How terrible it must be to love someone so deeply, even to become his wife, and still feel totally useless and unwanted.

"Allyson, please don't." I pushed the cart to the end of the bed out of the way and moved near to her. "I'm sure that David . . . cares for you."

"See!" she said, her brown eyes coming up quickly to accuse me. "Even you cannot bear to say the word *love*. You're too honest to lie to me."

"It isn't that at all," I said. "I just don't know you well enough, and as you pointed out before, David has changed a great deal since I knew him. I would not dare to try and tell you how your relationship with him should be."

"Well, I can tell you how I feel about him. I adore him . . . with all my heart. And that is why I want him to be happy. Even if it means finding someone else who

138

will make him so." She looked at me with a pointed, pleading look.

"Allyson, this is ludicrous. I will not listen to any more of it." I rose to leave her.

"Wait . . . please," she said. "I'm sorry. Stay only a few moments more."

I stopped, although I remained standing and did not return to sit beside her. "Then we must have no more of this nonsense about anyone taking your place."

"I shall only say one thing else . . . then I will hush,' she promised.

I was reluctant to stay, but she was like a willful little girl, pleading with her great brown eyes for me to listen. I shook my head and laughed, but allowed her to continue.

"I want you to promise me something, dear Julia." I was struck by the change in her. She had become suddenly very melancholy, even morose.

"Yes, what is it?"

"If anything should happen to me . . ."

I frowned again, preparing to tell her not to continue, but she would not let me, holding a hand up again to stay my words.

"If anything happens, please . . . you must promise you will help David . . . make it easier." There were tears in her eyes and her lips trembled slightly.

With a sigh I went to her and took her hand in mine. "Why are you talking this way? Nothing is going to happen to you! Your illness is not life threatening. I'm sure your doctors have told you that."

"That's what they say," she said tremulously.

I could not keep the vision from my mind as I'd seen it that morning, of the woman floating in the water. And a great dark well of fear fell about me, blocking out the delicate streaks of sunlight through the lace-curtained windows and bringing a chill to the rose-scented room.

139

I shook myself, knowing the last thing she needed was to see fear on my face as well.

"They have no reason to lie to you, Allyson. Now what is this all about?"

"I'm afraid here, Julia . . . I don't know why. David's family has never accepted me, but in Boston I had other friends. Here, I feel so alone, so unwanted. . . ."

I clasped her cold hands tighter. "Nonsense. The problem is you spend far too much time alone in this room. And it causes you to dwell on your illness. We must simply do something to correct that. Then I think you will feel much better."

Her smile was weak, although her eyes did brighten a bit as she looked at me with gratitude.

"Do you really think that is why I feel this way? So afraid . . ."

"I'm certain of it," I said, hoping I sounded confident.

"You are so kind to me, Julia," she said, smiling tremulously. "Yes . . . yes, I'm sure you must be right."

"Believe me, I am. And from now on we shall keep you so busy you will not have time to think of such dreary things. And before you know it you will be feeling much better and anxious to return home to Boston."

She seemed to feel better. But I stayed with her a long while, talking of the lovely weather and the plans for the cotillion. Only when she grew tired and I was sure she had recovered from her bout of melancholia did I agree to leave her. And I made a mental note to tell Monteen that we must plan some activities for her.

As I left I noticed that David had left the door slightly ajar. Directly outside, close enough to have heard everything Allyson and I had said, was Anna. She stood like a sentinel, her back against the wall, arms across her bosom. She made no effort to conceal the fact that she'd been blatantly eavesdropping. And she met my surprised look with a cool, haughty stare that sent chills down my spine even in the warmth of the August afternoon.

I was anxious to be away from her and took only a moment to fetch the medicine bag from the bathing salon before going upstairs.

As I walked along the hallway and up the stairs I felt the eerie silence of the beautiful house all around me. And there was a coldness, an unnatural air of hostility now, as if I were being watched. Suddenly the gracious, elegant home seemed different, no longer warm and welcoming, but rather like a dark stranger that lurks in the shadow of darkness to strike when one least expects it.

Chapter Twelve

I could hardly get to my room fast enough. I had thought earlier of joining Monteen and Mary outside, but all consideration of that idea was quickly dispelled from my mind by the haunting fear that gripped me. And all that was left was a cold, unreasoning dread that I could not shake.

I was actually shivering after I closed the door and locked it. I lay fully clothed on the bed, wrapping myself in the rose satin coverlet. I could hardly stop shaking as I lay with my knees drawn up, trying to get warm. Finally the tension I'd been feeling since coming to the Damron mansion, and the lack of sleep the night before, began to take their toll. And against my will I drifted off into a deep sleep.

I was dreaming. Visions floated before me as ghostly figures appeared in my mind's eye. I was trying desperately to see who it was and I didn't understand why I felt so alone and afraid. I wanted to run from the faceless shadows, but I could not move. My feet were leaden, my arms and legs so heavy I could not move them. I tried to scream, but no sound came. Then I saw the roses, white and lustrous in their perfect beauty. When I reached forward to take one in my hand, the thorns, like deadly needles, pierced my fingers. I looked down slowly in disbelief as the ruby-red blood dripped from my hand.

My heart was pounding loudly in my ears and still I could do nothing to protect myself from the shadowy apparitions that moved ever nearer to me. There was laughter surrounding me, a woman's hysterical strident laughter, the same I'd heard in the hallway outside my door that first night here.

From a great distance I heard a voice calling my name, loudly, insistently, as the pounding of my heart grew louder and seemed to fill the room where I lay.

Suddenly I was awake, throwing myself upward in bed. My heart was beating furiously, but it was not that which had wakened me. And it was not the sound of my heart I heard but a loud pounding on my door. And someone calling my name.

"Julia? Are you in there?" The loud rapping sounded once again.

I jumped from bed, feeling oddly disoriented. Monteen and Mary stood outside, both of them looking strangely at me.

"*Chère,* what is wrong? You look frightful. Are you ill?"

I motioned them silently inside. The light outside my windows had darkened and the sunset cast dusky golden shadows across the floor. I must have slept for hours.

"We've been knocking for the longest time, ma'am," Mary said, looking wide-eyed into my face. "Are you sure you're not takin' ill?"

"I'm fine," I said, brushing my hair back into some semblance of order. "I was sleeping very soundly. I . . . I didn't sleep well last night."

"Mary came up after our walk and we chatted awhile. But when I'd dressed for dinner and you still had not come to my room we thought we should check on you." Monteen still watched me cautiously.

I glanced at the mantel clock. "Is it so late already?

I can't believe I slept so long."

"Shall I help you dress, Miz Van Cleef?" Mary asked. Her eyes were still wide and sympathetic. I knew it surprised both of them seeing me so distracted. But I could hardly tell them about the silly dreams or the frightening thoughts I'd had recently. And I certainly could not tell them of the strange conversation I'd had earlier with Allyson Damron.

Whatever was wrong with me? It was as if I were slowly falling apart, losing a grip on my usual, practical behavior. It angered me that I should feel so helpless; and I suppose that helplessness made me remember the old determination I'd always had, the stubbornness that Richard had often teased me about.

"You must learn to trust, my love," he used to say. "Then you would not have to depend so vehemently on your own stubborn independence. Don't you know I will always take care of you and keep you safe?" But he had not been able to keep that promise to me. And I suppose it made me even more desperate than ever to control my own destiny.

"I would like for you to stay and arrange my hair, Mary. I'm sorry if I frightened you both, but I assure you I'm perfectly fine. I must have been so deeply asleep that I did not hear you at first."

"You're sure?" Monteen asked, stepping closer as if to examine my face. "I can have our dinner sent up . . . the three of us will have a quiet evening here if you'd like."

"Nonsense," I said. "I'm feeling much better after my rest. Now, you go down and join the others. With Mary's help I shan't be long."

Monteen smiled reluctantly, but she left, looking at Mary with a nod. I was sure there was a secret pact of some sort between them to look after me.

I bathed quickly in the copper tub behind the Chinese screen while Mary pulled a dress from the

145

wardrobe and arranged it upon the bed. Within a few minutes I was pulling the dress over my head, letting the delicate peach-colored silk flutter down my body to settle with a soft whisper upon its taffeta underskirt. The simple cut of the dress, with its pleated band just off the shoulders, had appealed to me the first time I saw it. And I guessed now that Mary's choice of it tonight was meant to flatter my pale complexion and reflect a bit of color to my cheeks.

Mary chattered happily as she brushed out my tangled hair. It was obvious how much she enjoyed being there at Stillmeadows. And I wanted to make sure my doubts did not change anything for her.

There was not much to be done in such a short time with hair as thick and straight as mine, but she managed to arrange it into an elegant, simple style, a smooth twist on top of my head.

I was feeling better already, so much so that I thoughtfully attributed my unreasonable fears of the afternoon to fatigue.

"I was afraid you might be catchin' a cold, like poor Miss Allyson," Mary said.

"What did you say?" I asked, looking up at her reflection in the mirror.

"Oh yes, she sent word to the kitchen just awhile ago, before we came up, that she'd have a bowl of soup in her room. She was feeling poorly and thought she might be coming down with a cold."

"That's odd," I mused. "She seemed perfectly fine when I left her this afternoon."

"Well, her sister said she was not feeling at all well. That's all I know." She stood back and looked at my hair. "I believe that will do it, ma'am. What do you think?"

My thoughts were elsewhere. "Wha . . . ? Oh, yes, that's lovely, Mary. You always manage to do things with my hair which I cannot."

146

"Perhaps I should go down and see about Allyson before dinner," I said almost to myself.

"Oh, I don't know 'bout that, ma'am. Her sister is probably standing guard like some old hound dog." Mary smiled at her own words and I was sure she must have heard the servants' gossip about Anna's strange, protective behavior toward her sister.

"Then I shall certainly go first thing tomorrow morning," I said, more to myself than to her.

As it was, all thoughts of Allyson vanished as soon as I entered the dining room. At least temporarily.

The first thing that caught my attention was the gaiety of the people gathered there, so different from the night before, when Allyson had seemed to put everyone's nerves on edge.

Monteen was seated at a small table near the front window with her cards spread out before her. Everyone was laughing and enjoying her entertaining comments. But most surprising of all was Anna's presence. I'd expected her to be with her sister. She was certainly not as gay and relaxed as the others. She never was. But her look for once was pleasant enough.

Anna's dress of pale yellow did nothing for her wan complexion, and the rows of frilly ruffles across her shoulders and again at the bottom of the skirt seemed incongruous with her big-boned, rather mannish figure. But tonight there was a touch of rouge upon her cheeks and she seemed highly restive and full of quick nervous movements.

But I gave not much thought to Anna, only too happy to see an appearance of normalcy in the household. I would welcome anything that helped banish the odd, uneasy emotions that would not seem to leave me.

James saw me first and with a low murmur of approval came to the doorway to take my hand and escort me into the room. For a moment the room grew silent and I feared I might be the cause of it.

Then Grace Damron spoke. "Julia, my dear. You look like a breath of spring. Come in, come in. Your friend Monteen has kept us pleasantly entertained until your arrival."

I was aware of David's gaze upon me and when I glanced toward him I saw his quick, subjective appraisal. His eyes had darkened and a smile played lightly about his lips as his gaze raked over me and down to where my skirt swept the floor. My breath caught in my throat and I had to look away, for I was certain everyone must see how unsettled his looks made me.

"But you should not have delayed your dinner because of me," I said. "Please forgive my being so late."

"Nonsense," Mrs. Damron said. "You're an important part of our gathering."

Millicent was resplendent in a shimmering rose-colored gown. She threw me a look that negated Mrs. Damron's gracious statement. But after all, could I blame her for resenting me, a stranger who had come to take some of David's attention from her?

It was growing more and more obvious to me that she and James were not happy. And the way she looked at David . . . the way she spent most of her day with him . . . made me certain that she was the specter in white, the woman who danced with such abandon beneath the large elm near the meadow.

And of course I could no longer deny that the lover she met had to be David. There simply were no other available men here except the domestics. And I could never imagine the haughty Millicent with one of the servants. So perhaps I could understand why she felt threatened by my presence and why her looks of resentment were often directed my way.

Anna, on the other hand, watched me with a sly

smile, her dark eyes positively aglow. I could not believe it was the same woman who watched so protectively and solemnly over the invalid Allyson.

Once we were seated at the table, conversation returned to normal. I tried to direct my looks anywhere but toward David. But it was impossible to ignore him . . . his tall, handsome good looks in his dark evening coat. The healthy golden color of his skin emphasized his electrifying eyes. I had never met a man who could make me feel the way he did. And so, under the circumstances, I knew it was wise to avoid him, at least as much as I was able to with such a man.

There was one moment when I pulled my eyes away from him that made me curious. I saw Anna watching him and on her face was a dreamy romantic look. It was so unlike her. Her thin lips were relaxed, curved into a wistful smile, and her eyes were soft and dazed, changing her mannish features into gentle curves. She was looking at him with complete admiration. I blinked several times, hardly aware of the talk going on around me or even of the delicious food before me. If David or anyone else noticed Anna's strange behavior, there was no indication. In fact David treated her as he always did, almost like a sister.

It was then, knowing I risked putting everyone in an ill mood, that I decided to ask about Allyson.

"Anna, I understand your sister is not feeling well tonight. Nothing serious I hope."

Anna turned her eyes from David and smiled. I was surprised at the white gleam of perfectly formed teeth. She really had a quite pleasant smile. "No, nothing serious. Only a cold. But I doubt she will be up to her treatments for a couple of days."

Monteen gave me one of her amused, exasperated looks.

"I'm sorry to hear that. Just when we were beginning to make a little progress," I said.

"Were you indeed?" David asked, directing his potent gaze at me.

"Why yes . . . ," I began. "She seemed stronger today and her attitude is growing more positive I believe."

He smiled enigmatically as he toyed with the rim of a crystal wine glass before him. Everyone at the table had quieted and seemed to wait with indrawn breath for his next comment.

"Actually Allyson has always been a very strong woman, both physically and mentally. She can do just about anything she sets her mind to."

I felt he was telling me that I did not know her as well as I thought. But I was not sure exactly of the point he wanted to make.

I looked at him with puzzlement. "If you're trying to tell me something, David, I'm afraid you'll have to be more specific."

"The doctors have already said there is no physical reason for her paralysis. And Allyson has been known to, shall I say, strain the truth a bit."

"David," Mrs. Damron interrupted. "What are you suggesting?"

"I only want Julia's opinion," he said coolly, without even turning to look at his mother.

"I understand that, dear, but it does not seem quite appropriate that we should discuss Allyson in such a way . . . with her not even here to defend herself."

"Oh, for goodness sake, Mother Damron," Millicent said. "You know how Allyson is. She's probably lurking outside the door now listening to every word and plotting her next sympathetic ploy. Besides, I'm sure Anna won't wait long until she tells her every word that is said." She threw a cold-eyed look toward Anna.

Mrs. Damron closed her eyes as if in pain, but only shook her head and sighed.

"What . . . what are you saying?" I asked again. "Do you think that Allyson is faking her illness? But why would anyone . . . ?"

"It doesn't matter what *we* think, Julia. I want to know *your* opinion . . . your professional opinion." David's voice was firm as he watched me and his hint of sarcasm angered me.

I glanced at Monteen, but she did nothing to help me; she only shrugged her shoulders and gave me a blank look. Of course she would do nothing to defend Allyson. She had never trusted her. Perhaps she too thought that Allyson was feigning her illness.

But I could not believe she would take such drastic steps to gain attention. Who would want to be so inactive and remain in bed all day? It made no sense at all.

I looked about the table, reluctant at first to speak about Allyson on such personal terms. But after all, this was her family; they knew her and lived with her. Evidently David did not mind that they hear whatever I had to say.

"Anna, surely you don't believe this?" I asked.

She lowered her eyes slowly and it was as if a shutter had been pulled over her plain features.

"No," she murmured, glancing almost apologetically at David. "I know my sister cannot walk."

I sighed, relieved that *someone* here believed in the girl besides me.

"My professional opinion, David, is that Allyson is a very sad and lonely young woman." If the comment sounded accusing, I did not care. My voice seemed loud, echoing slightly in the quiet room. "And like Anna, I'm positive that she is not capable of walking. The reason for that, however, is something I cannot guess."

"If you're insinuating that David is somehow the cause—," Millicent fairly sputtered with anger in her defense of the man she apparently loved.

"No, Millicent, I'm not," I said, cutting off her

151

words. I knew my voice was cold and as I met David's questioning look I didn't care that my eyes were equally cold. For he had angered me by the way he broached the subject, almost as if he were ridiculing my being here. I did not think it was fair to put me in such a position and it certainly was not fair to his wife.

He knew he had angered me. His sensual lips quirked in the slight grimace of a smile but he at least had the good grace not to mock me further. But I, with a stubbornness I could not quell, would not let it rest there.

"If you suspected Allyson of feigning her paralysis, why then did you ever consider the baths? And why did you ask me to come here?" My anger spilled over into my words.

"You misunderstand," David answered softly. "I've accused her of nothing." His voice was not as indignant as mine. "I only asked for your opinion as to her physical condition."

"She is sick! She cannot walk! And as I said before, the reasons behind this are something I cannot know. But believe me I intend to find out."

"I hope that you will," he said slowly, again running his fingers along the rim of his wine glass.

"I think you all do her an injustice. Perhaps she would not be so ill if she felt she truly belonged to this family." I knew as soon as the words leapt from my mouth that I had overstepped my bounds. But I was so angry that I did not care. Let them ask me to go . . . I was almost ready to do so anyhow.

"Mrs. Van Cleef!" Anna said. "I love my sister dearly and I, more than anyone, want to see her well again. But you have no right to speak to David this way. He has treated her with the utmost care and greatest of understanding." She was so furious she could hardly seem to get the words out fast enough.

I was shocked speechless by her defense of him.

152

"Oh, give it up . . . all of you. Can't you see that poor, sweet, vulnerable Allyson has done it again? She's already captured Julia's sympathy." Millicent's laugh was sneering. "And I would have thought you were much too sophisticated to be taken in by her so easily, Julia," she mocked.

"That will be enough, all of you. Julia has come here out of the goodness of her own heart. She sincerely agreed to help and I will not have her made to feel uncomfortable in this house. Not as long as I'm still mistress here!" Mrs. Damron's voice was stern, but not unkind. And I could not miss the fact that her attitude had changed drastically toward me since my eighteenth summer.

I could not believe she actually defended me . . . and I think that puzzled me even more than the family's irrational animosity toward Allyson.

For once Millicent seemed subdued and even a bit shamefaced. It was obvious that she genuinely cared for and respected her mother-in-law and did not want to upset her further.

"I apologize, Mother Damron," she said quietly. "And to you, Julia."

"Well, I, for one, would like to abandon this subject. Miss Valognes, why don't you continue your reading of the cards? I found it most entertaining." James spoke calmly, as if the distressing conversation bothered him not at all. I was beginning to see that he would avoid problems and confrontations whenever possible, many times by pretending they did not exist.

He had not uttered a word during dinner. In fact he was the only one in the family who'd had nothing to say about Allyson. And I noticed before that he was not as critical of her as the others.

Everyone was relieved at his suggestion and agreed readily that Monteen should again read the cards. She went back to the table, where the others joined her.

James stood back with me away from the others. He kept his voice low as he spoke. "I'm sorry my wife is so often rude to you, Julia. I'm afraid she's a very outspoken woman."

"Don't apologize, James," I said, smiling up into his kind, gentle eyes. "I'm a bit outspoken myself."

"That's not all bad, you know. Especially where my brother is concerned. He can tolerate almost anything except indifference." His eyes met mine and I saw there an empathy I had not expected. And I wondered if he had any idea that Millicent was in love with this brother he thought he knew so well.

Chapter Thirteen

David stood near the window also but he was not watching the cards as closely as the others. With a quick, unreadable glance toward me he picked up a glass of wine and walked out of the dining room, turning to go outside.

As my eyes followed him I had already forgotten James's presence beside me.

"I have a feeling you've misjudged him, Julia," he said quietly.

I glanced quickly at him. "What do you mean?"

"He really has Allyson's best interests at heart, you know. I think he wants her to be well so badly that he becomes frustrated. And he has not really gotten over losing the child. I've never known anyone who wanted a baby so desperately. I believe that's why he seems impatient and short-tempered with her . . . and with you."

Did James suspect that there were other, powerful emotions between David and me? Hidden feelings which caused us both to snap at each other? Oddly I felt I could trust James, might even speak to him about things I might not say to anyone else.

"He must love her very much then," I said quietly.

"I did not say that," he replied gently.

"But he . . . he must care for her. If he's as concerned

as you say."

"He wants a child . . . a family." James laughed softly, a warm murmuring sound. "Oh, my dear beautiful little Julia. You are so sweetly transparent. I can certainly see why my big brother is smitten with you. Underneath that elegant blond sophistication lies the heart of a young innocent. I can hardly believe you were ever married." His eyes twinkled as he stared boldly down at me with amusement.

I blushed, feeling very foolish. And just as he said, I felt like a young schoolgirl, noticing a man for the first time. But only I knew how close to the truth that was, for those wild, overpowering feelings of love had never been present in my marriage. I frowned at James and opened my mouth as if to protest.

James lifted his eyebrows, daring me to deny how I felt. But I could not. I could say nothing, feel nothing, except an overwhelming surprise that what I'd felt for David so long ago had never really left me. Even with all my years of denial.

"It's all right, you know. Your secret is quite safe with me." James looked at me warmly and with a great understanding.

"I . . . I don't know what to say," I stammered. I looked toward the card table, afraid that everyone would now know my secret. But they were all deeply engrossed in Monteen's nimble playing of the cards.

James took my hand and gently turned me to face him. "I only want us to be friends. You need not say anything to me . . . or explain. I, of all people, would never condemn you."

Something in his words made me look at him more closely. His sweetness toward me reminded me of Richard. But I did not really understand James's last comment. It was as if he had some hidden sin which he would like to confess. But before I said anything else he walked to the card table and stepped quietly behind his wife's chair, placing his hands upon her shoulders.

156

From where I stood I could see the door leading outside to the portico. And through the beveled glass panes I detected the glowing tip of a cigar where David stood, thoughtfully looking out over the lawn into the darkness.

I had to grapple with a strong inner feeling that urged me to go to him. He seemed so alone, so vulnerable. I needed to make my peace and assure him we would always be friends at least. But my instincts told me I must not—not now. And I had to remind myself that I was the one who'd said only last night that we must guard against being together.

So I joined the group gathered about the card table. Monteen had read each personal profile, except of course for David's and mine. Everyone was enjoying the diversion and none seemed upset with their readings.

"Do one for the house, Monteen," Millicent urged. "This place has so many ghosts from the past that it positively has a character all its own."

"Mais oui," Monteen smiled. "Houses certainly do have their own character and I suspect this one has more than most." She winked at me and I knew she was enjoying her evening.

She began to shuffle the cards, then placed them with a deft flick of her wrist, face up, on the table before her.

"This is a different method I shall use for the great house . . . a simple one. It is called the horseshoe spread. I learned it on a great riverboat, the *Mississippi Belle.*" Her smile was brilliant as she flashed her gold-flecked eyes at her audience. When she entertained in such a way Monteen was absolutely in her element. It was good to see her without the worried look she'd had recently.

Anna seemed as intrigued as a young child with a new toy. And of course Millicent was always eager for some diversion. Even Mrs. Damron leaned forward, placing her chin upon her hand as she watched each

157

move Monteen made.

Monteen had placed seven cards, six of them face up, in a V-shape. The last card of the V she placed face down. Her look grew more solemn as she pushed the card in the upper left hand corner forward, away from the rest.

"This card is influenced by the past. It affects some . . . not all in this room. A wrong was done . . . a small one, but one which multiplied and now involves more people than before. It has caused pain and suffering; it has caused even more mistakes to be made."

"Do you know what it was?" Grace Damron's voice sounded desperate as she leaned forward. Her face was pained and ashen.

Monteen looked up and stared for a moment into the woman's troubled gray eyes.

"No, I do not."

I sensed David's presence as he stepped quietly back into the room. We had all been so mesmerized by the game and by the excitement in the air that I don't think anyone noticed him except me. He stood in the shadows, away from the others, but close enough for him to see and hear what was happening.

He leaned a powerful shoulder against the wall and crossed his arms over his chest. His look and demeanor were ones of amusement and indifference.

Monteen pushed the second card forward. "This card indicates the present circumstances at Stillmeadows." She frowned and shook her head, then looked at me oddly. I could only describe the look as apologetic.

"There is much sadness in this house . . . much regret. It involves . . . all in this room."

I began to feel uneasy, for I hoped Monteen would not use anything I had told her just to further the entertainment. And I certainly did not want her to include me in her reading.

Millicent laughed, breaking for a moment the

tension in the room. "Of course there are regrets. You are being so general this reading could apply to any house or any family!"

"No, this is directly related to the misdeed I spoke of earlier. Some here are not aware of what I mean and yet it has affected all of you. Unless the truth is made known to all, I cannot speak in more than general terms."

Millicent smirked, twisting her lovely mouth into a distrusting look. "But *you* don't know the truth either . . . is that right?" James patted her shoulder, as a mother might calm a restless child.

"That is correct," Monteen said solemnly.

I could feel David's eyes upon me, but I did not look up to meet that gaze. For we both knew what Monteen had to be speaking of. Would I see a look of apology? Was he the one Monteen spoke of . . . the one who'd hurt someone? And was that someone me? Our differences were not something I wished to discuss in front of the whole family. And like Millicent, I could make no sense of Monteen's other statements.

She spoke then of correcting past mistakes. The next two cards she read told of the future and the action needed to make the corrections. But it seemed to depend on so many things that I, as well as the others, became confused at Monteen's rambling pronouncement. Perhaps I was the only one in the room who knew that was one of her most trusted diversions when anyone in the audience wanted to be specific.

Monteen reached the bottom of the V-shaped card design and now pointed out the fifth card, which led up the right side of the horseshoe.

"This card reveals your attitudes, all of you that belong to this house."

I felt a chill run down my neck and without thinking glanced at David. His eyes met mine with that mocking, amused look that so irritated me. And in their shadowed gray-green depths I saw his accusation.

159

But there was something else there that took me by surprise. There was pain, a deep hurt that he could not hide no matter how he tried with his cool, charming smile.

Was he sorry? Was that what he was trying to relay to me in that look? For a moment I felt a burgeoning hope within me. And I knew that I would gladly forgive his leaving all those years ago, if only he would ask it. It was something I never thought to admit, even to myself. For he had hurt me so deeply with his rejection and with his wish to marry someone of a higher status. I'd thought I would hate him forever. And yet, only a few days in his disturbing presence had proven how very wrong I was. And it was not an admission that made me feel proud of myself.

I frowned and looked away from his riveting gaze. By now Monteen was speaking about one of the other cards and I had missed part of what she said.

"... obstacles in the way. There are too many secrets, liaisons, that should not be. This must change before the aura of peace and happiness will return again to this house."

I saw James's fingers tighten only the slightest bit where his hands rested on Millicent's shoulders. I was beginning to believe more and more that he did know about Millicent and his brother and chose to suffer in silence rather than confront them. The look that Millicent quickly flashed from the corner of her beautiful violet eyes toward the man who lounged against the wall confirmed what I'd already guessed. And it made me feel sick inside.

The air was electric as everyone sat with bated breath, awaiting the reading of the seventh and last card. I was surprised that, with the very personal revelations, someone in the room did not come forward to stop Monteen. But no one did.

Monteen's beautiful olive skin was flushed and shimmering with perspiration. And I knew she believed with all her heart that what she saw in the cards was true. I was as frightened and confused as anyone gathered there that night. But I never once expected what the seventh card would reveal.

She flipped the card face up and a small gasp escaped her lips.

"Death."

The word hung in the room, echoing across the walls and seeming to glance off the cut glass vases and crystal chandelier. I could see the shock reflected on every face there. Even David pushed himself away from the wall as if he would move toward the woman who spoke, as if he meant to stop her from saying more.

Monteen herself looked surprised, as if she had not been able to control the words that came from her lips. Indeed she looked as if she'd just awakened from a deep sleep. Her widened eyes darted about the room and there was a look of stricken fear and regret in her dark eyes.

"Oh, my. I'm sorry," she whispered. "I should not have said that. I . . . I don't usually . . . shall I stop now?"

"No!" It was Anna who spoke, her look almost frantic as if she was compelled to hear the rest, to hear every last detail. "You must continue."

I was as surprised as Monteen seemed to be, for I knew this was one thing she never predicted. Her games, even as much as she truly believed them, must also have a light, entertaining air about them. For no one ever really wanted to know the grimness that the future life might bring. Even when Monteen did find the death card, she would always interpret it in some other, more positive way, such as a transformation, a rebirth. But tonight it was as if she had no choice, as if the word was propelled from her lips by some unknown being.

I went quickly to her, placing my hand over Monteen's trembling fingers that still held the card.

"No," I said. "That's enough."

I saw a hand reach out and deftly take the card from both our grasps. David threw it on the shining mahogany card table. His voice was quiet and dangerously commanding.

"Let her finish."

He stared at me, defying me to deny his order, challenging me to stay and hear what the death card would predict. I wanted to turn and run, to close my ears so I did not have to hear. But I could not; I was paralyzed by his intense gaze ... and by my own illogical fears.

Monteen drew in her breath. Then she closed her eyes and expelled the air slowly through pursed lips. Again the words seemed to come on their own, as if she had no will in the matter.

"Someone will die in this house ... an unnatural death. The evil of it shall be that it is done for greed. A greed of the heart." I shivered at her words, wishing someone would say something.

"It ... it's only a game," I stammered through lips that had grown cold and dry.

"Yes," Monteen said, smiling wanly, obviously anxious to quit the game. "Only a silly, childish game ... meant to frighten you ... but deliciously so." I almost believed her myself.

"So it was." Mrs. Damron rose slowly. She was pale and clearly shaken by what had just happened. But she hid it well. Smiling with an air of dignity, she turned and left the room in silence.

Even the exuberant Millicent was for once speechless. And whereas she usually could not seem to bear the sight of her husband, that night she clung to him, as if she were afraid for him to leave her side.

James was clearly flattered by his wife's newly found attention and with a passionate look he quickly spirited her away to the privacy of their own suite.

Anna rose and smiled toward David before she too left.

"Well, Miss Valognes, you certainly managed to give us all something to dream about." David had lit another cigarillo which he held near his lips. He squinted through the smoke at us, his look hard to comprehend. I could not tell if the glint in his eyes was from anger or his usual sarcasm.

"Yes, I know. I'm sorry."

He waved the cigarillo toward her and with a shrug of his broad shoulders dismissed her words. "Don't worry. I'm not superstitious. Good night, ladies," he said with a studied air of amusement. "Do have a pleasant evening."

Moments later, as Monteen and I ascended the stairs and hurried along the darkened hallway to our rooms, she gripped my arm tightly.

"Oh, *chère,*" she whispered. "I have never had this happen to me before. Never have I been in such a place, where the darkness lurks so frightfully near. I know now why I do not like it here . . . why I've begged you to go!"

"Stop it, Monteen," I said as we stood outside her room. "You're becoming carried away with this game and it's unnerving."

"It is good you feel that way! Now perhaps you will listen to me. Please, Julia, say that you will go back to the El Dorado right away!"

"Perhaps you're right," I said thoughtfully, worried not only about her prediction, but also about my own fears.

"Ah," she said with a sigh. "At least you will think about it now . . . yes?"

"Yes, Monteen. I will think about it."

She seemed relieved as we said our good-night. I hoped it would help her sleep well, but as for myself it only brought on more questions. Questions I feared would keep me awake the rest of the night.

After turning down the bedcovers and extinguishing the lamps except one dimly lit one near the bed, I walked restlessly about the room.

163

I walked to the window and pushed the curtains aside. There before me, like a flash of light in an ebony sky, appeared the woman in white—my own lady of the mists. She ran gracefully across the lawn, skirts whipping about her body, arms outstretched joyfully. She whirled and glided, running to the shadows of the great elm tree. But tonight I saw no one there to greet her.

I closed my eyes and pressed my hand over my face. "What is happening to me?"

A moment later when I looked again the woman was gone. There was no trace of her, or the path she had just danced across the grass.

The sound of my heart was loud in the silent room as my whole body began to tremble.

Had I really seen someone . . . or was it my imagination?

I strained my eyes, scanning the darkness of the tree limbs that swept toward the ground, the shadows that moved beneath the tree and played tricks with my vision. And now I was more afraid than ever and thought for once that Monteen was right and that we should leave this place.

For now I could not be sure if the woman in white had been real or imagined. I was certain that Millicent must still be with her husband in their room. Had I seen anyone at all, or was it some trick of the night lights? Perhaps it was only the hidden mists from the steaming baths hidden far beneath the earth's surface.

But even more frightening was a thought that came roaring into my mind like a firestorm: the thought that the vision I'd seen was not really Millicent . . . not really anyone living in this house . . . but the angel of death, come to fulfill Monteen's chilling prophecy.

Chapter Fourteen

I woke next morning sitting in a chair beside the bed, for I'd been afraid to lie down and sleep after the disturbing events of the night. My neck felt stiff and aching and my feet were numb with cold.

I was relieved that there would be no exercises that morning. But I did want to visit Allyson and make sure she was feeling better. So I hurriedly bathed and stood looking in the mirror with growing dismay at the dark circles beneath my eyes. My fair skin seemed even paler than usual, with no hint of color upon my cheeks.

I tied the straight fall of hair back with a satin ribbon and feeling somewhat better I dressed in a white muslin dress that was sprinkled with small apricot-colored flowers. I plucked the medicine bag from the dresser and hurried down directly to Allyson's room. It was empty except for a maid who was putting away clothes and straightening the bed.

"If you lookin' for Miz Damron, she's gone to take her treatment," she told me.

I looked at her with surprise, but I was happy Allyson was feeling well enough to go on with the therapy.

I was very late and when I entered the bath area I saw they had already finished the exercises and were helping Allyson into the steaming waters of the hot springs.

Monteen looked up at me and her face immediately broke into a smile of welcome. But as she came forward her look changed to one of concern.

Allyson seemed thoroughly relaxed as she lay back in the water. She smiled languidly and made a slight wave with her hand toward me. Anna was nowhere in sight this morning, so one of the maids had helped Monteen.

"How are you, *chère?*" Monteen whispered as she came to stand beside me.

"I'm fine," I assured her. "And sorry I'm so late. But I thought Anna said Allyson would not feel up to this for a few days."

Monteen shrugged and gestured toward Allyson. "She sent one of the maids to tell me that she was waiting."

"You should have told me," I said.

"When you did not come to my room at the usual time I assumed you were sleeping late. Besides, there is no reason Anna and I cannot handle things here. We know the routine and you might be free to spend some time outside, perhaps go horseback riding."

Her modestly lowered eyes did not fool me for an instant. "Monteen," I sighed. She exasperated me so at times with her not-so-subtle maneuverings. "Please stop playing matchmaker." I lowered my voice to a whisper. "There is nothing between me and . . ." I glanced at the pool where Allyson lay with her eyes closed.

"Oh, but I did not mean that you would ride with anyone in particular . . . only by yourself . . . just for exercise, mind you." But her dark eyes were wide and filled with amused innocence.

"Well, you certainly seem in fine spirits," I said. "After last night I'd have thought you'd be packing to go home."

"I'm convinced you will be ready to leave in a few

166

days and that makes me feel much easier. Besides, things seem better by the light of day."

"Yes," I said, wondering at her good humor. And I wondered if she had any idea, with her teasing, just how I really felt about David; or that even the mere mention of him sent my pulses racing wildly.

"I'm sorry if I've upset you with my teasing," she said, looking at me more solemnly. "I only meant to cheer you a bit."

"I know. I don't mean to be defensive," I said, forcing myself to smile at her. "Besides, do I look so badly this morning that you must resort to cheering me?"

If I expected my friend to flatter me, I was mistaken.

"You look tired. And it bothers me to see you this way." Her voice was firm and her gaze steady as she looked at me. "And . . . I suppose I feel somewhat responsible after last night."

"No," I began. "You're not."

"I wish I had never agreed to read the cards! Now I have cast a shadow upon the house and upon the festivities they are planning!"

"I'm sure none of them took it seriously," I said. "And your reading has nothing to do with my restless night." I meant to reassure her. But in my own heart I could not deny how disturbed I'd been last night, especially after I'd gone to my room.

"Still, I hope you'll consider leaving soon. Anna is very bright and capable and no one could be more devoted to a sister than she. Let her continue the therapy. If she has a problem she can always send word to us at home."

I had to admit that even the mention of home sounded like heaven to me at this point. The idea of my own house, the security of being with people who cared about me, brought to mind peacefulness and comfort. For even here in this beautiful house filled with light I had an ever-increasing sense of darkness and danger surrounding us. When I thought of the El Dorado and the happy bustle of activity there, the darkness was gone and I felt a strength and lightness I could not feel here.

"I think you're right," I said.

"Wha . . . you do?" she exclaimed, light leaping into her dark eyes. "You will agree to go home?"

I could not resist laughing aloud. "Perhaps not at this very moment. But yes, I have thought about what you said before. Besides, I feel something here in this house too . . . that even I cannot explain. Ever since the first morning when I saw the vision . . ." I glanced quickly toward the pool as if to reassure myself that the woman lying there was safe.

Seeing Allyson there so peacefully, I continued. "The dance is only a few days' time. I will think about leaving then. And that will give us more time to evaluate Allyson's condition and to go over anything Anna might have questions about."

She clasped my hand tightly, and a look of happy relief came into her eyes. *"A la bonne heure!"* she whispered. "Is good!" She put her hands together at her chest and glanced gratefully upward as if to heaven.

I was happy she did not question my reasoning for staying until the dance. For indeed, I did not want to tell her why. In my heart I knew I needed to linger these last few days here in David's home, where we'd first fallen in love; needed to be near him, to make the most of this last time that I could see him so closely, so intimately. And I could not resist one dance, one last night of being in his arms before I would have to force myself to say good-bye.

But I managed a smile at Monteen before going to help remove Allyson from the steaming water. By now Anna had joined us. She and Monteen worked well together and it amazed me that my friend could choose the dour, unsmiling woman as a favorable companion, especially since she could not hide the fact that she still distrusted Allyson.

It was while they were lifting Allyson from the water that I noticed her long-sleeved garment. It seemed curious, especially in the hot and humid weather. The loose-fitting blouse was of a lightweight material, almost like a muslin. And as the wet cloth clung to Allyson's arms I noticed a large, very dark spot on her skin beneath the blouse.

Quickly I pushed the sleeve up and gasped as I saw the ugly purplish bruise which was revealed.

Allyson looked up into my eyes and there was a look of alarm on her face as she reached to pull the sleeve back over the ugly mark.

"Allyson," I said, reaching for her arm again. I would not let her hide this from me.

Her eyes flicked toward her sister as if she was afraid of what Anna might say. But the tall woman's eyes were cold, almost black, as she watched me with no outward show of emotion. She had known all along about the bruises!

Pushing the sleeve up again I saw there were several large marks on Allyson's upper arm. And as I pulled back the cuff of the other sleeve, I saw there were also dark bruises on her wrist, as if someone's hand had clasped her there. Then I knew without a doubt why Anna had told everyone last night that Allyson was ill. But when Allyson had not wanted to miss her treatment she had thought to hide with long sleeves the evidence of what someone had done to her.

"What happened?" I asked. I reached for the medicine bag to find an ointment for her.

The room was quiet, with only the trickling of water making any appreciable noise.

"Oh, it was nothing," she said, smiling as though everything was perfectly normal. Her eyes held a glazed sparkle, as if she still was not quite awake. "I fell, that's all. I caught myself on my arms as I fell. It's nothing, really." Her voice sounded odd, detached somehow. I

169

looked at her curiously and wondered if she had been drinking again.

I did not believe her story. The evidence of fingerprints was clear, just as the conclusion seemed to be of who had done this to her.

David's face loomed before me as he had been yesterday in Allyson's room: so quietly furious when he promised to return . . . so they could speak privately, he'd said. But I had quickly dismissed it from my mind when she'd begun to babble, talking of David finding another woman, the companion she thought could give him something she could not. David had been more than angry. His face had darkened with a hidden rage and his eyes had stormed for her to be silent.

And later, she had spoken to me of a time when she might not be here. Had he actually threatened her? I could not believe it. My heart lurched painfully and I looked at her again as Monteen and Anna rubbed her skin dry with the large fluffy towels. Could it be she was actually afraid for her life? Had David treated her so forcefully before that she was frightened of what he might one day do to her? Surely nothing she'd said would cause this kind of a reaction in anyone. And it seemed doubly hard for me to believe that it might in David.

But I meant to know. I had to look into his eyes as I confronted him with this. Try as I might, I could not believe David Damron would harm anyone, especially a helpless woman . . . his own wife. But the doubts still nagged at me and I could not rest until I knew.

I handed the salve for Allyson's bruises to Monteen. When I started to close my bag I noticed that the contents seemed disarranged. I moved some of the bottles about but saw no evidence of anything missing. Still, for an instant I had an odd feeling about it. But I was much too preoccupied to worry about it and thought that later in my room I would check the list I'd made earlier just to make sure. Perhaps I'd done it when I gave Mrs. Woolridge the medicine for her husband.

"Monteen, I think I will take your advice and spend some time outdoors this afternoon. I'll see you tonight at dinner." Without waiting for her response I turned and marched from the room.

I had no idea where I might find David, but immediately I headed toward the back of the house. Beyond the French doors I could see Mr. Woolridge working with one of the men in the garden.

I stepped quietly outside, aware of the sweet smell of newly scythed grass in the warm breeze and as always the scent of roses. Mr. Woolridge was snipping away the golden-topped blooms of the faded marigolds, throwing into the air a pungent, earthy aroma that I especially liked.

"Good afternoon," I said.

He turned and, without straightening, looked at me with very pale blue eyes. His thin features held a friendly grin.

"Afternoon, young lady," he said. Mr. Woolridge, unlike his wife, made me feel immediately at ease. He stood up slowly and placed his hands at the small of his back.

"I surely do thank you, ma'am, for the medicine you gave the missus. It's done me a world of good."

"That's good," I said, smiling at him. "I'm happy it helped."

"Yes, it surely did that. Was there something I could help you with?"

"I was looking for Mr. Damron."

He looked about. "If you mean Mr. David, I believe he's still in the stables. Been spendin' a lot of time there since he got that shipment of mares a few days ago. He sure does love his horses."

"Yes," I said. "Thank you." I stepped onto the walkway where some of the thickly growing plants and shrubbery tumbled over onto the bricks. As I moved

171

out of the shadow of the house the sun's hot rays immediately struck me, burning my skin through the thin material of my dress. But it felt good and pleasantly distracting to be outside, to hear the birds that rustled in the tree limbs and scratched noisily beneath the thick azalea bushes.

I did not linger, for there was nothing that could delay me from confronting David and demanding an explanation for the cruelty he had inflicted on Allyson.

Inside the stables the air felt cooler and sounds of shuffling filled the air as the horses nuzzled their hay. I stopped for a moment, allowing my eyes to adjust to the dimness in the barn. When I heard a voice murmuring quietly just beyond me and around a corner, I stepped into the wide corridor between the row of individual stalls. The pleasant scents of hay and leather mingled with the faint smell of horses.

Near the end of the corridor David stood. His hand was outstretched to gently caress the nose of the magnificent chestnut I'd seen him riding before. My breath caught for a moment at the memory of his wild, daring ride down the mountain that day as Penny and I stood watching him. And I had to admit he was no less breathtaking today as he stood before me, tall and masculine, his long legs encased in trim breeches. The top button of his shirt had come undone, showing a glimpse of darkly burnished skin. In his left hand was the riding crop I'd noticed him carrying before.

He spoke softly to the animal and did not hear me approach at first. I was aware of the big horse's response to his master. His ears were perked to catch every murmured word and his nostrils flared as he nudged his nose against his owner's outstretched hand.

David heard me and turned slightly, watching but not speaking as I walked to him. I stopped almost three feet away, not wanting to move any closer.

"Good afternoon," he said quietly, his voice warm and welcoming in a way that made my face grow

172

flushed and heated.

Without preliminaries I blurted out my question. "Yesterday after I left Allyson, did you go back to talk to her?"

He lifted his eyebrows sardonically at the cool bluntness of my question. "As a matter of fact . . . yes I did." His eyes wandered over my face, probing as they looked deep into my own eyes.

"Why do you treat her so cruelly?" I demanded. "Have you changed so completely from the man I once knew . . . or did I never really know you at all?" My fists were clenched tightly at my sides as I challenged him, saying things I knew I should not say. I intruded boldly into an area of his life where I had no right to be. But I did not care; rather, I welcomed this confrontation. It had been building since he came to me at the El Dorado. There were so many questions between us that had never been answered. Those doubts hung like a dark storm cloud, accelerating rapidly every time we met.

"Obviously you've already answered that question." His eyes glinted in the dim light of the stables and I knew I'd angered him. But even that did not stop me.

The chestnut tossed its head from side to side, moving restlessly in the stall, as if it sensed the tension in the air.

"Don't evade me, David! I saw the bruises on Allyson's arms! How could you treat her in such a way? Your own wife . . . the woman you love."

My voice trailed away at the questioning look and the spark of annoyance that leapt into his gray-green eyes.

His lips twisted sarcastically as he stared at me. "I'm afraid I have no idea what you're talking about. Why don't you enlighten me?"

He stepped toward me. Instinctively I moved away, turning slightly so that he was standing between me and the long hallway of the barn.

He frowned, a puzzled look on his dark, handsome face. "Julia . . . are you afraid of me?" His voice registered surprise and underneath I could see there was also the hint of pain.

"No," I answered quickly. "I'm not afraid of you, though perhaps in all good sense I should be."

His eyes grew cold and hard. "Why don't you explain that remark? For I'm afraid I'm making no sense of this at all."

"Your wife's arms today are marred by dark, ugly bruises . . . obviously made by someone who brutally grabbed her. You need not deny it, David . . . I saw how angry you were and I saw with my own eyes the imprint of your fingers!"

He only looked at me, and there was still that oddly puzzled look in his eyes. His hand moved restlessly at his side as the riding crop he held whipped lightly against the side of his leg. He looked down, studying the toe of his boot thoughtfully. Then, pursing his lips, he looked up again at me as I stood accusing him, waiting . . . hoping for his denial.

"So . . . you think I'm capable of that." It was not a question, but a statement, a quiet, almost defeated statement.

Our eyes met, casting sparks into the air as if metal had struck metal. Could I have been wrong about this? God, but I wanted to believe he had not done it, wanted more than I wanted breath to hear him say he had not. But what kept him from making the denial, whether pride or stubbornness—or what I least wanted to believe, guilt—I could not know.

"David," I whispered, almost pleading with him to tell me the truth. Tears rushed to my eyes, causing his face to waver crazily before my vision. I wanted so badly to hear him say he had not hurt her.

David mistook my whispered pleading and moved toward me with swift determination. He threw the riding crop onto the hay-strewn floor and pulled me

174

into his arms before I could protest, before I even realized what he was doing.

And as always, the feel of his arms, the familiar scent of him, the perfect fit of his body against mine, sent my mind into a clamor. And as always, in the battle of my explosive feelings against my better judgment, I was powerless to step away from him.

"Julia," he whisperd, his lips moving against my hair. "Don't cry. I can't stand seeing you this way. Tell me what's wrong." His voice was deep, softly comforting. His arms tightened about me, strong and powerful as if he would never let me go.

Suddenly there was a new tension between us, something other than the anger and sadness. And it was no longer the sweet, innocent love we'd experienced as youths. This was an indescribable, wild, compelling feeling that rushed like a storm over both of us, daring us to try and weather its fury.

"No, David," I murmured, trying too late to pull away, trying to convince myself to do what was right.

"Be quiet," he whisperd, pulling me closer against the length of his strong, masculine body.

My knees grew weak, trembling as I tried to hold myself upright. But against my will, I was aware of how ideally my body fit to his, even while my brain cried out the wrongness of it. But it felt so right . . . how could I ever deny again just how complete I felt when I was with him?

His hand went to my hair, carefully pulling the ribbon from the back and brushing the straight length of it against my shoulders. I could only cling to him weakly, unable and unwilling now to make him stop.

His fingers gently wiped the tears from my cheeks and my lips. His eyes grew dark as he watched his fingers trail across my mouth, until slowly he lowered his lips to take their place. He kissed the corner of my lips, sweetly and with such gentleness that my eyes once again filled with tears.

There was no longer a battle between us, no longer any reason to quarrel. For whatever I had come to accuse him of was gone, erased from my mind by the sweet power of his hungry kisses.

And I was no longer an innocent young girl first awakening to a man's kisses. I welcomed his lips, his hands, everything about him as I clung to him, surprising even him with my passionate response. He pulled away only briefly and looked into my eyes and there was a look of wonder and delight as he read the welcome desire on my face.

We had moved slightly so that I was standing very close to a stall which was filled with hay. The baled stacks at the rear rose high toward the ceiling of the barn. Some of the hay had been removed near the front, leaving a stair-step pattern of hay bales. Without my realizing it, we had moved into the stall until the backs of my legs were against the hay.

I sank onto the sweetly scented grassy bench. David was beside me, touching my face, my throat, and my unbound hair. Slowly, his eyes holding mine, he unfastened the top buttons of my dress and pushed the material aside. His mouth was hot against the cooler surface of my skin as he trailed kisses to the hollow of my throat, and lower, to where my chemise barely covered my breasts.

I felt lost, unaware of time, or where we were. I did not even worry that someone would find us here, clinging to one another in a passionate embrace. There was only David and the ecstasy of his touch, the taste of his mouth on mine.

My unbound hair fell about my face, partially covering his as well, catching in the slight unseen stubble of his beard.

Suddenly, with a moan, and his breath rasping loudly in his throat, he pulled away from me. But his arms still held me. I moved nearer, as a freezing person moves to fire.

But his strong arms held me away as he slowly shook his head. There was such tenderness, such love in his eyes that I thought I should never forget the poignancy of that moment.

"I'm sorry." His voice was hoarse—a mere whisper. He stood up and moved even further away from me.

I looked up at him, hurt and bewildered. For I did not think I could bear his rejection again, could not bear being apart from him. Not now . . . not after this.

He saw the look on my face. In one swift movement he pulled me to my feet and gathered me again to his chest.

"Oh my darling Julia. Don't look at me that way. Never, ever think that I don't want you." He moved back so he could look down into my face. "I do. God in heaven knows how much. I've never been able to forget you, not for one day . . . or one hour. Your adorable face, your hair like silken clouds of gold . . ."

As if thinking better of his words he stopped and put an arm's-length distance between us, although his hands were still holding me firmly about my waist.

He took a long, slow breath and his eyes were dark, storm-filled with passion. "I could make love to you right here . . . right now. I know it's what you want as much as I. And you cannot imagine how happy that makes me. But then what? Do you think I'd be happy to carry on an affair with you . . . bring you disgrace when everyone found out? You're too good, too sweet for me to allow that to happen."

"But—," I began.

His hand, gentle against my lips, stopped my words. "Don't forget how well I know you, my love. I know how deeply you would grieve if you went against your beliefs and became a figure of disgrace. And I could never be responsible for that, for making you feel guilty every time you think of me. I want it to be perfect for us . . . and in time it will be. Our time will come darling . . . soon. I want you to believe that."

I was weak, limp with emotions so strong they threatened to overwhelm me and force me to do something shameful. I wanted to throw myself at him, beg him to do exactly what he and I both wished for. But I knew he was right. I knew it as surely as I knew I'd never love anyone as I loved this man. But he was married to someone else . . . someone I cared about and had vowed not to hurt. The deep crushing pain in my chest was almost unbearable as I turned and ran from him, ran away from the sadness in his eyes, away from the sight of the lips I'd just kissed, and away from the truth I knew he spoke. But the temptation of him engulfed me and I doubted I'd ever be left in peace again.

Chapter Fifteen

I ran outside. The sun, now in the west, was blinding as it settled like a halo about the house. I threw my hand up to shade my eyes from the glare.

Mr. Woolridge and the young man looked up from where they worked across the courtyard. I stood for a moment, unsure of where I could go, for I did not want to face them or anyone else in the household and let them see the tears on my face.

I went through one of the heavy iron gates in the stone wall and from there back to the east and away from the house. It was an area I had never explored.

This part of the ground was wilder, more dense than the manicured greens about the house. But it was obvious that it too was well tended. It looked as though it had been purposely cultivated to give a clean but natural and primitive look to the area past the barn.

The land here began to slope upward. Ahead of me was a steep ridge, dotted here and there with large outcrops of rock. And here were great towering trees, rugged oak and smooth-barked beech.

I walked quickly, not sure where I was going or when I would stop. Instinct drove me onward . . . that and the bursting energy I felt that was born of frustration.

A pathway leading into the rocky wooded area soon became apparent and without conscious decision, I took it. The back of my neck felt hot, damp with perspiration, and the white material of my dress felt sticky where it clung to my body.

Even when I was within the shaded shelter of the trees there was little coolness. But I didn't care. The walking felt good, the exertion distracting as I drove on along the path.

Only when I reached a small clearing did I stop and turn to study where I'd been. I was gasping for breath and my heart pounded in my ears and throat. But I welcomed the exhaustion that swept through me and caused my muscles to tremble. At least it deadened the ache in my heart, if only temporarily.

I allowed myself to cry then as I'd wanted to only minutes ago. I'd wanted to throw myself into his arms, crying and pleading with him. I had not wanted him to push me away or to protect me. All I wanted was his love. And I suppose I felt ashamed that he'd had to be the sensible one . . . the one to do what was proper.

And even worse than the humiliation was the guilt I felt. I was betraying Allyson, it was true, but I also betrayed myself when I'd so easily dismissed the troubling question I'd brought to David. I could not know if he had hurt Allyson or not, for as soon as he'd touched me I simply pushed them from my mind. And now I didn't know what to believe.

I cried until there seemed to be no more tears left, and I felt spent and weary.

Gradually as I stood looking down upon the house and the patterned garden I began to relax. I became aware for the first time of the beauty about me and of the sounds and smells of the forest. And at last the image of David began to recede.

Here, the rocks were craggy and dark, some of them covered with thick layers of moss. On closer inspection I saw that this was the opening to one of the hot springs which dotted the hillsides. It was possibly here that the water was piped to the house. And I suspected by the well-worn path and the smooth ground about the pool of water that this was one used by the servants of the house. Further evidence of that was a long-handled tin dipper hanging on a tree limb nearby.

Some of the rocks at the edge of the small pool were smooth, worn by years of use. And I guessed that here, as at the Corn Hole in shantytown, the people would congregate, sit and talk after their duties were completed, and soak their tired, work-worn feet. I could imagine it was a genial, even festive gathering, one where the servants might feel free to relax and be themselves, laughing and gossiping about the events of the big house below.

Steam rose from the gurgling water that trickled down the moss-covered slopes into the smaller pool. There was also a stream of water running beneath the slope from a large cavelike opening. Some of the rocks and surrounding foliage were stained by the different minerals found in the water, leaving streaks of rust brown and greenish yellow residue.

I bent and trailed my hand in the water. It was very hot here, much hotter than the pool in the house. But of course it would be cooled as it traveled the distance from the slopes to the house.

I walked back to the edge of the clearing that overlooked Stillmeadows. I'd never seen a more beautiful, calming sight. I sat on one of the large boulders to gather my thoughts and decide what I would do about David and all the conflicting emotions I felt about him.

It was surprising how much better I felt there, outdoors and away from the house. I studied the large white structure below me. It lay, like a gem, shining in the sunlight. It looked so lovely, so normal; and yet I was beginning to wonder if it held some strange dark magic. There beneath the blue Arkansas sky, listening to the pleasant trickle of the water and the rustle of wind in the great trees, I began to see, really see. There

181

was something wrong at Stillmeadows. Despite the polite well-to-do family who lived there, the expensive furniture, and the beautifully manicured lawn, there was something wrong, just as Monteen's cards had said. That realization left me with a dread of going back inside now that I could see the evil so clearly. And I could not help wondering how David, the man I still loved, was involved.

It was not like me to behave the way I'd done the past few days. I'd grown nervous and tense, short-tempered. More than that, I was afraid. More afraid than I'd ever been in my life. And I didn't know why.

The vision of the woman I'd seen drowned in the pool returned to me. And this time I did not try to shake the feeling that came rushing over me at the thought of it, did not try to force it away. Perhaps there was an answer in this vision somehow. I leaned back against the satiny bark of a beech tree and let the feelings come as they wished. Whatever was in my subconscious I knew I wanted to uncover it. And here in the serenity of the springs, with no one to see, I could let it happen and not be afraid of what others might think of me.

I could feel myself falling, plummeting through dark, empty, cavernous space. I felt the dark fear grip me again even as my mind urged me to open my eyes and banish the horror I felt. But I would not give in to that urge. I heard the laughter, a woman's voice, crazed and evil as I continued to fall. Then I stopped! I saw myself lying on a cold stone floor. I heard the dripping of water somewhere nearby. But that was all. The laughter had stopped. And there was no other sound, except my own breathing.

Suddenly there was someone before me, emerging from the shadows of the strange place where I lay. He stepped into the light and I saw dark hair touched with gold and eyes that glittered green in the darkness.

There was the deepest sorrow in his face as he looked

at me, and a longing in his dark-lashed eyes that tore at my heart. As I waited for him to take my hand and lead me away from the cold place, he closed his eyes. Then with a slight and sorrowful shake of his head, he moved back into the darkness. As he moved away from me he raised his arm and pointed into the gloom, directing my gaze there.

But I continued to watch him, not wanting him to leave me. "No, David, don't go. Please don't leave me here." I could hear my cries and see myself as if I were watching someone else.

Then he was gone and I looked to where he had pointed. And I saw it . . . the body of a young woman, dressed in white, lying on a raised bier. Her dress trailed gracefully to the floor, like a delicate covering for the platform. Her skin was as pale and lifeless as the dress she wore. Her hands were crossed against her breasts and in the dim light I could see the gleam of gold rings on her fingers.

I could feel it then, the terrible fear that was always with me. I had to see who she was, for I remembered the look of sadness on David's face and suddenly I was afraid the woman was me.

But I could never see her face clearly. There was a mist and the body seemed to move further away from me with each step I took.

"David!" my image cried. "David, where are you?"

The sound of a mourning dove murmured somewhere close to me. I opened my eyes, thankful the vision was over. But I felt weak and shaken by what I'd seen. It was the strongest premonition I'd ever experienced and I hoped with all my heart it would be the last.

Somewhere close another dove cooed, answering the one that perched in a nearby cedar. The sound, so melancholy and soft, caused a shiver to travel over my entire body.

All around me were the sounds of life on a typically

beautiful sunlit summer day. Cawing crows flew across the wide expanse of sky above me, while below, the sound of hammers echoed from somewhere near the house. People were busy working in the yard, presenting a vivid portrait of tranquility.

Yet I sat looking down as if I watched a play, for it all seemed so hollow and unreal. I shook myself, knowing I had to fight against the surge of fear that threatened me. I must not let it change me so completely. And I knew exactly what I had to do. I had to leave . . . forget my vow to help Allyson Damron and forget the man who'd come back into my life with such devastating force that it shook me to my very core.

The dance was only two days away; the morning after I would be back at the El Dorado and I knew that was for the best.

With the decision firmly planted in my mind I felt a slight easing of tension. And even though the premonition I'd just experienced was still nagging at me in the back of my mind, I felt a bit relieved. Surely, I told myself, nothing would happen in two days to make me regret my decision to stay for the dance.

I knew it would be best to avoid David and the rest of the family as much as possible until the dance. But there was one person I felt compelled to tell of my decision. I must explain to Allyson.

I brushed the leaves and twigs from my skirt and gazed around once more at the well-used springs area. Perhaps I might even come back here tomorrow, for it was a quite beautiful haven of peace.

The descent was even more rough and treacherous than the climb, for my leather slippers were not suitable for the rock-strewn path.

For a moment as I walked past the long stables I felt a familiar flutter catch in the pit of my stomach, and I had to fight the memory of David's handsome face and his passionate kisses. But I hurried on, letting myself into the garden by the same iron gate I'd exited a short while before.

I had intended to go directly to Allyson's room. But I saw that she was seated outside in the shade of a small dogwood tree near the white-rose garden. Her face was tilted upward, eyes closed as she relaxed. Anna sat nearby like a watchful nanny.

I felt an immediate lift in spirit at seeing her there. For surely this was a good sign if she felt well enough to venture out of her warm prison of a room.

Anna watched me approach, her eyes narrowed and alert. But I was already seated on a low retaining wall before Allyson realized I was there.

When she opened her eyes and saw me she smiled. She stared at me oddly for a moment with only the slightest frown between her brows. She seemed to be looking at my hair. I'd forgotten, after all that happened, that the ribbon was gone and my hair cascaded down about my face and shoulders in disarray like a young girl's. I blushed as I remembered how David had casually discarded the ribbon on the floor and brushed his fingers through my hair.

I smiled at her as I pushed the hair back behind my shoulders. But Anna, seated near enough to touch me, reached forward and plucked something from my hair.

I looked with dismay at the wisp of hay she held between her fingers as if it were a poisonous insect. Her eyes were cold and wary as she met my look, accusing me and condemning me all at once.

"I . . . I walked up the ridge behind the estate. To the springs . . ." But of course my stammering excuse was feeble, making no sense at all.

It did not help that David chose that moment to walk from the stables into the garden. But I knew then that there was nothing else I could say to explain. The guilt on my face must have been evidence enough.

Anna's eyes turned toward the man whose movement had caught all our attention. Twisting the hay between her fingers she looked first at her sister, then at

185

me. The fury in her dark eyes was obvious.

Allyson reacted coolly, just as she had done on other such awkward occasions. She reached forward and took the piece of hay from Anna's hand and dropped it unceremoniously into the dirt.

"Anna dear," she said quietly. "Why don't you bring us some cool lemonade?" The straightforward look she aimed at her sister left little doubt that she would brook no refusal.

Without a word Anna rose and went inside.

As David moved nearer he paused for a moment and looked deliberately into my face, wondering, I supposed, if I was still upset. He hardly even looked at Allyson. I wondered how he could study me with such questioning concern when his poor wife sat there seeing and reading that look. Embarrassed, I turned my eyes away from him.

I did not look up again, not even when I heard his muttered word, "Ladies," and his boots striking the brick walk as he too went into the house.

"Julia . . . I'm so sorry," Allyson said.

I quickly glanced up and into her face. "You're sorry? Allyson, how can you always be so noble, so . . . so . . ."

"Passionless?" she answered demurely.

"Nothing has happened between David and me. I need for you to know that." Sitting there facing her and discussing what I never thought we would, I felt relief that I could give her that assurance. David had made the correct decision for both of us in the stables earlier.

"It's all right," she said.

"No! No, it isn't all right! I want you to know that there has been nothing between us. I would never do that to you."

"But I've already told you—"

"Allyson—." I shook my head in frustration for I did not want her to even begin the subject she had

186

broached earlier.

"No, Julia, please listen. I appreciate your friendship and your loyalty. I can see now that you are not the kind of woman who could sacrifice her principles for a moment of passion. Even if I did not know, David has already made that clear to me."

"You and David . . . discussed this? Discussed me?" I was stunned by her blitheness.

"Well, of course we did. We have a very open relationship." She smiled patiently as if explaining something to a child.

"Allyson," I sighed. "I swear . . . I simply do not understand you . . . or your husband." I stood and walked, plucking leaves from the overhead branches of the dogwood tree. "In fact I don't seem to understand anyone in this house."

She laughed merrily, the sound drifting into the breeze and mingling with the rustling leaves.

"You don't understand how anyone could be dispassionate about a man like David?" She smiled merrily up at me, having the audacity to joke about it.

"How can you even discuss it?" I asked, sitting again on the low wall.

"I want the best for him. It's as simple as that. And obviously, in my circumstances, I cannot make him totally happy, so you—"

"Wait!" I said, raising my hand to stop her words. "This is not something I'm willing to discuss. It's impossible, it's embarrassing, and if you thought to somehow throw us together with your blessing, it simply will not work."

"All right then. I can see you are adamant about this. But you surprise me. I would never have taken you for such a narrow-minded moralist."

I looked sharply at her, stunned. The tone of her voice had even changed and her smile had become a crooked kind of sneer as she looked at me.

"But I will make a gift to you, Julia, here in the

187

perfect beauty of this summer day, while we are both young and full of life." She looked about her, waving her hands toward the skies. "If the day ever comes when I'm no longer in David's life, you both have my blessing, whether you want it or not."

"I don't!" I snapped. "I don't want your blessing! Can't you understand that?" I stood and looked down at her, my patience and understanding completely gone. How could anyone be so complacent, so uncaring, that she would make such extreme, ridiculous remarks? And how could any woman encourage another to conduct a liaison with her own husband?

"What is wrong with you, Allyson? Are you completely insane? I'm beginning to feel as if I'm in a madhouse!"

I ran from the garden then, from her smug martyred look and her strange disturbing words. I knew now that beneath her sweet-faced appearance lay a terrible sickness. And I wondered if she had always been this way or if the illness had somehow caused it. That day I glimpsed in her something that Monteen had hinted at before. It was almost as if another person dwelled within that quiet, docile being, hidden . . . waiting for her chance to shock the rest of us. And it was that person who insisted on giving her blessing to a union between her husband and me.

Chapter Sixteen

I managed somehow to spend the rest of the afternoon and evening alone in my room by pleading a headache, which wasn't too far from the truth. For after the events of the day and the premonition I'd felt at the springs, my head was indeed beginning to throb painfully.

I decided to spend the time rechecking the medicine I'd brought with me. I emptied the bottles and compared the contents to the list I'd made earlier. Something was not right. I checked and rechecked, but there was no mistake. The bottle that contained the opiate of poppy was missing!

Had I misplaced it somehow? Or had someone taken it? I could not believe the latter, even though I knew there was ample opportunity for anyone to have done so. But who? The bottle contained a powerful drug and one that, if overdosed, could be fatal.

I decided to say nothing to anyone until I could speak to Monteen about it. Perhaps together we could search for the missing drug.

The meal which Mary brought later helped my headache somewhat. But I still could not quite define the uneasy feelings I had about Allyson's words. I was irritated with her still and I could not for the life of me understand why she would say such outrageous things.

She had told me herself that she adored her husband. Was she only testing me . . . and my loyalty to her?

I supposed it was possible that they had simply never had a passionate love. But feeling the way I did about David, that was almost impossible for me to understand. I'd seen the way Allyson sometimes looked at him and I could not really believe there had never been passion between them.

Then my mind would turn the other way and I would wonder about the bruises and if they'd really been caused by David. After all, he never actually denied it. And it made me ashamed to admit that after he pulled me into his arms and kissed me I let the subject drop.

I walked to gaze out upon the meadow. The sun was only now beginning to disappear behind the distant blue mountains. But there was still enough twilight outside to see clearly. Without hesitation I left my room to venture outside for a few minutes before total darkness fell.

I hesitated before walking past the family dining room. But there were no sounds coming from the room; the Damrons had already eaten and departed. Quickly I opened the front door and walked across the portico and down the walkway.

It was quiet outside, with the stillness that sometimes comes at dusk. The large trees stood motionless and silent; there were no birds or butterflies flitting about the bushes as they did in the warmth of the day. The evening air was cool upon my bare arms.

I breathed deeply, aware again of how beautifully serene and perfect the estate was. Out over the still meadows, for which the house received its name, a slight fog had risen and settled upon the tall grasses. On the ridge behind the barn I could see the mists rising from the hot springs as the hot surface of the water met the cool night air. On past the one I'd visited were several other columns of mist rising from the trees like ghostly specters from deep within the earth.

I shivered and walked on down the circular drive, enjoying the new coolness in the air and the pleasure of the calm quietness around me.

Suddenly to my right I heard a rustle, as if something disturbed the tall grass of the meadow or the long-forgotten leaves of the past winter.

I stopped, wondering if I'd frightened some small night creature from its nest. My breath caught in my throat as I saw the tall figure of a man standing in the shadow of the elm. It was the same tree where I'd seen the woman in white dancing upon the grass, going to meet her lover.

My hand clutched my throat and I was powerless to speak, or to move. For if the man was David as I guessed then he must be waiting for Millicent. And I had to admit how badly it hurt to think that after our meeting in the stables, he would still come to her. I wanted to get away before he saw me, or before I was confronted by the sight of the two of them there together.

I turned sharply back toward the house. The interior lamps had been lit, throwing a soft golden glow through the long, sparkling windows out onto the lawn.

"Julia," the man's voice called behind me.

I hurried on, pretending I had not heard him call my name. Then I heard his muted footsteps as he jogged across the thick grass of the yard, and I knew I had no choice now but to face him.

But when I turned and the form grew nearer I saw that it was not David after all, but his brother.

"James," I said, breathing a whispered sigh of relief.

"Well, you sound happy to see me. What have I done to make me so lucky?" As he approached I could see his teasing smile.

"Just by being your charming self I suppose," I

191

answered, genuinely happy to see him.

"Or, by not being someone else?"

I looked away, hoping to channel his attention elsewhere. "It's a beautiful evening," I said. "I hope the weather continues so for the dance."

"I'm sorry," he said, ignoring my attempt at diversion. His words were more solemn. "I know I should not tease you about my brother."

I did not answer, not wanting to acknowledge that it did indeed disturb me to discuss David. His family seemed not to care in the least that he was a married man.

"Would you like to sit awhile and enjoy the evening before going back in?" he said. "I'm afraid I interrupted your walk and the least I can do is offer my company if you'd like to stay." He motioned to a white marble bench which sat back against a towering clump of lilac and azalea bushes.

I did not want to go back into the confines of my room so early, so I agreed. And I could not deny how curious I was about this quiet, good-natured man who seemed to blend so agreeably into the background of his odd family.

There was a large moon, not quite full, just appearing over the ridge behind the house. As if the orb's golden appearance summoned all the night creatures, crickets began to fill the air with their whirring calls. And in the forest beyond the meadow the low hoot of an owl drifted over to us. I shivered slightly as much from anxiety as the cool night air.

"You're cold," James said. He removed the dark jacket he wore and before I could protest, placed it around my shoulders.

"Thank you," I said. "It isn't really so cold. . . ."

"It can be frightening here if you aren't accustomed to the quietness of the country."

"Oh, no. I love the country. . . ." My voice trailed

away. How could I possibly explain to this man whom I hardly knew just how his home made me feel? I knew I could not possibly expect him to understand.

"I'm afraid we've all been a bit on edge since Monteen read the tarot cards for us," he said.

"Yes . . . I'm sorry for that. Our guests at the El Dorado find it quite amusing. I don't understand how it became so . . . so serious the other night."

"Perhaps because it was all true." His face was a dark silhouette against the sky as the lights from the house caste a glow upon his dark hair.

"Oh, you don't believe that . . . surely."

"Don't you? I could see a change in you that night. I wanted to say something to you before this, but to be honest, I did not know just how to approach you."

I looked at him with curiosity. He seemed so different tonight, not at all the carefree, joking young man he usually was.

He laughed softly. "I suppose I'm making no sense at all."

I waited, aware that he seemed to be gathering his thoughts.

"You're a very clever and observant woman, Julia. And I'm sure you did not need Monteen's soothsaying to tell you there is something wrong with our happy family."

"No . . . I suspected that all was not well, even before I came." I trusted him and saw no reason to be coy about my real feelings. Besides, I hoped he might help me learn more about David and the strange, uneasy alliance he seemed to have with his wife.

"I suppose it's always an unhappy situation when a marriage doesn't work."

"But why wouldn't it?" I asked, thinking he meant David and Allyson. "There seems to be everything to make it a happy one."

Something in his look made me wonder after I spoke

193

if perhaps he had meant his own marriage. I couldn't be sure.

"Did you love your husband, Julia?" he asked kindly.

"Yes . . . I did. But as it's been pointed out to me, perhaps not in a conventional way. He was my best friend. Ours was a warm, comfortable sort of love." I would not say more than that, because I was too embarrassed to tell him what was in my mind, about the wild, tempestuous love I felt for David.

"Ah," he said softly. "Friendship. I've often thought that all marriages should be based on friendship rather than love. Whatever it is we *think* is love."

"Perhaps you're right," I agreed. It was something I'd thought of before also. For I had not loved Richard in the beginning. It was from that warm and binding friendship that love grew. Why then did I feel so overwhelmed now by what I felt for David? It was certainly not the same thing I'd felt for my husband. I knew it was partly because I'd never stopped loving David even though I was married to someone else. Was it the same for him? I wondered. That was a question I longed to ask David.

"You look very sad tonight, here in the moonlight," he said softly. "Like a little girl with your golden hair down about your shoulders."

"Sad," I murmured. "Yes . . . I suppose that's mostly what I've been feeling lately . . . sadness."

"There are so many things I wish I could tell you, Julia. Things that might ease your feelings of sadness."

I looked at him curiously. "But why can't you tell me?"

"Oh . . . many reasons. Perhaps soon . . ." He looked away, up toward the house. "I can tell you that Allyson is not the person you think. Not nearly. It's you who should be with David."

I opened my mouth to speak, but he went on.

"No, don't say anything. There are things here you can't possibly know; things I cannot tell you . . . not yet. But soon, believe me, the path will be clear for you and David." He rose before I had time to react to his mysterious words. "And, if I'm lucky," he continued, "it will also solve my problems as well."

"But James—," I began.

"I'm sorry. I really must go now. There is something important I need to discuss with Millicent. Talking to you has given me the courage to do that." He looked down at me, his face in shadow. "Will you be all right here alone?"

"Of course," I said, still watching him curiously.

He walked quietly away and I watched him go up the steps and into the house.

So, he did know about David and Millicent. And if I interpreted his mysterious words correctly, he intended to confront his wife about her illicit affair tonight. But how would that clear the way for me? And what about Allyson? Now I was even more confused than ever and more certain that I did not belong here.

A whippoorwill sang its plaintive night song somewhere deep in the forest. It was a sound I loved, one that usually filled me with a certain peace. But tonight, alone in the shadow of the great house, I felt a chill run down my arms. It sounded so alone and so melancholy.

I rose and walked quickly toward the house. I realized I still wore James's jacket and pulled it from my shoulders to carry across my arm.

Just as I started up the curving steps to the covered portico I felt the eerie sensation of being watched. Above me on the porch someone stood in the darkness near the columns. I recognized Anna even before she spoke.

"It's a beautiful night," she said in her deep unmistakable voice.

195

I walked to where she stood. "Yes, it is. Quite lovely."

"James is a fine man." She nodded toward the jacket I carried. Her face was hidden in the filtered light from the hallway behind her.

Why was it that everywhere I went Anna seemed to be there, watching?

"Yes, he seems to be," I replied.

"And so is David. My sister does not realize how lucky she is." There was a spark of pride in her voice, of possessiveness even.

I could hardly believe she would stand before me praising David, not if she thought he had deliberately hurt her own sister. But at the same time, I could not deny the hope that leapt into my own heart. For I wanted to believe more than anything that the man I loved had not done such a cruel thing. If he had, how could I with any conscience continue to love him?

"But . . . but those bruises . . . the fingerprints on Allyson's arms," I stammered. "How can you . . . ?"

"She deserved it!"

"You don't think that! You can't possibly defend him if you think he intentionally hurt her."

"You don't understand," she said coldly.

"Then explain it to me."

"You don't belong here, Mrs. Van Cleef! And you never will. No matter what happens between David and my sister, he is too loyal to ever leave her; the scandal would ruin his family." Her voice, after her emotional statement, had changed to a low, emotionless drone.

"You'll get no disagreement from me that I don't belong here, Anna," I said. "That is becoming more and more evident to me each day. You'll probably be happy to know that I intend to go home to the El Dorado the day after the dance. I'm only staying that long as a favor to Allyson."

She turned her head then, and the light reflected

196

upon half of her plain features. I almost gasped at the sight, for it gave her the appearance of some monstrous gargoyle. One side of her smiling mouth was in darkness and the other showed her teeth, like some grotesque death mask.

"Good!" she sneered. "If you want to do what's best for David—and for yourself—that's exactly what you should do. And never come back here . . . never!"

Without another word she turned and walked down the steps and out across the lawn. Her dull gray dress reflected briefly in the moonlight before it blended and then disappeared into the darkness of the night.

Chapter Seventeen

On the morning of the dance Monteen and I went through the exercise routines with Anna and her sister for the last time. Anna was quiet, not at all the same as she had been that night on the front porch. She watched and listened carefully, showing the same care she always did where Allyson was concerned.

None of us made mention of the fact that this would be our last morning together until Allyson spoke.

"I do wish you'd change your mind and stay longer, Julia," she said. "But I understand your need to get back to your own home and your business. I only hope you will come back again for a visit . . . perhaps Christmas."

"Yes . . . perhaps I will." I felt guilty even as I spoke. For hearing it said aloud made me realize more than ever that I would never want to return to this house. Anna's pointed look made me certain of it. The frightening undercurrents that ran here beneath the polite, elegant atmosphere were just too strong to ignore.

Later, as had become our habit, Monteen and I took our lunch into the garden. She seemed extremely quiet and I asked her about it.

"What's wrong, Monteen? I would think you'd be feeling on top of the world today. After all, we're going home tomorrow morning. It's what you wanted, isn't it?"

"Yes . . . it is and I am happy about that at least. I only wish it could be tonight." I felt a stab of foreboding run through me when she looked away as if not able to meet my eyes.

"Why . . . has something happened?"

"Oh no, nothing like that. I'm just feeling a bit homesick, I suppose. Don't laugh, but I even miss our old staid and unimaginative Harry."

"Well," I said, smiling at her. "Perhaps absence truly does make the heart grow fonder."

"It's nothing like that!" she protested, giving me an expressive look of displeasure. "But I must admit that after the depressing atmosphere in this house, it will be good to be back to the simplicities of home. And I promise I shall never again complain of boredom, or declare poor sweet Harry to be dull!" She laughed and turned her head to look out upon the garden.

"Yes, I know exactly how you feel," I said. "There are so many things I'll tell you when we get back home."

She turned quickly to scan my face. "About David?" she asked eagerly.

"Yes . . . and his wife . . . and James." I sighed. "All of them seem so mysterious, so strangely at odds with the other, but I can't seem to put my finger on the exact problem. And I think that somehow Mrs. Damron is involved. She's not at all the same woman I knew before. She was so cold then and self-centered. And she ruled this estate with an iron hand. Now she's just a quiet shadowy figure who appears now and then. In fact I'm uncertain who *is* in charge here now."

"Oh, I have the distinct feeling that David Damron is the one. He's intelligent and alert and he's out and about the estate every day. He has a feel for the land. You can see it when he speaks of the place. Poor James is too embroiled in his domestic problems to be

200

interested in this house or the crops. Millicent seems to have the man dogging her steps everywhere she goes."

I was sure Monteen would understand James better if she knew what I suspected of his wife, and what I thought James already must know. But I made no mention of it and would not until we were away from here.

"Oh, yes," she continued. "David is definitely the one. You may have been too intent upon avoiding him to have noticed. But I have a feeling he will be staying on here at Stillmeadows, even after the summer's over and the rest have returned to Boston."

It was something I simply had not thought of. I suppose I looked at her as if she'd lost her mind. She laughed and shook her head as if to confirm that what she said was true. And she was correct about one thing: I had not noticed how David had taken over the running of the estate. It had seemed the most natural thing in the world to me, I suppose, his interest in the place. But the thought of his being here permanently, within such a short distance of the El Dorado, filled me with a strangely frightening joy. I had steeled myself to resist him while I was at his home, for I could see an end to it. But it would be impossible to avoid him if he became a permanent resident here.

We sat for a while before she spoke again. "By the way, I spent several hours yesterday discreetly looking for the bottle you said was missing from your bag."

"I suppose you found nothing," I said.

"Nothing . . . not a trace. Perhaps you should say something to David."

"No. I don't want to do that. Besides, I have a feeling it might have been Allyson. She acted very strange in the garden the other day. If she was not drinking that day, then it must have been something else. And I don't intend to become involved in their problems again."

Monteen nodded. "You're probably right. In any case we'll be gone from here tomorrow and it won't make any difference."

We saw Mary with one of her co-workers, strolling through the garden. They carried large baskets and were snipping flowers from various bushes and placing them in the baskets. They were both laughing, obviously enjoying their pleasant duties outside.

When they saw us they walked to where we sat in the shade of the vining wisteria.

"Good day," Mary said. "We're helping Mrs. Damron with the flowers for the dance."

"Yes, I see. The flowers are beautiful."

She held out the basket like a child proudly showing what she had gathered. There were dozens of long-stemmed tea roses, delicate pinks and the glorious white ones that grew so abundantly in the rich Stillmeadows soil. The other girl's basket was filled with feathery fronds of fern and blue strawflowers.

"Did Monteen tell you we will be going home tomorrow, Mary?" I asked.

She looked down at the ground. "Yes, ma'am. I been meanin' to speak to you about it." I knew immediately what she was trying so hard to say.

"You . . . you wish to stay here, Mary?" I asked.

"Oh, Miz Van Cleef. I love the El Dorado. And I love working for you and Miz Monteen. You've both been so good to me. Why, you've treated me like a sister. I feel so bad. . . ." She was almost in tears as she scuffed the toe of her shoe in the dirt.

I stood and embraced her. "Of course you're not to feel badly, Mary," I said. "We love you and want only your happiness. And if staying here will bring you that, then we would not think of objecting." Monteen murmured her agreement.

Mary's black eyes shimmered with tears as she looked at me with gratitude. "There's someone I'd like you to meet before you go home. His name is Joshua." She looked at the other girl and as their eyes met they giggled. I could not resist smiling also.

202

"I should like that very much," I answered. "I assume Mrs. Damron has given you a position here?"

"Oh yes, ma'am. Joshua asked Mr. David and he says I can stay as long as ever I like. And he told Joshua"—she hesitated and looked at the other girl, giggling again—"that when we get married we can have the rooms up over the stable. Oh, ma'am, they're ever so nice!"

"Married . . . well." Monteen stood up and embraced the girl. "That is wonderful, Mary. I'm so happy for you."

I hugged her again and watched as she and her friend walked on and continued searching for the most perfect blooms among the roses.

"I'd forgotten how it is to be young . . . and in love." Monteen's voice sounded wistful, and her eyes were envious as she watched the two girls.

"And so happily unaware that anything could ever go wrong," I added.

"Yes." Our eyes met and I knew we were both thinking of the men we'd loved and lost.

We sat down again, each of us adrift in our own silent daydreams. Suddenly Monteen laughed, a merry, ringing sound.

"Would you look at us? You're barely twenty-eight and I . . . well, I'm not *that* old. And we're sitting here like two old maids as if the world has passed us by!"

"You're right," I said. "And when we get back to civilization, we'll just have to do something about that, won't we?"

"Positively," she laughed.

"Let's go for a walk. There's a hot spring up on the ridge. I'll show it to you."

Monteen laughed as giddily as the young girls who searched among the roses. "Let's go," she agreed.

We ran and laughed, shouting to each other as we went. The weather was very warm again and far to the west was a bank of thick gray clouds which probably

203

would bring rain by evening. When we reached the top of the ridge, both of us were out of breath. The treetops at this level were swaying slightly, stirred by a hot humid wind that would probably soon engulf the whole valley.

Monteen went to the spring, immediately curious about this odd phenomenon of our mountains.

"Look, Julia, there's an entrance here at the side of the cave."

I climbed across the rocks to where she stood and we both peered into the black cavernous entrance. The air inside the cave was suffocating, carrying with it the heat from the steaming spring, a damp mustiness, and the heavy scent of iron.

"Can you see anything?" she asked.

"No, nothing. But I think it's too hot to go inside, even if we had a light."

"It isn't hot at all once you're inside." The voice behind us made me whirl about and I almost stumbled on the uneven, rock-strewn ground. It was Anna who stood below us in the small clearing where I'd sat yesterday.

"Anna!" I said, too surprised to say anything else.

The fun was suddenly gone from our adventurous afternoon. Monteen and I both walked the few steps down to where the homely-looking woman stood.

She held up a small water-jug. "I come here often and gather some of the mineral water to drink. The water from the springs seems richer than that at the house."

"Oh yes? I suppose it is," Monteen said. She was not as intimidated by the woman as I. In fact she often said she preferred Anna's company to her sister's.

There was an awkward pause while we all stood, not moving or speaking.

"Will we see you at the dance tonight, Anna?" Monteen asked politely.

"Oh yes. I would not miss it. I've heard many

204

exciting things about Mrs. Damron's end-of-the-summer ball."

"Good . . . good," Monteen said. "Well, we'll see you tonight then."

Anna did not make a move toward the spring. Rather she seemed to be waiting for us to depart. Perhaps, I thought, she had found this place to be perfect for a quiet retreat and had really come here to be alone. I could certainly understand that, since she rarely seemed to have a moment of solitude. Her entire day was usually devoted to her sister. So we left her there to pursue whatever pleasure she had hoped to find.

By the time we returned to the house, the whole place was alive with a frantic buzz of activity. I had not realized before that the house contained a large ballroom at the rear overlooking the garden. Even though I'd noticed a set of double doors just outside the bath area, I had never asked where they led.

Once these doors were thrown open, a short, wide hallway of rich parquet flooring was revealed, leading to a long, spacious room lined with tall windows. The windows were set almost to the floor so that once they were opened, one could walk through them onto a low-railed porch which overlooked the gardens. The whole effect was quite beautiful.

We looked about at the shining floors and the elegant blue velvet curtains pulled back with gold-tasseled ropes. Mary and the girls were busily carrying in large arrangements of freshly cut flowers, while several of the men servants polished the three crystal and silver chandeliers that had been lowered upon their chains almost to the floor.

"Oh, Julia," Monteen whispered almost reverently. "I don't think I've ever seen such a beautiful room."

The musicians began to arrive, placing their music stands upon the raised platform at the rear of the room. There certainly seemed to be nothing sinister or frightening about this room. I felt only a joyous anxiety for the guests to arrive and the music to begin.

"Monteen . . . the time! If we don't hurry we will be late."

Still laughing, we ran upstairs like schoolgirls preparing for our first cotillion. Each of us went to our room and began to prepare ourselves for the dance.

The dress I had chosen lay on the bed. It was not the newest nor the most stylish I owned, but it remained one of my favorites.

I tied a pannier about my waist. It consisted of several rows of stiffened ruffles at the back which would hold the dress out. I found it much more comfortable and not as exaggerated as the wire bustle that was currently in vogue.

I lifted the dress from the bed and slipped it over my head, letting the cool silken material fall easily to the floor. It was made of a delicate black French silk with large flat bows at the shoulder and short cap sleeves. From each bow, the material dipped low across my breasts and crisscrossed at the tightly fitted waist. Sparkling jet passementerie hung from the sleeves and also from the crossed material of the bodice. The front of the skirt fell straight in front and was pulled back at the hips to form a bustled short train which was layered with graduated flounces from hip to hem. The edges were trimmed with delicate black guipure lace.

I liked the soft rattling of the jet beading as I moved about and the cool feel of them upon my bare arms. The dress made me feel very feminine and presented the sophisticated air I'd tried so hard to cultivate.

My hair was much too straight for the cascade of curls that many woman favored. So I pulled it behind my ears and fashioned two braids down my neck and then looped them up in the back. When I'd pinned the ends in place at the back of my head I added a black silk bow which also dripped with jet beading.

I had just finished when there was a light tap at the

206

door. When I opened it, one of the maids made a small, polite curtsy.

"Mrs. Damron has asked to see you before you go down to the dance, ma'am. Her room is the last door on the right at the far end of the opposite wing." With that she turned and pointed down the hallway toward the other side of the house. "And also Miss Valognes asked me to tell you that Mrs. Penny Coulter has arrived and they will meet you downstairs later."

"Penny's here?" I had been so preoccupied of late that I had not even thought that Penny might come to the dance. But I was happy she had. "Thank you," I said as the girl walked away.

I could not imagine why Mrs. Damron would ask me to come to her room, but I hoped it would not take long, for I was anxious to see Penny again.

As soon as I was ready I made my way down the hall to where the stairway split the wings of the house. I walked past the banister toward the other end of the wing.

Just as I stopped at the door which the maid had pointed out, a door across the hallway opened.

My heart almost stopped as I watched David step into the hallway, his dark head bent as he closed the door. When he looked up and saw me, it was as if a million stars had exploded into the night sky. His eyes immediately came alive and I knew he was as happy and surprised to see me as I was him. We had said little to each other the past few days. And we certainly had not been alone as we now found ourselves.

The handsome, virile look of him in his black evening jacket struck me like a blow to the heart. His white shirt sported a high collar that framed his tanned, muscular neck. The narrow black silk tie he wore hung in a fashionable loose cascade. I felt breathless just looking at him and found myself totally speechless.

His eyes traveled from my hair down to my bare shoulders before lifting again to meet my awestruck gaze. There was a barely disguised flare of desire in the gray-green depths as he smiled slowly at me.

"Good evening," he drawled.

He came to where I stood motionless at Mrs. Damron's door. Not trusting myself to speak, I reached for the brass door-handle at the same time he did. It was only then that I realized he was also going into his mother's room.

The tension was broken and we both laughed. It was good to hear his deep, masculine laughter. The smile left his face and he lowered his head toward mine as if he would touch my lips with his own. Instead he spoke, so soft and quiet I could barely hear.

"You are too beautiful for words."

Before I could say anything the door opened and Mrs. Damron stood smiling at us.

"It's so lovely to hear laughter in the house again," she said. "Come in, children."

In her room large windows faced the meadow, just as in mine and Monteen's rooms. But since this room was at the end of the house there was also a window facing southward. Outside we could see the treetops twisting and bending under the onslaught of wind that seemed to be gaining strength.

Mrs. Damron's room of royal blue and ivory was lovely with its gleaming cherry furniture. Delicate Louis XIV chairs sat before the ornately carved white fireplace.

Mrs. Damron walked to the mantel and turned to face us. There was a certain stiffness and formality in her movements, as if she were a teacher about to discipline her pupils. I glanced at David but he seemed as curious and uncertain about why we'd both been summoned here as I was.

"Won't you sit down?" she said, pointing to the delicate chairs upholstered in stripes of pale gold, ivory, and blue.

I did sit, for I found my legs had grown unaccountably shaky and weak. Whether from my surprise encounter with David or from being here before his mother I could not decide.

David remained standing, his presence beside my chair seeming tall and powerful. "What exactly is this about, Mother?" he asked, his voice cool and skeptical.

Mrs. Damron stood straight and tall, an elegant and imposing figure in her gown of beige lace.

"There's something I've wanted to tell you, son, for a long time. And now that Julia has come back into your . . . into our lives, I could not wait any longer to say it."

David frowned at her and his eyes narrowed, but he waited patiently for her to continue. I had no idea what she was talking about, but the tone of her voice gave me a sinking feeling in the pit of my stomach.

"I've done a great disservice to you both. I think that when Monteen spoke of the wrong that was done, it was mine. And I'm certain that because of it your lives were changed dramatically. I can only tell you how very regretful I am and that I hope someday you will both be able to forgive me."

"What is it, Mother?" he asked sternly. "What is it you've done?"

"Let me preface this by saying that when Julia was here that summer, I was trying so desperately to keep our family together in the way your father would have wished. He had been dead only a few months, if you recall, having passed away that winter. I thought I was doing what was best for you, David, and for the Damron family." She looked at me apologetically. "But I've seen the last few years that I was wrong. We cannot control our children's lives, no matter what our good intentions might be." She looked at me. "Julia, when you came back here, so beautiful and sweet, so much the woman I would have wished for my son . . . I had to admit what a dreadful mistake I had made. And I could not believe what I had done."

David took a step toward her. "Tell us, Mother." There was a dawning awareness in his voice, as if he had guessed already what she would say. But I still had no idea.

She turned from his accusing glare and gazed out the south window. I could see how difficult it was for her to face him. Her muffled voice was barely loud enough for us to hear.

"That summer as I saw the two of you falling so suddenly . . . so deeply in love, I thought you were too young. And Julia, please forgive me, but I felt you were not the right sort to marry my son."

"I know that, Mrs. Damron," I said. My face burned with shame as I heard her words. For even now as I sat there before her, supposedly as an equal, in my expensive, original gown, I felt the pain again of being poor and unworthy. And it hurt . . . it still hurt terribly.

"I went to your father and . . . and I offered him money, a great deal of money. He was to use part of it to send you away to school. Away from Stillmeadows . . . and my son."

I could not suppress the gasp that rose in my throat. Her words explained so many things, so many questions. She had turned me against David and him against me. And all the while she told herself she was doing what was best for her son and her family.

David was furious as he tried to hold himself in control, unwilling, I knew, to berate his mother as he might someone else who had betrayed him. His fists were clenched at his side as he stood stiffly before her.

"David, my darling . . . I told you Julia had run away from here . . . away from you. And later that her father had arranged her marriage to someone else. None of it was true . . . none of it! And later, when you married Allyson, well, I thought it didn't matter. But now I know I was wrong . . . so very wrong."

"Yes, Mother, you were. And why now, so suddenly,

have you decided to *confess?*" His tone was sarcastic and bitter.

"David," I began. I hated seeing him this way, seeing the anger and pain I knew he must be feeling, just as I was. But I sensed that his mother was sincerely sorry for what she'd done. And I had the distinct feeling she had changed her view about me. Was it only because now I had money and was therefore considered suitable for the Damron family? And again, I saw the evidence of how little Allyson's presence seemed to matter.

"No, Julia, it's all right," she said. "I expected David to be angry with me and I don't blame him . . . or you."

"You didn't answer my question," he said angrily.

"All right. I will be blunt. I've seen your unhappiness, David. I've seen you change from a carefree young man into someone jaded and angry with life. And it should never have happened that way. I'm not blind to the kind of woman you married. Your marriage has become unbearable for you and therefore it is for me as well. For I've learned that the one good thing we have in life is love. It's all I should have wanted for both my sons. Money, position . . . none of it matters if there is no one in your life to love!" Her eyes sparked as she pulled herself proudly to her full height, her neck long and graceful. "And God forgive me, it's my fault that your life is without that. I robbed you of it."

But her contrite answer did not humble David, or appease him, not in the least. He made a noise in his throat, a rumbling grunt of derision.

"Well," he said quietly. "This is quite refreshing, Mother, though not totally unexpected. I wondered before if you had anything to do with Julia's leaving. You've tried to manipulate everyone in this family for as long as I can remember. And I suppose now we'll all just have to live with what you've done, won't we? But please forgive me if your grand scene of apology does not move me as you might have expected. It seems

211

you're a bit late."

I'd never seen him like that, so angry and bitter, like a wounded tiger, ready to lash out at anyone who came close to him. He turned on his heel to leave and if I'd not known better I would have sworn there were tears in his darkened eyes.

I stood and made a slight move to him. "David . . ." I wanted to help him, but he ignored me, walking on past. And I was lost, not knowing what to do.

Mrs. Damron stood by the window, her face reflecting great sadness and regret.

"Go after him, Julia. He needs you. I will make this all come aright for you both. I promise you that." Her words were said fiercely and with great determination.

But at that moment I was not thinking of her words nor what they meant. I thought only of David and I needed no further encouragement to go to him.

Chapter Eighteen

I ran out into the hall and stopped as I saw David standing near the balcony railing. His back was to me and his arms were pressed against the balustrade. He was bent forward as if he had been running and needed to catch his breath.

"David?" I said softly, walking to him.

He turned slowly, unable to erase the pain etched upon his face before he did. Seeing him that way, this man who was always so strong and confident, was like having a knife plunged beneath my ribs. And just as suddenly as the pain came the realization that all the bitterness I'd felt toward him, all the confusion, was gone. All I felt was a great rush of love and protectiveness. He had not abandoned me that summer! I was immediately ready to forget the past ten years and begin again. I was so relieved that I could not even feel angry toward his mother. And now it was I who was guilty of forgetting Allyson.

I moved toward him. "Oh, David," I whispered. "I'm so sorry."

Then I was in his arms . . . arms that closed about me in a grip so fierce it was almost painful. Then he took me by my arms and silently led me toward the doorway where I'd seen him emerge earlier. And I made no protest.

Once inside the room, he turned me to face him. I was pressed against the door by his lean, powerful body, long thighs that I could feel through the silken material of my dress. Then he lowered his mouth to mine in a kiss that burned like sun-warmed wine. It was hungry and passionate, with no preliminaries, with still a touch of the old anger I'd felt in him before. But I didn't care, I wanted him never to stop. Perhaps he thought to punish me or to recapture the years we'd lost; I did not care which. For I was ready and eager for his lips, his stirring touch.

His mouth moved to my throat while his hand deftly pushed the ribbons on my dress aside, sliding them off my shoulders. His lips followed, brushing hot kisses across my bare skin to the hollow of my throat. Then even lower to the tops of my breasts that strained against the confining material. I felt a wave of weakness course through me, down my body and into my legs, shaking me so badly I clung to him to keep from collapsing to the floor.

"Love, me, Julia," he murmured. "I want you to love me."

"I do . . . oh, David, I do love you," I answered.

"And I've never stopped loving you," he said.

Everything was so right, the feel of his body against mine, his hands that moved and touched, setting every inch of me on fire. And his mouth . . . nothing could have felt or tasted more glorious to me than his kisses.

He lifted his head as we both struggled for breath. His eyes, thick lashed and heavy, gazed into mine with a green fire. Then slowly and reluctantly he stepped away.

"David?" I reached forward to touch his arm, but he pulled away. "What is it? What's wrong?"

His shoulders lifted and he took a long, shuddering breath before turning back to face me with blazing eyes.

"Everything, dammit! Everything is wrong. For ten years I've known who to blame for losing you, for my life being a failure. It was easier to tell myself I didn't love you if I could denounce you. God . . . sometimes I hated you and loved you at the same time. I even married a woman I did not love and all the while it was as if I was punishing you for my own failure. And now . . . now I find the person I should have blamed was my own mother!"

I knew exactly how he felt . . . exactly. I felt a certain void now that the resentment I'd clung to slowly loosened its grip. And I, like David, still needed someone to blame, someone to hate for this terrible helpless feeling that coursed through me. And perhaps it was even worse, knowing that we'd lost so much precious time . . . time from our lives that could never be replaced. And all because of his mother's and my father's interference.

But I also knew, even through my regrets, that I could bear anything except seeing him hurt this way. And I knew he would have to find a way to forgive his mother for what she'd done.

"Don't hate her, David. You must let it go . . . we both must do that. I can't bear seeing you hurt for one more moment."

I walked to him silently and placed my hand on his arm. I looked up into his face, so much dearer to me now than ever before. And I felt the hot, bitter tears upon my face as they streamed from my eyes.

His hands shot forward, gripping my shoulders as he pulled me possessively to him. I felt a tremble move through him as he growled, deep and low in his throat. "I'll never let *anything* or *anyone* hurt you again! Do you hear me? Never!"

His fierceness frightened and thrilled me at the same time. And I sensed that same wild anger still surged through him as it had the first night he came

215

to my room.

His mouth came down on mine hard, hotly searching. And I wanted it, wanted him with a fierceness that shook me with surprise. For I'd never known there could be such sweet agony as this love I felt for him. Richard's kind, patient lovemaking had never prepared me for this.

When finally he pulled away he stood looking at me with amazement upon his beautiful face. And I knew it was for the powerful feelings we both felt.

"David," I gasped. "Love me . . . make love to me."

"Don't tempt me so, my darling," he whispered. And I remembered his vow in the stables to protect me and I knew he had not forgotten.

He moved away from me and raked his fingers through his hair. I put my arms about his waist and laid my head against his broad shoulders, unwilling to be apart from him for a second. He turned and put his arms around me, holding me close to his chest so that I could feel the beating of a heart; I could not be sure if it was his or mine. And at last his anger seemed gone.

"I'll never stop loving you, Julia," he said, almost with defeat.

"I think I finally believe that," I said. "But I can't stay here any longer, not like this. Tomorrow I will return to Hot Springs as planned." My voice cracked as I said the words.

"But not for long, my love," he said, pulling me close again. "I swear, it will not be for long."

His fierce promise puzzled me. For I knew there was no way we could be together as long as Allyson was his wife. But his face was stern and determined and I did not question what was in his words.

"You go downstairs now, sweetheart. I will join you shortly." He kissed me again, tenderly, and brushed his thumb across my cheeks, erasing any trace of tears. I did not know what he intended, but I trusted him and did as he asked. And as I left him I felt such a rush of tenderness for him and gratitude that the questioning resentments of the past were gone. At last I was free to love and trust him again. We might never have a life together, but I was thankful at least to be free of the terrible rancor of the past.

I took just a few moments to go to my room and compose myself a bit and to splash my face with cool water. Then I went downstairs to join the party.

Almost immediately as I entered the ballroom I saw Penny and Monteen off to the side of the room, engaged in deep conversation. I went to them and put my arms about both of them. They turned to me, not with welcoming smiles as I'd expected, but with looks of consternation.

"What's wrong?" I asked, feeling a new fear grip me.

"Julia," Penny said, smiling at last. "I'm sorry. I have not even said hello. And how beautiful you look." She stood back to look at my dress just as I noted her appearance as well.

Her emerald green satin gown looked wonderful on her petite rounded figure. But I could not admire her for long after seeing the worried look on her face.

"What is it, Penny?"

"Oh, I'm sure it's not as bad as I've imagined. There's been an outbreak of influenza in town; several people have even died. Mother's taken the children to my aunt's out in Little Rock. But many of our employees are ill. And many of yours as well, I'm afraid. Even your poor Harry is taken with the illness."

"Oh, no," I murmured. "Then we must go home immediately . . . tonight." I felt a stab of regret, for I'd longed for this night, just one special moment when I might dance with David. And after our meeting I could hardly bear to leave him.

"Julia," Monteen said, touching my arm and looking into my eyes. "I'll go and pack and leave with Penny

217

right away. There's no reason for both of us to go flying out in the middle of the night. You stay for the dance. Then you can drive your buggy home in the morning just as you planned."

"No, Monteen, you know I can't do that."

"And why not? Is there anything you can do that I cannot? Are a few more hours going to make any difference at home? Trust me, *chère,* and let me do this one thing for you."

What she did not say was that she wanted me to have this night as much as I did. For even though I had not said as much, she seemed to know how much it meant to me.

"She's right, Julia," Penny said.

"I do trust you, Monteen." I looked at her for a long moment, then I sighed. "All right, you go ahead. And I'll leave very early tomorrow morning."

"Good," she said. "I'll see you then. Penny, tell your driver I shall be out in a few minutes."

Monteen turned to me. *"Dieu vous garde,"* she whispered.

"And God keep you as well, Monteen," I replied.

We embraced and I turned to Penny. "Now, Penny, you take care of yourself. I wish we had more time to talk."

"I will take care. And we shall have plenty of time to talk once you're home. I can't wait to hear all about your stay here. I'll see you tomorrow. Try not to worry."

When I turned my attention back to the dance floor I saw James with Millicent clinging to his arm. They were coming straight toward me.

"Where is Monteen going in such a hurry?" Millicent asked, arching her dark brows.

"I'm afraid she's had to leave early. There's been an outbreak of influenza in town and her help was needed at home."

"Oh, that's too bad," Millicent said. "But I understand from Allyson you had intended to leave tomorrow morning anyhow." Her look indicated she hoped I would still do so.

"Yes . . . I still plan to," I replied.

James, politely silent, allowed his gaze to wander freely over my face and down to the black dress I wore. There was a tiny smile on his face and I wondered for a moment with alarm if I looked as disheveled as I felt . . . if he had somehow guessed what had transpired between David and me.

"Black becomes you, Julia," he said in his most gentlemanly tone of voice. "You look stunning."

Millicent's eyes turned as cold as a winter sunset. It puzzled me how she would manage to appear so jealous when she herself was involved with her brother-in-law. Again I wondered about her less-than-happy disposition and thought that except for that she was probably the most beautiful women I'd ever met.

Her gown of French muslin was a soft pinkish shade of purple. It fit her to perfection, as only an expensive original creation would do.

"Your dress is beautiful, Millicent," I said. "The color is quite unusual and becoming."

"Why . . . thank you," she said slowly, obviously wary of my compliment. "The color is called amaranthus."

"You're very lucky, James," I said. "Your wife is the loveliest woman here tonight."

"You'll get no argument from me on that," he said. He turned to her and looked deeply into her eyes. The words he spoke had the sound of an apology and I wondered at it. Especially when Millicent gazed up into his face with a newfound adoration, her eyes shimmering with tears. I was stunned. There certainly seemed to be a great change in both of them.

Then, almost as if I had ceased to exist, he took her

219

hand and led her onto the dance floor. I smiled at them with curiosity.

"My, don't they seem a happy couple tonight?" Anna had come to stand beside me as she pushed Allyson in her chair. Both of them watched James and his lovely wife. But where Anna's face showed amused derision, Allyson was clearly angry. I'd never seen her look the way she did that night.

"Anna!" she snapped. "I don't wish to sit here in the middle of the dance floor. I'm sure I must look perfectly stupid. Kindly push me over toward the windows where I might get some air!"

Anna did as her sister commanded and I, out of curiosity, followed. I took a chair next to Allyson. But she paid little attention to me. Her dark eyes were focused on the dance floor and it seemed to be James and Millicent she continued to watch. They certainly seemed to have captured her full attention.

"How are you feeling, Allyson?" I asked, trying to draw her into conversation.

She turned to look at me, clearly distracted. "I'm afraid I've felt little change since the treatments began. But I will never forget your concern and your kind help." Her words were polite enough, but I felt a certain dismissal as if she, too, was ready to see me go.

"Well, actually there has not been enough time to say whether or not you will improve. And with Anna helping you, who knows, perhaps one day soon you will get better."

"I don't think so," she said coldly, surprising me. She didn't seem at all like the poor complacent girl I'd come to know.

She glanced at Anna and when their eyes met, there was something there, some spark of animosity, I thought. Had they quarreled? But I quickly dismissed that for I could not imagine the subservient Anna ever causing anger in her sister. She was simply too devoted.

When David appeared at the entrance doorway I could not quell the ripple of excitement that shot through me. He stood for a brief moment, his chin up, eyes alertly scanning the crowd. He was taller than most of the men about him and his handsomeness would certainly make him stand out in any gathering. Then his restless eyes found mine and I felt a tingle much like that in the summer air during a lightning storm. He nodded imperceptibly, but did not move toward me. I knew he was still trying to maintain a proper decorum.

Mrs. Damron wandered about through the crush of people, chatting and putting everyone at ease. She looked as serene and lovely as a queen, with no hint about her of the turbulent events that had just taken place between her and her son.

I saw her dance several times and often she would bring the gentleman, usually a neighbor, over to meet Allyson, Anna, and myself.

I danced with James, enjoying his pleasant chatter and graceful maneuvering across the floor. Later I danced with some of the young men who were acquaintances from Hot Springs.

All evening the winds outside continued to roar and buffet the house and gardens. There was the distinct feel of a storm in the air, but as often happens in such hot weather, it seemed a long time in coming. But I enjoyed the wind and walked outside to watch its fury as it whirled through the treetops and whistled around the eaves of the great house.

It was there that David found me, moving to stand very close to me in the shadow of the porch. The wind ruffled his hair and brought the clean, masculine scent of him drifting toward me.

"Aren't you afraid out here alone, with the wind howling so wildly?" he asked quietly.

"No . . . the wind doesn't frighten me," I said,

glancing up at his profile in the dark.

"You could at least pretend a little fright, so that I might offer my masculine protection." I knew he was teasing, but at the same time I was afraid he might take me in his arms.

"David . . . ," I began, warning him as I stepped slightly away.

He laughed and also stepped back as if to see me more clearly. "Don't worry, ma'am. I shan't cause a scene and embarrass you"—his voice dipped before he continued—"although believe me that's exactly what I would like to do."

"What will I do without you," I asked suddenly, unable to hide the desperation in my voice. I had wanted so much to be strong this one last night, but it was becoming more and more impossible.

"You will never be without me," he said softly. "I'm going to divorce Allyson. It will come as no surprise to her. After all, it's something she and I have discussed many times before, even before you came back here . . . before I saw you again. She's clearly not happy and I shall settle a large amount of money for her and Anna. She can have anything she wants. And believe me, that is very important to her."

"She can have anything she wants—except you," I said.

"Oh," he laughed scornfully. "What has she been telling you? She never wanted me. The Damron name perhaps. But no, she never really wanted me, never seemed to take the time to know me. . . ." His voice sounded sad and full of long-forgotten hurts. It made me think that he had once cared for her, at least in the beginning, no matter how much he protested that he had not.

"I'm sorry," I said.

"No, don't be," he said gently. "I accepted it long ago. It was a mistake . . . as much mine as hers. It

222

would have ended before now except for . . . for the child. But then that was not to be either." He gazed out into the garden, squinting into the dark wind-tossed night.

"Let's go back in," he said. "I want to dance with the most beautiful woman here."

"Do you think it's wise? I don't want to—"

"I don't care if it's wise," he said with a soft fierceness, turning to stand dangerously close to me. "Allyson's gone to her room and as for the rest of our guests, I don't give a damn."

His words were sharp and bitter. And I think for the first time I saw what a terribly empty life he must have had. My heart ached with love for him and I wished I had it within my power to take away all the unhappiness he'd ever known.

We went inside to join the other dancers. And if anyone noticed that we danced the last three dances of the evening together, nothing was said.

The last dance of the ball was a slow, lilting waltz. While some of the couples moved to the perimeter of the dance floor so that they might whirl and glide exuberantly about the floor, David swept me toward the center. There the pace was slower, a mere excuse to remain in the arms of someone you loved.

I dared not look up into David's beautiful eyes as we danced. For that would surely have caused tongues to wag. Yet I was not sure I could resist the urge to reach up and kiss his sensual lips.

I could have cried when the music ended. For on this day I'd learned with such joy of heart that David loved me and always had. But I had no idea what the future would bring for us. I knew little of divorce, except that the parties of such were usually scorned by society. And I knew, even if I had not said it aloud, that a scandal in the Damron family would never be tolerated. And as much as I loved him, I did not want to

223

alienate David from his family.

We stood for a moment in the middle of the dance floor as the other guests around us talked and said their good-nights.

"Tomorrow morning when you go, I will saddle Samson and ride with you," he said.

"No," I replied. "There's no need for you to do that."

"I want to. Do you really think I could say good-bye to you tonight . . . here among all these people? I want every possible minute with you."

I thought of the long beautiful drive across the mountain, where the huge trees overshadowed the road for miles in a dark, intimate tunnel. And the thought of him being there beside me excited as well as comforted me.

"Then I will see you early . . . around six o'clock. Will you be awake at that hour?" I asked.

"I doubt I shall sleep at all." His lids opened slowly and I could see the pain he tried to tease away. And suddenly I wanted to cling to him and never let him go.

But the evening was over and many of the guests were leaving hurriedly, hoping to make it home before the threatening storm came.

I stood for a moment at the front door with David and his family as they told each guest good-night. David made no indication, either by word or deed, that he was angry with his mother. But several times I saw her watching him with a worried little frown.

Finally everyone had left and Mrs. Damron turned to me. "Julia, shall we go up?" she asked. I knew she did not think it proper for me to remain alone with David any longer.

I glanced toward him, but he only nodded, his eyes serious as he indicated I should do as she asked. And I knew we would have our time alone tomorrow morning.

"We'll walk up with you too, Mother Damron."

Millicent seemed quite amiable for once.

"You go ahead, darling," James said quickly. "I think I'll fetch a book from the parlor and then I'll join you." Millicent looked disappointed as he kissed her briefly on the cheek but she said nothing. Her small white teeth bit her lips and a frown wrinkled her brow.

"Are you coming, David?" Mrs. Damron asked.

"In a while, Mother. I'm going to see if Allyson's still awake."

I knew without his being able to say it that he intended to broach the subject of divorce to her.

It was a strange moment, for I felt distinctly that everyone present knew exactly what was going on between us. And I was glad to end the evening and be away from their speculating looks.

Chapter Nineteen

It was not surprising that I could not sleep after all that had happened that day. And the wind grew more furious by the minute, rattling the windows and howling like a thousand wolves about the house. I walked around the room, restlessly touching the various objects and gazing at the vague misty water-color paintings on the wall. After a while I thought of what James had said about getting a book from downstairs.

Without another thought I pulled a robe on over my long nightgown. There were no lights coming from downstairs so I took one of the lamps from my room and tiptoed down the hallway.

I walked slowly, holding the wavering light away from me so I could see the steps. I went into the parlor where I'd earlier seen a row of books on the sideboards, and set the lamp on a nearby table. There was a heavy thump outside; it sounded like it was on the front porch. I stood listening for a moment, then decided the wind must have blown a limb onto the roof.

But I heard it again and this time I thought I also heard the murmured sound of voices. Leaving the lamp on the table I stepped into the darkened hallway. There *was* someone there, on the porch, just outside the door. I stepped back, intending to go back into the parlor.

But it was too late . . . the door opened and a woman in white stepped into the hallway. I knew immediately that she was the woman I'd seen dancing across the lawn. My heart stood still as I saw the shadow of the man behind her. Many thoughts ran through my mind and I wondered if David had wanted only to say good-bye to his lover, or if he never intended to give her up at all. With a small ache in my chest I had to admit it was something I had not been able to ask him about. Perhaps I had not wanted to know.

The opened door transported the full fury of the storm into the entry hall and the wind blew the newly fallen rain inside. The lamp I'd left in the parlor illuminated me there in the doorway. There was no way I could hide now.

"Who is it?" the woman asked.

"It's . . . it's Julia," I answered. "Millicent?" I could hardly bear seeing them together, wondering if he had kissed her, held her as he did me. Wondering when he had last made love to her.

I heard her strike a match and light one of the candles kept near the door. When she turned to face me, I gasped as if I'd seen a ghost.

"Allyson!" I looked at her from the top of her hair, now wet with rain, to the tip of her shoes, where she stood on two perfectly sturdy legs.

There in the flickering shadows of the candle's light she looked like someone from another realm. Her eyes glittered and her mouth was opened in a sneering, mocking laugh. She looked nothing like the helpless creature I'd come here to help, the girl I thought I knew. She threw her head back and laughed softly as she stood defiantly before me with her hands at her waist.

"Well, well, if it isn't our sweet, saintly Julia! She's found me out!" She laughed again. "And where were you going at this hour, my dear? To meet my good and noble husband somewhere? But no, you and he are both too high-minded for that, aren't you? God, but you deserve each other!"

But if the man with her wasn't David . . . ? I looked up into the eyes of the man standing behind her. He was obviously embarrassed and could hardly meet my disbelieving eyes.

"James!" I whispered. It was all beginning to make sense to me at last. His mysterious words about happy marriages, his vow to talk with Millicent, and then their seemingly newfound love. I had been wrong about everything and it left me feeling confused and uneasy and so glad I had not said anything to David or accused him of meeting Millicent.

Allyson's laughter rang out in the hallway. She was not the same person I knew. There was no remorse, no shame in her at all. Her laughter was raucous and shrill like some cheap girl in a tavern. Only the roar of the storm outside, now fully upon us, kept her from being heard elsewhere in the house.

James stepped toward me, his hands outstretched as if to explain. His voice was low and filled with a desperate kind of pleading. "Julia, please listen to me. Try to understand."

"No," I said, stepping back into the doorway of the parlor. "I don't understand. How could you do this to Millicent . . . and to David?" I glanced toward Allyson, who stood gloating, her eyes twinkling with real joy. "You could walk all along? You put David—this family—through such worry for your own sick little game? And James . . . you knew it?"

"But that was part of the fun, sweets," Allyson said breezily. "Watching everyone's reaction . . . like yours. Oh, you were so concerned about me, even though you were in love with my husband. It gave me quite a bit of amusement, you know, thinking up clever things to make you feel even more guilty than before." She laughed again.

"You are despicable!" I said.

229

"Yes, aren't I?" she laughed. "And clever. Who would ever suspect a poor crippled girl of having an affair right under everyone's nose. And my dear sister-in-law, whose beauty could not help her hold her husband . . . she must have doubted her own sanity. I mean she knew her darling James was meeting *someone*. Was it you? she must have wondered. Perhaps the exciting Creole, or one of the servants? Oh, it was simply too delicious to resist!" She swung her arms about, turning herself around in a bizarre dance.

"Shhh," James cautioned. "Allyson, you're going to wake the entire household. You're drunk!"

"Of course I'm drunk, darling! But you never complained before. In fact you found it very exciting, didn't you?" She trailed her finger flirtatiously across his face and down the front of his wet shirt. "How else could I stand being cooped up here in this godforsaken place all day? Pretending to be so good, so sacrificing. Hah! You know I did it all for you . . . and it was so exciting . . . so beautiful." She moved drunkenly to him, holding her arms out to touch him. "If it were not for the nights my darling boy . . ."

"James, we must get her to bed before she brings everyone down here." I took her by the arm.

"Yes," he said with relief. "Yes, that's exactly what we must do. Come along, Allyson . . . please."

I looked at him with amazement. He was pathetic in his pleading, deferential manner. He saw my look and pulled his eyes away, unable to face the contempt I could not hide.

Allyson was much drunker than even he knew and he seemed not to know how to handle her. When we finally got her to her room, Anna met us at the door.

She looked at us for a moment. "Well, you've certainly done it now!" she told Allyson. "When they tell David the truth about you, he'll kick you out without a penny. Here," she said to us, taking Allyson roughly by the arm. "I'll take care of her now."

"James . . . James," Allyson whined. "Come put me in bed, my darling love."

Anna pulled her ungently into her room, but Allyson began to thrash her arms about wildly, pushing Anna away. But the bigger woman quickly overpowered her and guided her into the room.

We did not follow them in, but the scent of the roses drifted out to us and for a moment I thought I would be sick.

"We can talk in the parlor," I said to James.

Once we were inside with the door shut I turned to face him. Light flashed through the windows, illuminating the room for an instant as brightly as daytime.

"Do you want to explain what's been going on here?" I asked. I was shaking so badly I could hardly speak and my teeth chattered.

He did not sit down, but paced the floor restlessly.

"God, Julia. You must believe me. I had no idea that it would all lead to this. Allyson was always a flirt . . . but when she had the accident, I believed, like everyone else, that she was paralyzed. She was so sad and depressed. She asked me to come and talk to her, spend time with her. Of course, how could I refuse? What harm was there in that? And then, just before we came home, she revealed to me that she was faking . . . had been all along. She did not want children and she thought this way she would be free of that at least. It seemed like such a lark at first . . . so exciting. I became completely caught up in the game, and in her. She made me feel good about myself again . . . like a man." He looked at me, his gray eyes large and filled with guilt. But I could find in my heart little sympathy for him now.

"But how could you, James? I mean you have Millicent. She is so beautiful. . . ."

"Beautiful!" he scoffed. "What is beauty when it's matched every day by contempt, by scorn and ridicule? My God, I could do nothing to please her! She always compared me to David and nagged me about being more responsible, more like him."

"But James, I'm so confused. Tonight you and Millicent . . . you seemed so happy."

"We were! That's what I'm trying to tell you. The other night after you and I talked I realized I had to end this charade with Allyson. It was Millicent I wanted, her I've always loved. When I saw the love between you and David I knew it could be that way with my wife and me . . . it used to be once. I told Millie that night how much I needed her and how much I wanted her kindness and her approval. I told her things I'd never said before . . . about how hurt and rejected I felt when she was in one of her little moods. And I learned that it was only a defense she had erected. . . ." He waved his hand in the air. "Oh, it's a long story. I confessed to her about Allyson, but she had already guessed there was someone and she was suspicious about Allyson's illness all along."

"But she forgave you?" I asked, guessing that he would say yes.

"Julia, she was so hurt. I could not believe it. And then she apologized to *me!* Can you imagine that? She blamed much of it on herself . . . and Allyson too of course. But, yes, she forgave me and we made a vow to each other then to begin our life anew."

"Then what was tonight all about?"

"When I told Allyson it was over, she insisted that we meet once more . . . to talk, she said. But she had been drinking and she became more and more furious! I don't flatter myself that it was because she loved me so deeply. Allyson simply cannot tolerate not having her own way. She threatened to tell David. And that's the one thing I cannot face, Julia! I can't face him if he knows what I've done. David has always been the one to take care of everything . . . to take care of me! He's my best friend." He sighed, sat in one of the chairs, and lowered his head to his hands. His quiet sobs were muffled by the fury of the raging storm.

I reached forward to touch his hair. He was like a little boy, so lost and forlorn, so in need of forgiveness. And as for myself I could not condemn him for what he'd done. I felt so sad I wanted to cry with him.

"So," I sighed. "David does not know Allyson can walk . . . nor does your mother."

"No," he said. "But I think Anna has known all along and has been protecting her sister's secret."

"Oh, yes," I said. "I can see it all now. It makes everything so much clearer. That would account for her protectiveness. So . . . what will happen now?"

"I don't know. But I do know one thing—Allyson must not be allowed to hurt this family any more. She's already made David's life a living hell, and he does not deserve that! And I swear one thing: No matter what I must do, I intend to see she never hurts anyone else!"

His face in the dim lamplight was a painful grimace and his eyes were still wet with tears.

"Oh, James," I said. "What a confused dilemma you've made for yourself." I was more thankful than ever to be leaving Stillmeadows. Yet now, I felt a great need to protect David if I could.

For, like James, I could not bear to see David hurt further. I only hoped that James would be able to persuade Allyson to give up this farce once she was sober. Then perhaps David need never know what James had done.

I rose, suddenly so tired I could hardly hold my eyes open. "I'm going to bed now, James. I probably shan't see you before I go, so I'll say good-bye now."

He stood and took my hands. "Julia, you're a good person. And I promise you that I'll do what I can to help you and David."

I nodded, still uncomfortable with having my feelings for David known to everyone. After all he was still married to Allyson.

Later I lay in bed for hours listening to the rushing

wind and the steady rainfall. Toward morning the thunder moved on to the east, although the rain continued to fall heavily. It was a pleasant soothing noise, but even that did not lull me to sleep.

I was up early just as I'd planned and anxious to be away from Stillmeadows. And although I knew that driving in the rain would be slow and unpleasant I could hardly wait to see David alone. I was already dressed in an amber poplin traveling suit, and was checking to see that I had everything.

It must have been almost six o'clock when I heard the screams.

They came from somewhere in the house, downstairs in the hallway, I thought. The woman's screams echoed through the silent house and seemed to hang in the air for several minutes.

I ran into the hall outside my door and saw David coming from the other wing. He was just at the stair landing. He hesitated only a moment when he saw me, then hurried down the stairs. And I was close behind him.

The downstairs hallway seemed to be filled with people as all the house servants had come to see what the shouting was about. One young woman came forth to clutch at David's jacket lapel.

"Oh, Mr. Damron, come quick . . . in the bath . . ."

David broke away in a long-legged stride and when I reached the open door to the baths, he had stopped and was looking with disbelief toward the tiled pool. The young maid who had screamed looked up at him, her eyes large and frightened, her hand covering her trembling mouth.

Then I saw what had caused the stunned expression on both their faces; it made my head feel light and seemed to expel all the air from my lungs.

There before me was the scene I had envisioned . . . come to horrible reality! In the water lying face down was the woman in the white dress; the only difference

234

was that the water was tinged pink with blood.

David ran forward and down into the water, pulling the woman's limp body over. I walked to the edge of the pool and looked into the pale, lifeless face of Allyson Damron. And in her clenched fist was a perfect, long-stemmed white rose.

David was on his knees in the shallow water. With a choked cry of disbelief he cradled his wife's lifeless body in his arms and stroked the dark wet strands of hair that clung to his jacket.

I began to cry and my body shook violently, but I could not move, could not find a way to comfort him. I'd never felt such burning agony, not only at seeing this brutal death, but at seeing David so shattered, and so obviously grieving for a woman I thought he no longer loved.

I heard a commotion behind me as the rest of the family came into the room, pushing their way through the crowd of people who stood gaping at the terrible scene.

James came to stand beside me. He too was stopped cold by the sight. "My God," he whispered. "Is it . . . ?"

I nodded. "It's Allyson."

He immediately moved forward into the water and put his arm about David's shoulders. Then he motioned back toward the doorway. "Some of you men . . . come and help us lift her out of the water." His voice was quiet and authoritative as all the while his attention seemed totally focused on helping his brother.

Mrs. Damron was there, as well as Millicent. They seemed too stunned for words and only stared helplessly at the unbelievable scene before us.

When the body was being carried away, Anna appeared. Poor Anna. I had almost forgotten her. When she saw her sister's dead body she simply fell to pieces. Her crying and screams could be heard reverberating about the cold tiles of the room. Each one was enough to pierce the heart.

But it was left to the servants to comfort her, for the rest of us did not move from David.

His eyes were pained, stricken with such grief and incredulity. He stumbled slightly as he came out of the pool, but James was there, with an arm about his waist.

All of us moved forward as he stepped out of the pool. But when Mrs. Damron and Millicent went to him, I did not. I was still the outsider and I had no right to comfort him or cling to him, much as I longed to. I'd known all along that was true, but never had I felt it so strongly as on that terrible dark morning.

"I'm all right," David said to them. His voice was steady now and the terrible pained expression was gone from his face. He was once again master of the estate, strong and self-assured. But I wondered if I'd ever be able to forget the way he had looked as he pulled Allyson's limp body to his chest.

"James, send someone into town to bring Sheriff Moreland," he said.

"Yes," James said. "I'll take care of that. You should go up and change out of those wet clothes."

James left and I could hear his voice in the hall. "All of you go back to whatever you were doing. Everything is going to be taken care of." There was a murmur as they all moved away.

"David, what happened? Have you any idea?" Mrs. Damron looked frightened.

He shook his head, his look dazed. "No, I don't. There was a cut on her head, perhaps she tried to walk and stumbled into the pool, striking her head as she fell." He pointed to her wheelchair which sat close to the pool's edge.

"Oh, dear," Mrs. Damron murmured.

But Millicent's amethyst eyes lifted to mine where I stood a few feet away from her. There was a silent warning within their beautiful depths: warning me no doubt that I must not reveal Allyson's devious secret.

236

For if I did, the whole truth would emerge about James and Allyson. I nodded, knowing that now was not the time to tell David such a thing about his wife and his brother. But in my heart I made a soundless vow that I would tell him soon. It was not right that this should be kept from him, not now. There must be no more secrets between us, for they had already darkened this house and shattered too many lives, just as Monteen's cards had foretold.

And suddenly I remembered not only Monteen's reading of the tarot cards but my earlier premonition. But there was another vision I'd seen . . . the one of myself locked in a cold stone cell while David walked away and left me there alone.

I looked across at him, staring at him now with fear. For something else came violently to mind, something David had said last night: He had promised that *no one would ever come between us again.* A chill ran up my neck as he turned and looked into my eyes, as if he sensed my look at him. There was not enough time for me to hide the horror I was feeling. And I knew he saw it.

He frowned and a look of quiet anger flashed across his features. He did not like what he saw in my eyes, yet I was powerless to hide it. And the words kept running over and over in my mind. *Was David, the man I loved, capable of murdering his wife so that we could be together?* Could he have been pretending the terrible grief I just saw?

For I knew, felt with every ounce of my being, that Allyson had not fallen into the pool by accident. She had been murdered.

237

Chapter Twenty

I put my hand to my temples, trying to stop the thoughts that whirled through my head. I didn't know what to do, or where to turn. I jumped as Mrs. Damron walked behind me and placed her hand on my shoulder.

"I think under the circumstances you should not go home, Julia," she said. "I'm sure the sheriff will want to speak with all of us. At least until he can determine that there was no foul play involved in Allyson's death."

I looked up into her attractive face. This morning, as usual, she appeared calm and serene, clothes just so, not a hair out of place. But this morning I did not expect her to be quite so peaceful . . . and it puzzled me.

"Yes," I said numbly. "Of course I'll stay."

"Good. I have no idea what's to be done. I suppose we must wait until Sheriff Moreland is here," she said. Her only sign of nervousness was the clasping and unclasping of her hands in front of her as she spoke.

"Mother Damron, why don't we all go into the parlor and have some coffee or tea," Millicent suggested.

"Yes, dear," Mrs. Damron said with a touch of relief. "That's a splendid idea."

Millicent, with a new air of concern, hooked her arm

through her mother-in-law's and walked her toward the door. Over her shoulder she called softly, "Coming, Julia?"

"Yes . . . yes," I said absently. I looked at the empty wheelchair and the bloodied water of the pool and I shuddered, more than ready to leave the room.

The rain continued to fall, enclosing the house in a thick gray curtain of water. The house was dark and silent and everyone who'd been in the hallway before had simply vanished. I wondered what they were saying as they moved quietly about the house and whispered their feelings to one another. Was I the only one to wonder about David . . . I who should have been his most ardent defender? I remembered the way he'd looked as he held Allyson's lifeless body to him. Could that anguish have been feigned? No, I told myself, surely it could not have been.

We sat in the parlor before the fireplace with only the sound of rain against the windows and the ticking of the small mantel-clock. The click of cup against saucer seemed loud and offensive and I finally gave up even trying to force the hot sweet tea down my throat.

Mrs. Damron sat as if in a trance, her face solemn and thoughtful as she gazed out the windows. Millicent seemed ill at ease and her violet eyes were dark with worry as they darted about the room. What was she thinking? Was she as worried about David as I?

Just then there was a light tap at the door. It opened and a familiar face peered across the room at me.

"Mary," I said, rising and going to her.

Her eyes were big and full of terror. "Are you all right, ma'am?" she asked.

"Yes, Mary, I'm fine. Is . . . is something wrong?"

Her long slender fingers plucked at the sleeves of my dress, pulling me closer to her.

"There's somethin' I want to tell you. I . . . I don't know if it means anything or not."

"About Allyson?"

"Yes, ma'am," she whispered.

From the room Mrs. Damron spoke. "If you know something about what happened this morning, Mary, you must tell us."

Mary looked at me, uncertainty flickering across her sweet face.

"It's all right, Mary," I said. "Come in and tell us what you know. There's no need to be afraid."

I stood close beside her as she spoke. She twisted her hands before her nervously and her speech was slow and hesitant.

"It's just that . . . I heard someone say Miz Allyson must have fell from her chair . . . into the pool."

"Yes . . ."

"Well, I don't see how that could be. I mean, I was workin' early this mornin', helping with breakfast in the kitchen. I came back into the main house through the French doors. Miz Allyson's room was open . . . I looked in to see if she was all right, but she wasn't there."

"Did you see her at all?" Millicent asked.

"No, ma'am, I didn't. But what I wanted to say was . . . her wheelchair was in her room. I was surprised, for I never saw her when she wasn't in it, except of course when she was in bed."

Millicent glanced at me, a knowing look on her face.

"That is very odd," Mrs. Damron mused "Then how did she get to the bath? About what time was this, Mary?"

"It was a quarter of six, ma'am. I just happened to look at Miz Allyson's clock when I stopped at her room. And I also noticed the light was on in the bath area too." She shivered, thinking I'm sure of what might possibly have been happening at that very moment.

"Mary, dear, when the sheriff gets here I want you to tell him exactly what you've told us," Mrs. Damron said.

241

"Yes, ma'am."

"Thank you, Mary. You did the right thing," I said as I walked with her to the door.

It seemed an interminable wait for Sheriff Moreland. There was not much conversation; we could only wait. But I was not anxious to go up to the quiet solitude of my bedroom and I sensed Mrs. Damron and Millicent also felt the need to be in the company of others. So we waited together, quietly and thoughtfully, not even bothering after a while to try and make polite conversation.

I wondered about David. Where was he? What was he thinking? I wanted so badly to speak to him alone.

When at last we heard sounds at the front of the house Mrs. Damron went to look out the front window. "Good, it's the sheriff," she said, walking to the front door to let the man in.

Sheriff Moreland was a big man, well over six feet tall with wide, bulky shoulders. He wore a dark pin-striped suit with a vest that stretched across the broad expanse of his stomach. A watch fob dangled there from a shiny gold chain. Underneath his rain slicker he wore a jacket that reached almost to his knees. Pinned to the lapel of the jacket was a large brass star. He made quite a dashing figure with his large black mustache and pomaded hair.

"Sorry we're late, Mrs. Damron, but we had to find another place to cross the creek. Water's out of its banks and across the bridge on the main road."

Mrs. Damron ushered him in and another man followed close behind him. I recognized him as Dr. Ballard from Hot Springs. He came almost to Sheriff Moreland's shoulders and was a frail-looking man, weighing not much more than a woman might. He too wore a mustache, but it was liberally sprinkled with gray, as was his thick, unruly hair.

"I wasn't sure exactly what took place here, Mrs. Damron," the sheriff said. "But I thought it best to bring Tom along."

"Yes, it's good that you did. Both of you come in, and take off your wet coats," Mrs. Damron said. "If you'll come into the parlor I'll have some fresh coffee brought in."

"Thank you, ma'am," the sheriff said. "Sorry we're drippin' water all over your floor."

"Oh, think nothing of that," she said and I knew she meant it sincerely. I had learned that much about her since coming back. She put her guests' comfort before everything. Even this sad and somber occasion did not change that.

"If it's all the same to you, Mrs. Damron, we'll . . . uh . . . take a look at the body now. If you'd like to wait in the parlor, we'll join you there as soon as we can."

"Oh yes . . . of course," she said. "And here's my son now. He can take you."

David came from the rear of the house toward us. His hair was damp and I had a sudden vision of him riding his powerful horse through the thundering rain with that same wildness I'd seen before.

"Allyson was David's wife," Mrs. Damron clarified.

The men offered David their condolences and with what I thought was a great deal of tact they made their way to the room where Allyson lay.

So we were to wait still a longer period of time. Mrs. Damron took the opportunity to order coffee and sandwiches brought in and to assemble any of the servants who had seen or heard anything unusual. That of course included Mary.

Finally everyone arrived. The small parlor was crowded, with Mary and the other household servants standing around the walls. David stood at the fireplace, leaning an elbow on the mantel. He looked tired and irritable, and when our eyes met there was still a question in his look as if I'd hurt him somehow. As for myself, I felt more confused than ever and I wondered how much longer it would be before David and I could

243

be alone to speak about what had happened.

Sheriff Moreland, with fingers hooked into his vest pockets, took center floor and began to put together the story as he saw it.

"Dr. Ballard has determined that Mrs. Damron's death was no accident." There was a low murmur about the room. "I take it that comes as no big surprise to anyone here?" No one answered. "We've both decided that the lady did not fall into the pool, but was probably placed there after her death, probably to make it look like an accident." His eyes wandered over the people in the room.

"Now, Doc Ballard is going to tell you what he's found. Being careful, of course, not to offend the delicate sensibilities of the ladies present." He said his last words to the doctor, who nodded agreeably.

Doc Ballard stepped forward and in a voice that was surprisingly deep and mellow, told us what he thought had happened. He spoke softly and with sensitivity, but still, hearing his words was shocking.

"Mrs. Damron, I believe, had been dead no longer than thirty minutes when she was found in the pool. There was a gash on the side of her head, but it probably was not what killed her. It's even possible the cut did result as she struck the side of the pool after being dropped into the water, since there was not that much blood."

Millicent made a slight noise and placed a lacy handkerchief to her mouth.

"Uh . . . sorry, ma'am," the doctor said before continuing. "There were bruises on the dead woman's throat and her larynx had been crushed. She died as a result of this injury and from suffocation."

When he said the word bruises, my eyes instantly sought David's. He was staring at me and there was that odd look of anger and defiance in his eyes. *Just as there had been the day I accused him of causing the bruises on Allyson's arms.*

244

I groaned slightly beneath my breath. I pulled my eyes away from David's, for I did not want to believe what all this meant, did not want to remember his promise that no one would ever come between us again.

The doctor made a slight bow and stepped back. Then again the sheriff moved to the center of the room.

"I'm sure I don't have to say it, but I will anyway. . . . We are now conducting a murder investigation. We will need to question everyone here as well as the other household help. Sorry for the inconvenience, ma'am," he said toward Mrs. Damron.

She only nodded and I saw that for the first time she was shaken, her face ashen. Was it because there was to be an investigation or because of Allyson's shocking death?

The sheriff continued. "I'd like to speak to each of you, one at a time now." Then he turned his gaze toward David. "Mr. Damron, I believe we'll start with you."

I closed my eyes and had to fight the nausea that threatened to overtake me. Please, I prayed, please don't let it be David.

The rest of us filed out of the room in complete silence after being told to stay close by so that he could find us.

From where I waited in the hall, I could see the room where Allyson's body lay . . . her bedroom, filled with the scent of roses. I watched with growing sorrow and despair as two of the maids went in with washbasins and towels to prepare the body for burial. And I saw too when Anna walked slowly into the room with a white dress draped across her arms.

"Poor woman," Millicent said from where she sat near the stairs. "I don't know what she'll do now that Allyson is gone. She devoted her whole life to her and now . . ." She shrugged her shoulders as if there was nothing else to say.

245

The others about us seemed occupied with their own conversations. Mrs. Damron and James spoke quietly near the front door.

"Millicent," I said quietly, "I intend to tell David that Allyson could walk. I think he has the right to know."

She looked at me for a moment, then sighed. "I think you're right, Julia. He should be told . . . if he hasn't found out on his own."

She looked at me apologetically. She probably had not meant to imply that David might have killed his wife. But it was the only conclusion I could reach.

"Well . . . I . . . I'm glad you agree," I said.

"Surprised? You shouldn't be, you know. David has been the best friend I've ever had. He's listened to me, tried to make excuses for his brother's wandering eyes. This was not the first time he's had to defend him, you know. But more than that he understood me, cared about me when no one . . . well, he never condemned me for my outspoken ways or my selfishness."

I suppose I must have shown surprise at her words.

"Yes, I know I'm selfish." She looked at me rebelliously although I had not said a word. "But David saw through all that and he never judged me. And now, no matter what, I'm going to stand by him. And in case you've wondered, yes, I do love David. But the love I feel for him is purely platonic and much too important for a casual affair."

"I . . . I don't know what to say, Millicent," I stammered. "I suppose I should start by saying I've misjudged you."

"I suppose I make it easy for people to do that," she said quietly.

"I'm sorry," I said simply.

She lifted her eyebrows in a sort of self-mockery. "Well! David said you were a person of integrity. But personally I could never understand how he felt that way after what you did to him."

So, he had not told her about what his mother had

done. But probably only because he had not had a chance to talk to her since the dance.

"That was all a mistake," I told her. "And David and I have resolved all the misunderstandings of the past."

"Indeed? Well, please forgive me if I'm not suddenly overjoyed for you, Julia."

"Why?" I asked.

"Well, you see, the sheriff seems to suspect David of Allyson's murder. But I happen to know for certain that you had as much reason as anyone here to want her dead. Simply coveting another woman's husband would be suspicion enough, it seems to me."

I was stunned. Of course she was right, but I had been so worried about David that I had not even thought that I too would be a suspect.

"I had nothing to do with Allyson's death," I said. "And the sheriff will probably learn that it was your husband that she was meeting secretly. So perhaps you also had your reasons for wanting Allyson dead."

Millicent smiled and gave a derisive snort of laughter before rising and walking slowly to stand beside her husband.

Her words set my mind thinking about other suspects, other reasons for wanting Allyson dead. And suddenly I felt hopeful that my first fears about David were wrong. My eyes went quickly to James, and I scanned his features. There was nothing there to give away what he was feeling. And he did not seem too grieved by the death of a woman whom he knew so intimately. But his concern had certainly seemed genuine when he came in and saw David holding Allyson in his arms.

But, I reminded myself, Allyson was trying to use their affair against him, trying somehow to hang on to their exciting relationship by threatening to tell David. And that was the one thing James had declared he could not tolerate. And with a chill I remembered his telling me last night in the parlor that Allyson would

247

never hurt anyone again. I watched him closely before my eyes swung to his lovely wife, who stood looking up at him.

For all Millicent's cool disdain I thought she was very shaken by what had happened. James seemed to think she took the news of his affair with Allyson very well. But I wondered. Could she have confronted Allyson herself this morning, knowing that James had been out somewhere in the rain last night? Surely she would have guessed where he'd been. But even if she had confronted Allyson, could she have killed her in a jealous rage? I found it hard to believe the lovely woman was capable of such an act of violence.

The day seemed to drag by in a quiet dreary grayness. The rain still fell as heavily as it had during the height of the storm. All through the house were hushed murmurs and soft shuffling of people going about their chores.

Once during this time I heard a cry of anguish from Allyson's room. It must have been Anna grieving for her sister. Mrs. Damron, with a compassionate look, walked down the hall as if to comfort her.

I wasn't sure how many people the sheriff had questioned. David, the first one, was in the room for a long time and did not speak to any of us when he came out and walked out the front door.

As it grew later into the afternoon Mrs. Damron mentioned that she'd have the staff place a light buffet meal on the sideboard in the dining room. We were to eat when and if we pleased.

As the servants began carrying trays of food past us, the aroma of food drifted into the hallway, making me realize how hungry I was. Soon the hall between the dining room and parlor was empty except for myself. It was then through the glass of the front door that I saw David's tall figure where he stood on the front portico. He seemed intent on watching the heavy screen of rain.

While no one was watching I went out to him. The

248

air was still warm and full of such heavy moisture that even standing beneath a shelter, one's clothes became damp.

I moved to the balustrade beside him. He glanced briefly down at me, his face cold and expressionless.

"Are you all right?" I asked.

"Yes, I'm fine." His words were clipped and impersonal and it was hard to believe this was the same man who'd held me so passionately the night before.

"Poor Anna is so bereft. . . ." I knew my efforts sounded forced. But I had no idea how to draw him out, for I knew he'd seen the doubt in my eyes earlier. But that had only been fear; and now I realized that David could never have done such a thing.

"We all show our grief in different ways." Still he gazed through the curtain of rain and out toward the meadow.

"Yes . . . my . . . my father never got over his grief . . . when my mother died."

He did not answer.

Finally I could stand it no longer. "David . . . please. Talk to me. Won't you just talk to me?"

At last he turned to me, but the look on his face was full of bitterness. "Why would you assume I need to talk? You knew I didn't love Allyson . . . she was a devious woman with little regard for the happiness of others. Allyson was too wrapped up in what *she* wanted to ever give anyone else a passing thought." His eyes moved away, staring again straight ahead of him.

"You don't fool me, you know," I said softly. "I saw your reaction this morning . . . saw the pain you obviously felt. There's no need to pretend you didn't care . . . not with me anyway." I spoke quietly and it sounded like the apology I wanted it to be.

His jaw clenched several times and his mouth was drawn tightly together. "I didn't kill her, Julia." The words were said so softly that I barely heard them through the pounding rain.

"I know you didn't," I said.

He turned to me, teeth still clenched. But it was the agony in his changeable eyes that wounded me.

"Do you indeed?" he snarled. "Is that why I saw such fright in your eyes before?"

"I . . . I don't know. . . ."

"It's all right . . . there's no need to try and protect my feelings. Those lovely blue eyes can hide nothing, you know. It was there for everyone to see. You think I killed her so that I could come to you a free man. And I can hardly blame you for thinking that."

"David—," I began.

"Damn it, don't deny it!" His eyes blazed with a quiet fury before he sighed heavily and turned away from me. His fists were clenched upon the top of the railing.

"David . . . I'm sorry. I won't deny that it worried me . . . when I remembered your words about us being together. And that day in the stables, you never denied that you had hurt Allyson. . . ."

He looked at me, a frown of disbelief forming between his stormy eyes. "I didn't think I had to deny it—I thought you knew!" He closed his eyes and shook his head slightly. "I've *never* touched Allyson in a violent way . . . though God knows there were times when I wanted to."

"I know that now. But there have been so many mysteries, so much I wasn't sure about. And just for a moment I was afraid it might have been . . ."

"Well, you were wrong." Now he only sounded weary as his shoulders slumped with fatigue.

Nothing had ever made me feel so guilty . . . and this time I had done it to myself. And it made me wonder if there was something within me that pushed me to be unhappy, to make such blind mistakes with the people I cared about. At that moment I thought I'd lost him forever. For how could I ever expect his forgiveness for doubting him?

"I *was* wrong; I admit that." My voice was tight with

barely controlled emotion. "But I want you to know that I love you, David Damron . . . more now than ever . . . more than anything or anyone in the world. And you were right about my marriage. *You* are the only man I've ever loved." I paused, biting my lips against the tears that threatened to choke me. "I . . . I have a hard time trusting. This is the first time I've ever actually said those words out loud. But that is a fault within me and I never wanted you to be hurt because of it. I hope you will be able one day to forgive me."

He watched me silently as I walked away, leaving him there surrounded by the drumming rain, to grieve alone for his wife. And I could only pray that after the grief he would be able to think of me with forgiveness for my doubts.

More than anything I hoped the love he felt for me would return. For in truth I did not know how I could live without that one most precious thing in my life now that I had found it.

Chapter Twenty-One

I went back inside and stepped into the dining room. There was no one else about except one of the maids who had come to check on the food. So I took a plate and helped myself to the various dishes from the sideboard.

"What may I bring you to drink?" the girl asked.

"Hot tea will be fine," I told her.

She hurried down the hall while I sat at the long, empty table to eat.

"Well, Mrs. Van Cleef. You are the only one remaining that I have not yet spoken to."

"Sheriff Moreland," I said, turning to see him enter the room. "Shall I come now?"

"No, no." He waved a large thick hand at me as if it was of no importance. "You finish your dinner. As a matter of fact, I've grown quite hungry myself." He eyed the heavily laden sideboard. "And if you don't mind, I think I will join you."

"Please do," I said. And although the man was a virtual stranger to me, at that moment I welcomed his company and his diversion.

I watched as he amply filled his plate with food. He sat across from me and with great enjoyment began to eat. When the maid came in with a pot of steaming tea the sheriff barely looked up from his plate.

"Sheriff, would you like tea?" I asked, holding the pot to his cup.

"Yes, yes," he said. "Tea will be fine."

I thought I'd never seen anyone consume as much food, or indeed enjoy it so thoroughly. The maid's eyes widened with surprise when she saw that the tray of hot biscuits was empty. Then briskly she went off to bring more.

After he'd eaten a third portion of the delicious pork pie he gave a low groan of satisfaction and pushed himself slightly away from the table. He took his cup and settled back to enjoy his tea. As he did so he crossed one very large booted foot across his opposite knee.

"Now, Mrs. Van Cleef. I've heard many things about you since your arrival back in Hot Springs. Caused quite a stir in our little town. Beautiful young widow, with lots of money . . ." He looked across the table and winked. His actions and his words were beginning to make me a little uncomfortable.

"But I didn't know you were on such friendly terms with the Damrons. Seeing as how they've been gone nearly ten years now." His face was friendly enough, but his keen black eyes watched me closely. I knew my interrogation had begun.

"I worked here one summer. David and I became friends."

"I see. And were you also friends with his wife, Allyson?"

"As a matter of fact . . . yes, I was." I smiled at him. And I was glad I did not have to lie about that.

"Hummm. Did you like her? Now that might seem a silly kind of question, but you see, I've found that almost no one in this house really *liked* the young woman. Curious . . . very curious."

"Yes, I did like her. However, I confess I did not know her well at all, only for the short time I've been here. And the last few days I think I began to realize

254

that she was not well liked, as you say. And perhaps I was even beginning to see why."

"Oh? And would you care to elaborate on that?"

"I can only give you my observations, sir . . . and my own personal opinion."

"Yes, I understand. Do go on."

"I believe Allyson was a very unhappy person who spent much of her time trying to amuse herself by manipulating everyone around her. She liked playing jokes on people . . . sometimes cruel jokes. And she seemed to delight in always coming out on top . . . if you understand what I'm trying to say."

"Pitting one person against the other, so to speak."

"Yes . . ." I hesitated only a moment before glancing into his piercing eyes and continuing. "But outwardly she liked to appear sweet and gentle, even martyred I think."

"Martyred? And why do you think anyone would wish to appear so?"

"I'm not sure. Perhaps it gave her some sort of pleasure seeing others so obviously fooled. Perhaps she craved sympathy. As I said before, I did not know her well at all."

I met his frank stare and studied carefully his knowing smile, the eyes that twinkled beneath bushy brows. He was enjoying this. And I felt he knew more than he was saying.

"Yes," he said. "In case you're wondering, ma'am," he drawled, "you aren't the first person to tell me such things today."

I was surprised and I'm sure my face must have reflected it. I'd have thought the Damrons would probably try to protect Allyson's reputation as much as possible. And I could not help wondering which of them had given the sheriff his information.

"You seem surprised," he said.

"Well, yes, I am a little."

"You do have an idea who killed the woman, don't

255

you, Mrs. Van Cleef?" Quickly he changed from a dawdling backwoods sheriff to a man of keen perception. Now I was sure he'd been toying with me all along.

"I . . . no, I don't. I can honestly say that I'm at a loss to know who did it, or why. Allyson Damron might have had her faults, but surely nothing to cause her death."

He set his teacup down and leaned his head back, watching me through narrowed black eyes.

"I believe you," he declared suddenly, slapping the palm of his hand against his thigh.

I laughed. I could not help it. His mannerisms were so dramatic that they were almost comical.

"So, let me see if you will agree with this, ma'am." He laced his thick fingers together and lifted them to his chin. "Suspect . . . David Damron. Rich, powerful, influential . . . married to a woman who often embarrassed him, lied to him, perhaps even made a cuckold of him. Even his mother says he did not marry her for love, but for convenience."

I said nothing, neither agreeing nor disagreeing.

"And he finds himself thrown together with a beautiful widow . . . someone from his past. Someone he might even have loved once. He asks his wife for a divorce, they quarrel—he kills her. I'm certain the murderer did not intend it to happen." He lifted his eyes suddenly and gazed into mine. "You agree so far?"

"David did not kill Allyson," I said.

He ignored me and went on with his spiel. "Perhaps you're right, perhaps not. So let's talk about James Damron . . . a nice loving son, unambitious, always passed by in deference to his dynamic older brother." He stopped and looked at me smugly.

I could not believe his words, nor that he'd found out about James so quickly.

"Spoiled, immature . . . and having a fiery affair it seems with his brother's wife . . . who by the way was

256

not a cripple."

His method was to shock, I could see that. And even though I knew about all of it, the words certainly did have a shocking dramatic ring. I was most shocked that he'd already discovered Allyson's paralysis to be staged.

It was his turn to laugh now and I could see the delight it gave him to finally have shaken my outward confidence.

"More than anything James wanted to keep his relationship with Allyson Damron secret from his brother. But he also wanted to put an end to the affair, having discovered like everyone else what a devious, manipulative person Allyson really was. She threatened to tell David. Did he kill her?"

It was all true. And I knew it. "No . . . I don't believe that." But my words sounded weak and unconvincing.

As I expected, my words did not deter him. He went on. "Or Millicent Damron," he drawled. Was he never going to stop? "A strikingly beautiful woman betrayed —nay, humiliated—by her husband, aware that the man she loved had a mistress in her own home! Furious when she finds that this woman is none other than her own sister-in-law, flaunting it right under her beautiful nose! She must have been bitterly angry, scorned. Dangerous situation . . . yes, very dangerous. Perhaps she confronted this mistress. Perhaps she even murdered her."

This time I made no comment but looked coldly into his shrewd eyes.

"So you see, Mrs. Van Cleef. I have a real dilemma on my hands. I have a suspect at every turn." He hesitated. "Perhaps there are even others. What do you think?"

I was growing steadily more impatient with the man and his theatrical tactics, especially since he was so obviously enjoying himself. I had been as honest with

257

him as I could and yet he continued to taunt me with his sarcastic insinuations.

"I think, Sheriff Moreland, that you are struggling. And I think you have no more idea of who really killed Allyson Damron than I do."

His eyes opened wider and he nodded, a little smile upon his lips. "You are very astute, ma'am, very cool." He pushed himself up from his chair and stood for a moment as if studying me. "But I promise you this . . . I will find the murderer. It's only a matter of time. This family won't be able to use their wealth to hide from the law." His heavy footsteps echoed down the hallway as he left the dining room.

I sat there for a long while thinking about all the things he'd said, about all he had learned. And I had to admit I was still as puzzled as ever about who could have killed Allyson. I was pouring myself another cup of tea when Mrs. Damron came in.

"Julia," she said. "I was wondering where you were. Did you speak with the sheriff yet?"

"Yes, just now."

"It's just all so horrible," she said, sitting across from me.

It had grown dark outside and the candles were the only light in the dining room. They flickered across Mrs. Damron's serene face. She looked about the room as if seeing it for the first time.

"I'm sure you'll be relieved to be back at your own home and away from this place. What an uncomfortable time you've had here."

I thought to myself that the word uncomfortable would not quite describe what I felt. "There's no reason for me to stay now," I said.

"Yes . . . sadly that's true. I only hope the rain lets up during the night. We planned to have the funeral service tomorrow morning. Allyson's parents are dead, you know, and she had no other relatives except Anna . . . and us of course. We thought it best to go ahead with it."

"Yes, I agree." I wondered how David felt, how he would feel tomorrow at his wife's funeral. I still could not believe this horrible thing had happened to him.

"Well," she sighed, and rose as if she was very weary. For the first time she seemed tired; she seemed her age. "I'm going to my room. I probably shall not sleep . . . I doubt any of us will. But I feel the need to be alone for a while."

"I understand," I told her. "I think I will go up soon too."

"Julia, there's one other thing. When I spoke to you and David earlier . . ." I looked into her troubled gray eyes and nodded my understanding of what she meant. "When I said I would make things right for you and David, I never meant . . . I mean I hope you don't think I would actually harm Allyson."

"No . . . no, of course not," I answered her. "I've thought no more of it."

She smiled, obviously relieved. "Good. Well, good night then, dear."

But after she'd left I sat thinking of her words and of the sadness I felt. A woman was dead and it grew more obvious every hour that it was a relief to many in this house.

I continued to sit at the table, unwilling to go up to the dark quiet room. I'd grown to dread being alone there. Only when Mary and one of the other girls came in to clear the dishes away did I rise to go.

"Are you all right, Mary?" I asked. "I know you've been working hard since early this morning."

"Oh, I'm fine, ma'am," she said. "But what about you? Miz Monteen will skin me if she thinks I'm not taking good care of you."

I laughed for I could just imagine Monteen's instructions to Mary about that subject. I assured her I was well and she drew closer to me, whispering so the other girl would not hear.

"I wish you could get away from here, ma'am. But the sheriff, he says the road into town is flooded . . . and if it rains all night again, it might be another day or two before anyone can get through."

Her sweetness and concern moved me and I hugged her briefly. "Don't worry about me, Mary. This will all be over soon. The rain will end, the sun will shine again, and I shall go home safely to the El Dorado."

Later I stood in the hallway and looked toward the back of the house and the shadowy corner near the garden doors. Lamps had been set on tables at either side of the entry to Allyson's room. A spray of white roses hung upon the dark panels of the door.

I walked slowly that way, dreading it and yet acknowledging that it had been in my mind all day to go there.

One of the young male servants sat dozing peacefully near the door, his chair leaned back against the wall. My footsteps woke him and he brought the chair down to the floor and stood up.

"It's all right," I assured him. "I only wanted to . . . to step inside for a moment. Is anyone else in there?"

"No, ma'am. I think everyone's gone to bed." His dark face was open and friendly and he looked at me as if he knew me. Suddenly I realized why he looked so familiar.

"You must be Jess . . . Mary's cousin," I said, smiling at him.

"Yes, ma'am." He seemed pleased by my words and my recognition.

"Well, I'm very happy to meet you, Jess. Mary often speaks of you."

He smiled shyly.

"Has anyone else been here?" I asked, wondering how Anna was feeling.

"Oh, yes, ma'am. Near 'bout all the family's been here. Mr. David, he just left. He was with her for quite a spell, he was." He nodded, his large dark eyes alert and sympathetic.

"Well, I shan't be long. Please sit back down."

I pushed open the door and felt an instant lurch in the pit of my stomach as the familiar scent of roses assailed my nostrils. Allyson's roses.

The room was dimly lit, but the stark whiteness of the bed and the figure in white lying upon it drew me like a beacon.

As I looked down at her, so still and pale, I felt a cold wave of fear travel up my neck and to my head. Death had always been a mysterious, terrifying entity to me, and I now felt the total finality of it.

Tears stung my eyelids and closed my throat. But my grief was not only for Allyson and her untimely, violent death. It was for all of us, for the ones who were left to wonder why this had happened. And for David. I could not bear to see this vital, energetic man in his present sad, vulnerable state.

"Oh Allyson," I whispered. "Was this what you tried to tell me that day? Did you feel death coming?" I could not stop the tears that blurred my vision and ran hotly down to tinge my lips with their salty taste.

Searching blindly for a handkerchief, I opened the drawer of the night table beside the bed. When I pulled a white lace-trimmed one from inside, there was the rattle of glass against wood as something fell inside.

Reaching inside, I retrieved the bottle and opened my hand to read the label: Elixir of Poppy, Prop. of the El Dorado Spa. *The missing bottle from my medicine cache!*

I looked down at the dead woman with a new sadness as I held in my hand further proof of her excesses. This was probably what she had taken last night that had made her so wild and uncontrollable in the hallway with James.

She had lied so much, deceived all of us; and now I must add stealing to her pitiful list of sins. But I could not hate her; even now all I felt was a great well of sadness for such a wasted life.

And I was also afraid. Afraid for the man I loved. Afraid that the evil that lurked quietly in this house would somehow come for David and take him away from me forever.

Chapter Twenty-Two

Sometime during the night the rain stopped. But the next morning the sky was still a dark slaty shade of gray. A heavy mist of fog draped everything, completely obliterating the mountains and the meadow. Even the treetops were hidden, as was everything more than a few feet above the ground.

The fog seemed to muffle each sound, and so it was an eerily quiet procession that left the house at midmorning. There were only a few carriages, all of them draped in black. Because of the weather there were not many people there other than family.

The neighbors who did arrive were those who lived nearby and did not have to ford the creek.

Almost at the end of the long circular drive was a narrow, little-used road which wound its way through the dense stand of trees. As we went only a short way, the road became more rocky and sloped upward. It snaked around the base of a small hill, moving up on the opposite side to a small, neatly kept cemetery.

We stood about the open grave as the pastor spoke briefly. There were no pious messages, no hypocritical sermon about the goodness of the woman who was being laid to rest. And I thought perhaps that was the saddest note of all.

The gathering looked like a large flock of ravens in

our black clothes and large black umbrellas which had been opened to ward off the heavy mist of fog.

I could hardly pull my eyes away from David during the services. He was solemn, but nothing like he had been the moment he found Allyson in the pool. Only once did his hooded gray-green eyes turn to meet mine. I felt such a rush of love as I looked at him and smiled. He looked away, not returning my smile, and the ache within my heart grew even larger than before.

Sheriff Moreland and Doc Ballard stood at the back of the group across the grave from me. The larger man's eyes roved over the family and I knew he was still trying to decide who the murderer was.

The ceremony was over quickly. But just as we turned to get back into the carriages, Anna threw herself to the front of the group. She fell upon the wooden casket, clawing at the fastening with her hands. I thought I'd never witnessed such grief in anyone.

Both James and David stepped forward to pull her away. We could hear their murmured words of comfort as they spoke to her. She did not fight them, but clung to David tightly. Then she threw back her head and in a loud and shrill keening cry, called her sister's name. The sound of it sent shivers up my spine and prickled the hair at the back of my neck. I was afraid she had suffered such a mental blow that she might never fully recover.

Once back at the house we saw that a meal had been prepared and placed on the sideboard, much like the one the evening before. I filled a plate and along with some of the others moved across the hall to eat in the smaller room. There was a low fire burning in the grate, for even though it was the end of August there was a touch of autumn in the air. The warmth from the crackling flames felt comforting somehow as I wondered if I would ever feel dry or warm again.

Most of the guests seemed to be intent on spending

the rest of the day. And although everyone was respectfully quiet, there was food and drink and people chatting in small groups, much like a party.

I saw David slip quietly away and watched him as he turned toward the back of the house. I guessed he was escaping to the comfort of his horses and the stables.

I waited until I thought no one would notice my leaving and I too went down the hall and let myself quietly out the French doors.

The sky seemed to have lightened some, although the heavy fog still clung heavily to the trees, blocking out what little light there might have been.

I walked hurriedly through the garden to the stables. Heavy rain-soaked bushes and flowers grabbed at my black skirts as I passed. I could feel the wet coldness permeate through to my skin.

It felt cozier and much warmer in the hay-scented barn. I could hear David's voice as he spoke softly to the horses.

"David?" I called as I drew nearer.

He was feeding an apple to the big chestnut horse he called Samson. But he glanced briefly my way and I had a feeling he'd been expecting me.

I stopped before him. "David . . . are we never to speak to one another again?"

He looked coolly at me as a brief smile moved across his handsome features. "What are we to speak of? How I wished my wife dead so that we might be together?"

"David!"

"Oh, let's be honest . . . isn't it what we both wished? What difference should it make how it happened?" His voice was hard, unrelenting, and I knew it was guilt that made him speak so harshly.

"No!" I swore. "It was *never* my wish and I don't believe it was yours either." This time he did not look at me and I began to see why he was so angry and bitter.

"Is that what's wrong, David? Are you feeling guilty because you're free of her and it was what you wanted?"

He sat down heavily on a bale of hay, his long legs stretched out before him. Then he looked up at me. "She was my wife . . . we lived together for five years. She even carried my child, Julia. And God help me . . . I can't even feel grief as I should. I only feel relief that it's finally over. What kind of man does that make me?"

"The man that I love," I whispered. I went to him and put my arms about him, cradling his head against my breast. He did not pull away.

"Oh, David, my darling. You must not think this way. You are the dearest man . . . the most decent man in the world. You're still in shock . . . we all are. It's just that everything is so . . . so complicated."

I sat down beside him and looked into his pain-filled eyes. "I have something to tell you, something about Allyson that you should have been told sooner but . . ."

"I think I already know what you're going to say," he said.

I stared at him in surprise. "You knew that Allyson could walk?"

"Not until yesterday. James told me and he also told me about his affair with Allyson. I'd suspected for some time that she could walk. That's why I questioned you so when you first came. I thought perhaps there was some way you might be able to tell."

"No . . . there wasn't. She completely fooled me as well."

"I knew James was meeting someone. It was only a matter of time before I'd have known for sure. Poor Millie had come to me . . . heartbroken, although it wasn't the first time James had engaged in such behavior. But she sensed that somehow this time was different. James was like a man obsessed. I could see that his mind was never where it should have been. And something about Allyson's manner made me suspect her. I think she wanted me to know. It was part of the game for her; she got some perverse thrill out of

266

flaunting it."

"David, I'm sorry."

"Don't pity me," he said wryly. He stood up and moved away from me. "We'd hardly come home from our honeymoon before it began . . . the lies, the disappearances, the elaborate excuses. But she had Anna to protect her lies. Poor Anna, I suppose Allyson used her most of all."

"Yes, I think that's true."

"But it was my fault as well. I was not the most attentive of husbands. I was cool toward her; I could hardly be otherwise." He turned to me then and looked down into my eyes, his gaze deep and searching. "I've never loved anyone but you."

It was so good to hear him say the words that I'd thought were lost to me forever. But as much as I wanted to touch him, he did not pull me into his arms, or kiss me. The moment was too sad for that, too poignant and full of painful memories and regrets. So we both held back, reluctant to touch.

"I want to tell you something else, Julia. Something no one else knows, although I suspect Anna might." He suddenly turned quiet and thoughtful again.

"What, David? What is it?"

"You asked me before why I was so cold to Allyson. You were right, I was cruel to her and I did not even care. But neither did she, except when you came. You became her audience then and she loved playing the poor mistreated cripple for you. By the time we came here I'd lost all compassion for her. I was almost certain she had faked her accident and her reason for it made me sick. So sick I could hardly stand the sight of her."

"What reason?" I asked slowly, seeing the tenseness in his jaw.

"To make it look as if the accident caused her to lose the baby. My own child. And the paralysis later was the perfect opportunity, I suppose, for her to continue her little game. As it turned out, I was right."

"What are you saying?" I asked with growing disbelief.

"One of the maids in Boston was a particular favorite of Allyson's. She did everything for her, her clothes, her hair; and I suspect she also covered up for her on more than one occasion. But when she too began to see how truly sick Allyson was, she came to me." He paused and took a long, slow breath. "She told me that my wife had obtained a potion from one of the old gypsy women down at the docks. An extract prepared for a woman who did not wish to have a child."

I could see in his eyes even now the horror and disbelief he still felt. And I knew how very much losing the child had hurt him. I began to understand why he could not stand to be in Allyson's presence. For truly I could not imagine a happy, healthy woman doing what Allyson had done. Especially if she was married to a man like David.

"And do you believe it was true?"

"Yes. I know it is. When I confronted Allyson she admitted it . . . with great delight. She never wanted children; they would only be a burden to her. My money, it seemed, was enough to make her happy. But she would never admit that the accident was faked, so I brought her here." He stood then and restlessly ran his hand down the painted wooden rail of one of the stalls. "I let everyone believe the story she had told. Mother would have been devastated, especially since she blamed herself for my disastrous marriage." He stood restlessly before me, his head arched back as he looked upward. "God, how I hated her! If ever I'd intended to kill her, believe me it would have been then."

My heart leapt as he spoke. There was so much anger in him still that it frightened me.

"But I didn't kill her. And I can't bring myself to believe it was actually someone here at Stillmeadows." He looked steadily down at me.

"So you have no idea either who did it?"

"Not an idea really ... more a fear that I might know." He turned and looked at me. "I'm afraid it might have been James."

"James?" I murmured. I didn't want him to know that I was also afraid of that very thing.

David came back to where I sat. His hands were on my shoulders, pulling me up to stand almost touching him. His stormy gaze held me, his look unwavering. It was a moment I thought I'd never forget. All the intensity and passion we both felt came together and with it the lowering of his guard. In that moment he allowed me to see and to feel his love as never before, with no holding back, no false pride.

"I love you, Julia. I will always love you. Do you believe that?"

"Yes," I smiled. "I do believe it. And I love you, my darling. You are my first ... my only love."

"If this is ever over ..."

"Shhh," I whispered. "It will be ... and we have time ... the rest of our lives."

I felt a shudder course through his strong body and he pulled me tightly against him. His hands were gentle as he traced the outline of my face and lips. He lowered his mouth to mine in a sweet yet provocatively lingering kiss. It was strange to feel such complete joy in the midst of sorrow, but I knew I'd finally rediscovered my only love. I knew that I'd never really glimpsed true happiness until now. And I knew that after the sorrow of those days we would find it together.

He raised his head and saw my tears. "Oh, love, don't ..." He pressed warm kisses where the tears had moistened my face. He kissed me until we both were breathless and jolted by the surging power of our feelings.

He looked at me for a moment and smiled. "You make me so happy."

I heard a noise near the front of the barn and turned to look.

"What is it?" he asked.

"I . . . I thought I heard something . . . someone."

He stepped away from me and looked into the dusky shadows ahead. "Hello . . . is anyone there?" he asked. There was no answer, only the shuffling of one of the animals in its stall.

He took me in his arms again and smiled down at me. "You'd better go back now. I don't want anything to cast a shadow on what we have and I don't want anyone insinuating things about you which aren't true. You must go home as planned. I want to do this exactly right . . . for you, my love."

"Yes," I whispered in agreement. For it was exactly what I wanted as well and proof of his genuine love for me. His saying it made me feel secure.

"Go then. I'll see you at dinner." As I left, he pulled me back and with a low rumble of laughter kissed me once more. "I seem to have a problem letting you go." His voice was lighter than it had been in days. "Everything is going to be all right," he said as if finally believing it himself.

"Yes," I said.

When I left him there I gave no further thought to the noise I'd heard. In my state of mind I thought of nothing except the magic I felt and the happiness that blossomed within my heart. And in retrospect I know I was probably as unguarded and fearless as I'd been in my entire life.

The rain had stopped for good now and the fog was beginning to lift from the trees. I even caught a glimpse of blue far away in the southern skies. I walked through the garden, letting my mind wander freely, as I touched the flowers or bent to smell the thick profussion of still-wet pink fairy roses. I sat at the wisteria-covered bench where Monteen and I usually ate lunch. I missed her and was anxious to be back home. And I was excited knowing that David and I might finally be able to build a life together.

When I looked up, Anna was moving through the garden toward me. I guessed she too was seeking peace and solace here in the serenity of the flowers.

She was more friendly than usual and she seemed at last to have her grief under control.

"How are you, Anna?" I asked.

"I shall be all right," she said firmly. "Mrs. Damron has kindly offered me a home here for as long as I wish. I could not hope for a more generous family."

"That's good," I said. She continued to stand. She looked uncomfortable and hot in her black long-sleeved bombazine dress. "Would you care to sit down awhile?" I asked.

"No, actually I thought I'd walk up the hill to the springs. But I hate to go alone . . . I suppose I'm still a little frightened by what has happened."

"Yes, I know how you feel. Would you like for me to accompany you? I think a walk would be just the thing before dinner. We could even ask Mary or Millicent to come with us."

"There's no need to bother them. But if you would go with me . . ."

"I'd be happy to." So I rose and we walked to the end of the garden as Monteen and I had before, and I followed Anna in the slow climb up the hill toward the hot springs.

Anna seemed quite animated that day and I thought it unusual. And she was especially cautious, looking about us all the while as we moved through the trees.

"Is anything wrong, Anna?" I asked once. "You seem nervous."

"No, nothing," she assured me. Then she moved on up the slope ahead of me.

When we reached the top I walked to the tree at the overlook. Below, Stillmeadows was beautiful beneath the lingering gray skies. The dark light made it appear

271

by contrast even brighter and more pristine than ever. I imagined it with horses in the pastures as David dreamed and with children playing in the yard, scampering happily through the gardens. I smiled.

"What are you thinking?" Anna asked.

"Oh, I was thinking about children and how much happiness they can bring to a family."

She said nothing, but continued to watch me with her narrowed black eyes.

"Have you ever been inside the cave?" she asked.

I turned and looked at the opening Monteen and I had found before. I felt a small twinge of alarm for I was not comfortable inside caves or dark enclosures.

"No . . . I'm not sure I would like it." Some instinct made me reluctant to go inside the dark, steamy cavern with her.

"Of course you'll like it! It's really quite beautiful. Come along . . . we'll only peek inside and then we'll go back down to the house."

A warning nagged somewhere in the back of my mind but I ignored it. What harm could there be in humoring her today? If I could provide a bit of distraction for her, I told myself, I should be more than willing to do so.

I followed Anna along the rocky, moss-covered edge of the pool to the opening of the cave. Being a tall woman, she had to bend almost double to get through the narrow doorway.

I could feel the heat from the springs as the heavily scented mineral air assailed my senses. I fought the feeling of suffocation and continued to follow her.

To my surprise I saw there were steps carved into the rocks leading down into the cave. There the opening grew larger, forming a huge room where water glistened on the walls. Anna reached into a rocky alcove and brought out a small corroded brass lantern. From a metal container she took a match and lit the wick of the lamp. The smell of oil mingled with the damp scent of the cave.

The light shimmered upon the wall, revealing layers of glittering quartz. It was breathtaking, just as she'd promised.

Anna turned to me and the lamplight reflected in her eyes like an animal's in a darkened forest. "Now, aren't you glad you came?" she asked.

"Yes, this is beautiful . . . and it is cooler here just as you said."

She only smiled, oddly, I thought, her eyes glittering in the lamplight.

There were several narrow passages leading from the main room. Anna silently started along one of the paths, but I had seen all I cared to.

"Anna, wait . . ."

"It's just a short way . . . something special I want to show you."

So I followed reluctantly, growing more uneasy with each step.

I followed her along narrow walkways, through twists and turns. By now I knew I could never find my way back out alone. And I was growing more and more alarmed.

"Anna, please . . . I think we should go back now."

"It's just around this corner," she said over her shoulder as she hurried along even faster.

Then I sensed we'd entered another large room. Anna held the lamp high and I saw the walls of the round cavern. They were smooth and gray like the walls of a prison.

I gasped and felt real terror grip my heart. My pulse raced, beating in my ears until it shut out any other sound. The gray-walled prison of the room was exactly like the one I'd dreamed of, the room where I'd felt myself dying.

Anna turned then and I saw in her eyes what I should

273

have seen all along. There was a crazed look of triumph there . . . a madness unlike anything I'd ever seen before.

"Anna . . . why are we here?" I asked, my breath coming in short gasps.

"Don't you know? This is your *tomb*, Julia . . . this secret room which was once known only to the Indians. It's where you'll spend eternity!" Then she laughed, her coarse, deep voice loud in the stillness of the enclosure. And I knew she intended to kill me.

"But . . . why? Why do you want to hurt me?"

"You stupid woman! You couldn't wait one whole day after my poor sister's funeral to go running to her husband. I saw you there in the barn today you know. And it wasn't the first time! Remember the day I pulled the hay from your hair? You wallowed there with him like a whore! But it's not his fault. He's confused, he doesn't know yet who he loves. And when he sees that you've abandoned him yet again . . . he'll turn to me. Then he'll see . . . everyone will see how I'll care for him!"

"You're in love with David," I said numbly. Why had I not seen it before?

"Yes I love him! I've loved him from the first moment I saw him! But he married Allyson. Hateful, deceitful person. I tried to tell him about her then, but he only laughed at me. He told me it did not matter because he wanted children more than love and it was not important."

"But Anna," I said, trying to remain calm, hoping to soothe her, "you don't have to kill me. You can tell David how you feel . . . let him be the one to choose."

She stepped forward, eyes blazing. "Shut up! Shut your whining mouth! Do you think I'm a fool? Men lust after beauty and I know I could never compete with yours. But you don't really love him . . . you're just like Allyson! I told her and told her." She began to pace now like an enraged animal and her voice was

274

harsh and cold, devoid of anything except hatred. "I have to make David see that . . . that he's better off without her . . . without you!"

"Anna, please . . ."

She whirled at me, striking the side of my head with the heavy lantern. I saw flashes of light and felt the cold hard floor as I collapsed upon it. The air swooshed from my lungs and I could only gasp, unable to move or speak. The blow had extinguished the lamp and I could see nothing . . . there was absolute darkness all around me.

I heard Anna's voice as she stood above me. "She killed his child. . . . She hurt him time and again. She was nothing but a deceitful harlot! Cheating with David's own brother. I warned her . . . I did warn her. But she laughed at me. She laughed and told me I was too ugly to ever have a man who would love me. She said David would never love someone like me. Then she waved one of her damned roses in my face and I hit her! I hit her and hit her and I choked the words out of her lying throat. I had to make her stop laughing!" She was completely, violently out of control now and absolutely insane. I lay perfectly still, hoping she'd think I was unconscious.

She kicked at me and I cried out as the blow glanced painfully off my ribs. Then I heard her shuffling footsteps going out of the room. And I was completely alone in a black void where not even the tiniest amount of light penetrated. The feeling that swept over me then was one of pure terror. It shook me from head to toe and I could even taste its galling bitterness on my tongue.

Chapter Twenty-Three

I don't know how long I lay there in the darkness with the numbing fear holding me prisoner. I had to think . . . had to plan what I would do to escape—if indeed there was an escape.

But as I sat there thinking of David, his words of love came back to me and I knew I had to try and find a way out of the cave. I would never give up and risk losing him forever. I couldn't!

As I stood up shakily I wished I had paid more attention to the many intricate twists and turns leading to the room. I remembered that the sound of trickling water left us at the last few turns. So I reasoned that when I again heard the water I could follow it until it reached its exit point at the opening of the cave.

My head pounded where the lantern had struck me. I could feel the sticky wetness of blood matted in my hair. But the disorientation I felt as I groped slowly along the black pathway was the most frightening aspect of all.

It seemed like hours until I heard the faint sound of running water. I stopped, trying to get my bearings and decide which way to go. It must have been at that point I made the mistake. For within minutes as I moved on, I could no longer hear the water and by now I was so disoriented I had no idea which way to turn. My eyes felt sore and strained from peering so intently into the gloom. I felt along the walls and the floor until I found a flat place to sit. Then I slid to the ground, exhausted, and dizzy from the pain and the constant battle to find my way through total darkness.

I must have slept then, for how long I could not say. Waking was one of the most horrible feelings I've ever experienced. It was as if the world had disappeared and I'd been swallowed up in some dark, frightening void. I even began to feel strangely unreal, as if I were losing my mind.

I had no idea what time it was, or how long I'd wandered inside the earth. I didn't know if it was daytime or night, raining or clear. The more I thought about it the more afraid I became until finally I began to cry, my sobs echoing eerily off the damp walls about me.

I woke several times during the next few hours, drifting in and out of an uneasy sleep. But I yearned for sleep to shut out the whirling thoughts and the sound of animals that scurried about in the cave. And most of all to shut off the hopeless despair I was beginning to feel.

I had no idea how long I'd been there when I heard the first faint sounds of voices. At first I thought I was dreaming, hallucinating, for I knew there could be no one else in the cave. Then a new tingle of fear coursed through me as I thought it might be Anna returning to make sure I was dead.

But I realized the voices were those of men and with a growing hope I thought they sounded familiar.

"I'm here!" I managed to cry. My throat was so dry that it was only a raspy croak.

"Julia?" The voice that rang clearly through the dark corridors was David's. I knew it had to be him. But was I dreaming or was he really there somewhere in the cave?

"Julia! Answer me. We're trying to find the direction." It was David . . . I was certain of it now and my heart filled with an almost hysterical joy.

"David," I called weakly. "I'm here. I'm here." I heard my voice go on and on calling to him and crying. I could not seem to stop crying.

Suddenly ahead of me there was a flash of light. I could see it coming near to me, but I could not move. I could only lie there weakly, weeping with relief.

"She's here," the voice said. "Hurry!"

Everything seemed to blur into some great faraway distance. I do remember strong arms beneath me, whispered words soothing and comforting me as I was lifted up and held tightly against his warm body. But I have no recollection of being carried from the cave, no remembrance of seeing the outside world again at last. The only other thing I remember is David's deep, strong voice telling me he loved me and urging me to hold on to him.

They tell me I slept for twenty-four hours. It had been early morning when David and the others found me, sometime before dawn. So in sleeping I missed one whole day and night.

When I first woke in my bed that next morning I could not remember where I was or what had happened to me. I saw Mary dozing in a chair beside me. And I heard the songbirds in the trees outside the windows.

I was aware of a slight ache in my head and ribs and I was tired . . . so tired I could hardly keep my eyes from closing again.

"Mary," I whispered.

Her eyes flew open at once and she slid from the chair to reach forward and take my hand in hers.

"Oh, ma'am," she said. "How do you feel? Does your head ache? Are you hungry?"

I laughed, then grimaced, for my head did indeed ache at the slightest move. I reached up to touch my hair and felt a thick bandage wrapped around my skull. Then it all came back to me in a rush; Anna's mad ravings—the lantern—the dark overwhelming fear of

279

being alone in the black cavern. I shuddered at remembering.

"Don't move," Mary said. "I'm going to find Mr. David. He only just left a few moments ago."

It was only a short wait until David burst through the door and came quickly to my side.

"Julia . . . how are you?" There was a hint of dark stubble upon his face and his eyes were tired, as if he had not slept. His shirtsleeves were rolled up to the elbow and I wondered if Mary had brought him from his shaving stand.

"I feel fine," I said, turning my hand over in his so that I could clasp his warm fingers between mine.

"Are you sure?" he asked anxiously as he studied my face with great tenderness. "You seem so pale."

From behind David someone cleared his throat. It was Dr. Ballard who peered around David at me. His look was very kind, but amused.

"Mr. Damron, if you allow me to get close enough to see the patient, I believe I can answer those questions for you."

David nodded, his face still serious, and stepped away, giving Dr. Ballard room to get to the bed. The doctor hesitated a moment, then turned to look at David and Mary.

"If both of you will just step outside, this won't take but a moment."

David's gaze held my own and I could see his reluctance to let me out of his sight, even for a short while.

I smiled and lifted my hand toward him. "Go ahead . . . I promise you I'm all right."

After they'd left Dr. Ballard placed a stethoscope to my chest and asked me to breathe deeply. He helped me into a sitting position and placed the device on my back, listening silently for a few seconds. Making no comment he placed the instrument back in his bag and turned to begin removing the bandage from my head.

His hands were so cool and gentle that I never felt frightened or ill at ease.

"Hum . . . ," he murmured. "Your head wound appears to be healing nicely." He placed a cool hand on my forehead. "No fever. Are you in pain anywhere . . . any dizziness?" He peered intently into my eyes.

"No . . . my head aches only a little, when I move."

"To be expected," he murmured. He pulled the quilt back up to my breasts and sat down beside me. "Well, you appear no worse for the wear. I will only prescribe something to eat and a bit more rest. You may even be up and about your room if you feel up to it."

"Oh, yes I do. And thank you, Doctor."

"You're a very lucky young woman, Mrs. Van Cleef. It seems the fates were with you, or you might never have been found."

"Yes, I know." I frowned thinking of the place Anna had called my tomb.

He chuckled as he picked up his bag and rose to go. "I should say fate *and* Mr. Damron. That man was intent on moving heaven and earth to find you. And he would not let any of us rest until we did!"

I smiled, so thankful for David and for his strength and love.

"And speaking of rest, ma'am. The roads are once again clear. You are on the way to a full recovery and if you have no further questions, I intend to go home and take a bit of a rest myself."

"I have no questions," I said. "And thank you again for everything you've done for me."

"It was my pleasure. Good day, Mrs. Van Cleef."

I could hear his voice in the hall as he spoke to David and Mary, assuring them that I was fine. When the two of them came back in, their smiles reflected the relief they must have felt.

"Julia, I'm going to leave you in Mary's capable hands. She's going to help you bathe and change into your clothes. And I will personally go to the kitchen and order your breakfast." His voice was light and teasing and it was good to see the look of worry leave his face.

At the door he turned. "After you eat, I'll tell you everything. I imagine you have many questions."

"Yes," I nodded.

As Mary helped me with my toilet she chatted as usual in her soft, sweet voice.

"Miz Monteen's here. She came as soon as she could. I thought she was going to kill that Miss Anna with her bare hands before the sheriff took her away. She was a regular wildcat, she was," she chuckled. "She wanted to stay up here with you last night, but Mr. David, he wouldn't hear of it. Wouldn't allow nobody in here but himself, and Doc Ballard of course. He only left this morning to bathe and change clothes ... after I promised at least twelve times to call him if you so much as moved." She chuckled again. "My, my, never seen no man so besotted with anybody as he is with you." Her eyes flashed merrily at me. "Don't you tell him I said that either! He'd tell me I was too fresh for my own good!

"Well," she said after brushing out my hair. "We're finished. And I best get outta here before that man of yours come bustin' in and tells me to git."

She handed me a soft, deep blue morning robe and held onto my arm as I moved to sit in one of the chairs near the windows.

Before she left I reached up and hugged her, realizing how lucky I was to have a sweet, vivacious friend like her in my life. "Thank you, Mary."

She must have gone directly down to tell Monteen I was awake, for within seconds the door opened and the dark-haired woman peeked in cautiously.

"Monteen," I said happily. "Come in! I'm so happy you're here."

She opened the door, revealing for the first time the man standing in the hallway behind her.

Harry looked pale, from his illness I supposed, but

282

on his face was the happiest smile I'd ever seen there. I realized at once that it was not entirely for me, but for another reason also.

As they came toward me, Monteen in her ruby red suit and Harry in a conservative gray tweed, his hand was firmly and possessively at her small waist.

"Well," I said. "What's this?" At last it was my time to tease her and see the hint of a blush beneath her olive skin.

She smiled and lifted her chin, ignoring my question as she came to sit near me. "Are you all right, *chère?* Oh I was so worried. I knew I should have made you leave here that night!"

"Now, Monteen, don't blame yourself for this. It was my decision to stay. You know you could not have changed my mind."

"Yes," she sighed. "You are inclined to be stubborn. But are you sure you're all right?"

"Only a slight headache," I said, pointing to the cut on my head. I looked up at the tall man standing so quietly and patiently behind Monteen. "And you, Harry, how are you?"

"Much better. I guess I was never as sick as some of the others."

"He's still very weak," Monteen declared, looking up with shining eyes over her shoulder at him. "He should have stayed home in bed, but he insisted on coming out here with me."

I looked with bemusement at them. The two were so completely different and yet so obviously intoxicated with each other. There was an animated spark about Harry I'd never seen before, and Monteen, a vision in her red suit, was fairly aglow.

"Seeing you two together does my heart good," I said.

They both smiled, first at me, then at each other.

"Kismet," Monteen smiled. "We cannot change what the fates have in store."

She stood up to go, as she did leaning back ever so slightly against the tall, slender man behind her. Again his hand touched her waist as he looked down at her upturned face.

"Is that not so, darling?" she asked.

"That, and a little persistence," he said softly.

I laughed as a warm color touched her cheeks again. It was delightful seeing my friend so happy and so much in love. And even I could not have wished for a kinder, more gentle man for her.

"But we must go, *chère,*" she said, bending to kiss my cheek. "I'm sure David is anxious to have you all alone to himself."

"Now don't worry about me," I said. "There is no longer any danger here at Stillmeadows. And David will see me safely home as soon as I'm able."

"Of that I am certain. You are a lucky woman, Julia," she said, shaking a finger at me as she left.

It was only a few seconds before David returned, carrying a handled oblong silver tray. He placed it on the table and then in a move that took me completely by surprise, he knelt at my feet and put his arms about my waist. I ran my fingers through his dark hair, captivated by the golden streaks that shimmered there in the morning sunlight.

"Oh, God, Julia," he sighed. "How would I live if anything had happened to you?"

I smiled at him, tenderness melting my heart. My eyes burned with tears before David reached up to brush them from my lashes.

"Here . . . what's this? Tears have no more place in our lives, darling."

"They're only tears of happiness," I said.

He pulled my head down so that he could kiss my lips. His touch was sweet and gentle, as if I were something quite fragile and extraordinary.

"In that case," he said, pulling his lips away from mine and grinning at me, "I suppose you shall spend many hours in tears . . . for I intend to make you the happiest woman on earth."

"I can't wait," I whispered, leaning to kiss him again.

With a soft groan he stood up and pulled the other chair close to the table between us.

"You will have to wait awhile at least," he said lightly. "Until you've eaten every bite of the breakfast I've brought."

"Only if you eat with me," I said, smiling at him.

"Oh, the nagging begins so soon!" he taunted.

The food he'd brought was delicious and I was starving. He watched me with amusement in his eyes as I ate everything he'd brought, washing it down with two cups of tea.

"If your appetite is any indication, then you certainly must be better."

"I am," I said. "Now . . . tell me what happened and how you knew where to find me."

He sat back in the chair and turned his gaze out the windows. The only indication of his suppressed emotions was a muscle that moved slightly in his jaw.

"Well, I must tell you, Anna fooled me completely. I had no idea it was she who killed Allyson. Would not have guessed it in a million years. When you disappeared and did not return by dinner, I had no reason to suspect her. I was at a complete loss to know even where to begin.

"But once the word spread through the house that you were missing, Mary and Mrs. Woolridge remembered seeing you in the garden with Anna. That struck a chord of warning in me, because I had seen Anna earlier at dinner and she said she had not seen you at all.

"James became extremely angry with her when she denied seeing you. The more he tried to force her to tell what she knew the more deranged she became. She came to me, pleading with me to believe her, to trust her. She said the strangest things . . . that only she

285

could take care of me as I deserved. And that Allyson was never good enough for me. I felt as if someone had struck me between the eyes. And I wondered how I could have been so blind that I suspected nothing before."

"So it was Anna who finally told you?" I asked.

"Yes. I took her aside away from the others. And I began to agree with everything she said about how she would love me and take care of me as no one else could. And I began to see that she was totally insane. It didn't take long to gain enough trust so that when I asked her very gently if she killed Allyson, she admitted it. She swore that she didn't intend to kill her. There was a fight and I believe Anna did it accidentally."

"Yes," I said. "That's what she told me too."

"By that time I was in a panic, wondering where you were and if you were still alive. I wanted to shake her until she told me where she'd taken you. I've never been so scared in my life." There was still a hint of that worry in his eyes now as he relived it.

"Then she told me where you were. It seems you did hear someone in the barn that day. Anna overheard everything we said. Then in her crazed mind she reasoned that with you gone, I would turn to her."

"This is all so unbelievable."

"We locked her in her room. I had one of the men guard her. Then, Sheriff Moreland, Doc Ballard, James, and I began to search the various pathways in the cave."

We were silent for a while, looking across the yard to watch the meadows where the sun was beginning to paint the treetops with gold.

"I always loved this place beyond anything," he said. "This land. But the memories here are so painful now for both of us. I want to build a new home . . . one just for us . . . a place to make our own remembrances." He turned to look into my eyes and in that look there was a promise that no matter what my answer, he would take care of me and protect me from any other harm. And I wanted with all my heart to be able to do the same for him.

"A house of my own," I said aloud. "A home with warmth and love. And children . . . lots of children. Oh, David, do you know how many times I've dreamed of such a thing?"

"Tell me, darling," he said, pulling me from the chair into his arms.

"A thousand times. And do you know who I always pictured there with me, in that house filled with such warmth and love?"

His lips were tantalizingly close to mine as he whispered. "Who, my love?"

"You, my darling David. It was always you."

Dear Reader,

Zebra Books welcomes your comments about this book or any other Zebra Gothic you have read recently. Please address your comments to:

Zebra Books. Dept. WM
475 Park Avenue South
New York, NY 10016

Thank you for your interest.

Sincerely,
The Editorial Department
Zebra Books